Tempting Her Dragon Bodyguard

A Dragon Protectors Novel

Michelle Miles

TEMPTING HER DRAGON BODYGUARD

Cover Design by Erin Dameron-Hill

ISBN: 978-1-7333887-9-5

Tempting Her Dragon Bodyguard

A Dragon Protectors Novel

Dragon Lord Jaxson Lane has spent a lonely existence drifting through the human realm with no real purpose. With the Hidden Lands cursed and his clans dying, his friend and ally, Logan, discovers the Drakana's sinister plot to use a blood ritual in the hopes it will heal their ailing world. The key to that blood ritual is Zahra, the eldest noblewoman of the ancient Fire-Drakes and a woman Jaxson once loved now promised to another. Seeing Zahra again rekindles the fire burning within him and one kiss is all it takes to drive her back into his arms, even though he tries to resist her. Now with the Drakana after Zahra as their target, Jaxson will keep her safe by any means necessary.

Lady Zahra Veritor's betrothal to the son of one of the Council of Five leaders is not a happy one. The only man she's ever loved has been absent from her life for years until a chance encounter brings them together once again. When her life is suddenly in danger, Jax is the only man she can turn to for help…and the only man she's ever loved. As he protects her from the men who want her, tempting him back into her arms becomes her mission. But their game of seduction is cut short when she is injured and nearly killed. Now her only chance of survival lies with the only man she can truly trust—her dragon bodyguard.

⤙ 1 ⤚

After the deep freeze of winter, summer finally thawed out New York City bringing tourists from all over the world as well as the sweltering heat. Jaxson jockeyed for position through the jam-packed streets as he made his way towards Hell's Kitchen. He had been in the city long enough to know it wasn't the place for him. He needed to get back to the Hidden Lands where he could breathe in fresh air and hear the soft twitter of birds instead of car horns and sirens all hours of the night.

But the Hidden Lands were dying, and the air wasn't fresh anymore. It had turned toxic. At least, toxic to most of the shifters. For others, it didn't seem to affect them at all. The Dragon's Breath hiding the Whispering Mountains of his homeland had turned poisonous. In the last few months since he'd been living in the city, he'd witnessed more and more clans abandoning it and entering the human realm.

Except his father. As a member of the Council of Five, Lord Nyles Lane was determined to stay behind to care for his ailing wife and keep order amidst chaos. A dangerous thing, Jaxson knew. When he offered to return home, his father ordered him to stay. He set up a tiny apartment on the Upper West Side and found work doing freelance security jobs for the wealthy. It kept him fed and mostly out of trouble.

His friend, Logan, needed all the allies he could get. Taking over the Council of Five as Chief Magistrate hadn't been an easy task. He'd had to fight the usurper, Lord Archer Drake, for control and nearly lost his life in the process. Killing Archer allowed Lord

Herrick to take his place to continue to threaten Logan's claim as Chief. When Logan asked him to meet with him, he assumed it had something to do with the recent unrest in the Council as well as the dying Hidden Lands.

All this swirled through Jaxson's mind as he headed into Bar Inferno, the local hangout for the supernaturals in the city with the exception of the vamps. The bar was off limits to them.

Logan had called him that morning and asked to meet there for a late afternoon lunch. He'd agreed only because they hadn't really spoken in the last few months since Logan had been in the human realm.

He arrived first and took a secluded booth in the back of the bar. Minutes later, his usual drink arrived. He clutched the bourbon in one hand and his smartphone in the other while keeping a watchful eye on the door.

Logan entered a few minutes later, gave him a quick wave of hello. He paused to speak to Meg, the bartender, and then made his way over. He slid into the booth across from him and plopped a thick folder with papers spilling out of it onto the table next to him.

"Thanks for meeting me," Logan said.

"Anytime." Jaxson downed the bourbon and eyed the folder as the alcohol burned down to his gut. "It sounded urgent."

Before Logan could reply, Meg arrived and dropped off his drink. "You guys want the usual?"

Jaxson nodded as Logan said, "Sure."

They had been customers often enough she knew what they always ordered.

"I'll get you another drink, Jax." She bounced off before he could reply.

"You know I'm determined to break the curse on the Hidden Lands," Logan began, jumping right into it. "I've been reading through my father's notes and journals every chance I can get when I go back."

"So, you have been back?" Jaxson asked.

He nodded. "Several times. Bree came with me a few times before she had the baby."

"Have you been back since the baby was born?" Jaxson asked.

Logan was the proud father of an adorable little boy named after his father, Elijah. Half human, half dragon-shifter, the boy was growing faster than the average human and already into his toddler phase.

"Only once to grab my father's journals." He glanced at the folder. "I can't risk my family's safety in the Hidden Lands until I know the curse is broken and the air is safe again."

Jaxson's second drink arrived. He palmed the highball, clutching it until his fingers ached. He hadn't been back to the Hidden Lands since he stepped through a portal of his own making. It wasn't that he didn't want to go back, he knew as Logan did it wasn't safe. With the air turning more and more toxic, and more and more dragon-shifters dying, he didn't want to risk it, either. Nor did several of the clans judging by how many abandoned the realm. Truth be told, he was ready to go home. The fast-paced city that never slept exhausted him.

"You plan to return for good?" he asked.

"When this is all over, yes," Logan said. "Your father sends his regards."

He hadn't spoken to his father since he stepped through the portal, nor had he seen his mother. "And my mother?"

"Your father says she's well."

But how well? When he left, she was quite ill. His father insisted it was nothing serious, but he suspected it had something to do with the air. He'd wanted to bring her with him, but she refused because she didn't want to leave her home or her husband. Jaxson wished he had insisted.

Logan flipped open the folder, fluttering the pages. Jaxson could see copied pages from a handwritten journal. Someone, likely Logan, had scrawled notes along the copies. He flipped through them until he came to the one he wanted and stopped.

"I got help from one of the clan elders to help translate my father's journals. He has specific notes about the Hidden Lands and the curse. It requires the Blood Stone and the tooth from the cold-drake, both of which I have."

"I know that already," Jaxson said, sounding more agitated than he intended.

Logan cut him a glance but said nothing. He dropped his gaze back to the page, his tanned finger going down to the bottom. "I also need a scale from a fire-drake." He sat back in his chair and gave him a pointed look.

A tingling sensation flickered through him as he met Logan's gaze. He knew there was more to it than simply any scale from any fire-drake. He shifted in the booth, the vinyl crunching under his weight, and said nothing.

Logan laced his fingers together on top of the papers. "The scale has to be from one of the Rindhara bloodline. Like the tooth had to come from one of the Gildhara bloodline. It's very specific to breaking the curse."

His mouth went bone dry. "And why is that?"

"The tooth will have to be ground down to infuse the Blood Stone with the power. The scale gives it the energy it needs along with three drops of blood from three specific bloodlines—the Gildhara, the Rindhara, and an elemental. The ritual requires all of that plus a chant, which I have yet to translate. Once all that's complete, the curse will break, and the Hidden Lands will heal."

"Allegedly," Jaxson said.

Logan raised his brow in question. "Why allegedly?"

"Do you have proof that this chant will break whatever curse is on the Hidden Lands?"

His mouth thinned into a straight line. "No."

"Then how do you know it will work?"

"I have to believe it will. If it doesn't…" His voice trailed off.

Jaxson knew what he implied. If it didn't, then the Hidden Lands were lost forever. He stared at Logan, his hand tightening even more around the glass until his fingers ached.

"What does this have to do with me?" As if he didn't know the answer already.

"I traced the Rindhara bloodline, Jax."

They stared at each other, the din of the bar fading into a muffled hum. All he could hear was the blood rushing through his ears. All he could feel was the sudden erratic pounding of his pulse.

"And?" His voice rasped when he spoke.

"There is only one clan of fire-drakes left. One ancient, noble clan. One you know well."

Jaxson downed his drink in one gulp in response. The alcohol burned down to his churning gut. He didn't want to hear this. He didn't want anything to do with this conversation. Logan was one of his oldest friends, though. He couldn't bolt from the bar without looking like a total ass.

"It took me some time to trace the bloodline, but I finally did it," Logan continued. "I wasn't sure about it until I found this."

He shoved papers in the folder aside and turned one around toward him. It was a family crest, the symbol that of an orange dragon, upright with wings open and the tail curling around a sword on a red shield. Jaxson knew that crest without even looking at it. He never knew, though, the bloodline was that of the Rindhara. Not until today.

"Again, why are you telling me this?" He tried for indifference but wasn't sure if he pulled it off.

"You know why." Logan's glinting stare hardened.

It was as he thought, but Logan wasn't willing to say it out loud. Annoyance pulsed behind his eyes as he stared at his friend.

"What are you asking me, Logan?"

"You know what I'm asking." He leaned across the table, dropping his voice. "We need her. She's the one with the third and final relic."

He shifted in his seat and knew Logan wasn't lying. His dragon magic told him as much. He puffed out a heated breath. "For fucks sake, Logan. I haven't talked to her in years."

"Then it's time to get reacquainted." Logan sat back in the seat, flipping the folder closed.

Before he could respond, the food arrived. The young female server delivered the two plates and then hurried away before either of them could reply. Likely she could sense the tension between them.

Jaxson stared down at the hot wings and fries, suddenly no longer hungry. His stomach burned with the heat of the bourbon, his chest ached with the gaping hole that was left there, his mind scorched with fervent denial of even thinking her name. He had pushed her so far out of his thoughts, he couldn't quite recall her face.

No, that wasn't true. He had thought of her and often. More often than he wanted to admit. They had been young and stupid and so incredibly hot for each other. But that was a long time ago. He had lost all hope of ever seeing her again, all thought of ever getting her back. Even if she was his mate.

"Jax, I know you don't want to talk to her." He fiddled with his fork, likely trying to decide how to ask him whatever it was he wanted to ask him.

"But?" he prompted.

"But I need you to talk to her, to convince her to help us."

"No." His tone was abrupt and succinct.

Logan's brows flew up in surprise. "No?"

"You can't ask me to do this."

He huffed out a breath and flipped open the folder again. He turned several pages until he got to the yellow 3x3 sticky note attached to one of the papers. He could see flowing handwriting he knew wasn't Logan's. It had to be Bree's. He pulled the note off the paper, held it, looking down at it.

"I tried talking to her, but she didn't want anything to do with me. She has an address in Phoenix, but she has another place on Fifth Avenue. Right here in Manhattan."

"Convenient."

"She's in town on business."

"Also, convenient."

He dropped the note next to Jaxson's plate. "Her address and phone number. I'm asking you, as a friend, as your Chief Magistrate, Jax. Talk to her. We need her."

For fucks sake. He stared down at the perfect handwriting, the blue ink stark against the yellow paper. Heat sparked up his spine. The handwriting wasn't Bree's. It was his mother's. Questions. So many questions swirled in his mind.

"Where did you get this information?" Jaxson demanded.

"I can't reveal my source."

But Jaxson knew. Somewhere along the way, Logan contacted his mother. He hadn't a clue how she got it, though.

"What makes you think she'll talk to me?" Jaxson asked.

His mind pounded with the last memory he had of them together. The last time he kissed her. The way she smelled, looked, tasted, felt. The blood pounded hard through his veins, pulsating at a rapid pace. It made him light headed. He plucked a fry from his plate, holding it between his thumb and forefinger.

"If you can't get through to her, then no one can. Besides," he paused, swallowed hard, "I can still smell her on you."

Again, not a lie.

Jaxson squeezed the fry, the guts of the potato squishing out of it and breaking the crispy exterior. He tossed it back onto his plate and pinned Logan with his best warning glare. "Don't."

Logan knew, as he did, she was his mate but they had never spoken of it.

"I don't know what happened between you two—"

"And you never will," he cut in.

"But you're the best chance I have at getting her to hand over a dragon scale."

Tense silence descended between them as they stared each other down. Logan was his oldest friend but he had never shared the truth with him. It had been too painful, too awful to even think about. Jaxson had been paying the price since that fateful day when he walked out of her life forever. He hadn't seen her since, nor had he ever planned to see her again.

He clenched his jaw so tight, his back teeth ached.

"I smelled you on her, too," Logan added. "I thought you should know."

His heart nearly stopped. The blood rushed out of his head so fast, he saw dark pinpricks of light.

The mating scent was strongest shortly after ka kladou, the dragon mating, and eventually faded but would always remain there as a faint undertone. Knowing Logan could still smell him on her meant two things. One, he was close enough to her to smell it. And two, the mating bond was still strong between them. Strong enough to reignite it.

"You saw her. That's how you know she's here in Manhattan."

"I tried to talk to her but she wasn't interested. She slammed the door in my face."

He couldn't help his curiosity. "How does she look?"

"Find out for yourself."

A little glimmer of hope sparked deep inside him at the thought of seeing her again. He knew, in time, that would ignite into a hot, burning need. He doubted she would even want to see him, talk to him. Their parting hadn't been a good one.

Jaxson inhaled a deep breath through his nose, let it out through his mouth. "Fine. I'll talk to her. But you're going to owe me for this."

"I'll buy you the finest bottle of bourbon I can find, okay?"

"Think bigger." He flashed his friend a grin, his tone teasing, but deep down he was serious.

Consideration flickered over Logan's face. "When all this is over, there will likely be an empty place on the council. It's yours if you want it."

The idea took him aback as he looked at him across the table. He thought for a minute Logan was kidding. If he had been, he would have been able to sense it. There was no hint of a lie. There was no hint of a playful smile anywhere on his face. His tone was sincere. His offer was an honest one.

"You don't have to answer now," Logan added.

"I'll think about it."

"Good. Now, let's eat." He picked up his triple decker sandwich and took a healthy bite.

But Jaxson couldn't eat. Not with the name Zahra Veritor staring at him in his mother's graceful blue-inked script.

… 2 …

Zahra perched on the edge of the Bethesda Fountain in Central Park and tilted her face to the late afternoon sun, the heavenly warmth pressing into her skin. Nothing made her feel more recharged than spending an afternoon soaking up the rays and letting it fill her. The only thing that would make it better was if she shifted into her dragon form and let her scales take in the sun.

But she couldn't do that here. Hell, she couldn't do that at all anymore. Her shifting powers had deserted her years ago around the same time as when she got her heart broken. She had lost all her dragon magic, her ability to shift, everything. She hadn't felt a glimmer of her powers since.

Behind her, water spilled down from the angel sculpture, the sound soothing and rhythmic. It was a crowded afternoon with lots of kids, moms, and tourists but she knew it was the only chance she'd get to spend it in the sun since she'd be working the rest of the weekend. As a freelance photographer, she was often hired for high-profile weddings and paid a nice sum for it. This weekend was the wedding of a financier to his socialite girlfriend at the Ritz. Even though she didn't fit into those circles, she did enjoy the food.

As she glanced around, the saw a man she knew making a path straight for her. Tall, broad-shouldered, dark hair with bright green eyes and stubble shadowing his jawline. He had been working for her father for decades. He was an ever-present shadow following in her father's wake.

Her tranquil afternoon was about to be ruined. She straightened and tried to hide the scowl that wanted to erupt on her face. She was never very good at hiding her emotions. With a huff, she stood and slung her Louis Vuitton handbag over her shoulder. No sense in delaying the inevitable. She headed right for him, making eye contact and making sure he knew she saw him coming.

He halted halfway to her and let her close the gap between them. She folded her arms over her chest and glared him. Bastian worked for her father back in the Hidden Lands. She hadn't stepped foot there in a few years. Not that she had planned to return anytime soon. She had no interest in politics or contact with her estranged father. For all she cared, he could die a slow death and take all the pompous entitled Council members with him.

"What do you want, Bastian?" She gave him her best death glare.

"Your father wants to see you," Bastian said.

"Good for him. I don't want to see him."

She started to walk around him but he grabbed her arm. "You don't have a choice."

The way his fingers dug into her upper arm showed he meant business. She glanced down at his hand and then back up at him. "Take your hand off me."

"I will if you agree to come with me."

Surprise flickered through her. "He wants to see me now?" When he nodded, she added, "I'm not going back there."

"He's here in the city," Bastian clarified.

"Here?"

What the hell was her father doing in Manhattan? He rarely, if ever, left the Hidden Lands. Whatever he wanted to see her about must be important. She could admit it piqued her curiosity but it still didn't mean she wanted to see him. She pulled her arm free of his grasp.

"Doesn't matter. I'm still not going."

This time she managed to step around him, the click of her kitten heels on the pavement was the only sound she heard as she walked away.

"He thought you might say that," Bastian called. "So, he said if you refused, he would make sure you wouldn't have contact with Nemea again."

She halted, her back to him. Her little sister was her only link to her realm. She'd kept in contact with her throughout her years from her home in the human realm to make sure she was all right. She had no idea her father knew of their secret messages. What else did he know? She'd have to be more careful about what she put in those messages. Even though Nemea was good at reading between the lines, she didn't need her father meddling in her life. She looked at Bastian over her shoulder, knowing she had no choice.

"Fine. Let's go."

Ten minutes later, they were in Hell's Kitchen at a place she'd never even heard of—Bar Inferno. They arrived at the kickoff of happy hour and found her father tucked away in a corner booth alone nursing a gin and tonic. Bastian stood next to her as she paused at the edge of the table, looking down at him with indifference.

It had been a few years since she'd seen him. Haggard was a good way to describe him. Haggard and old. His once black hair was dusted with gray. Those brown eyes that once held mirth and humor now were filled with fatigue and weariness. One thing that hadn't changed was the look of disdain on his permanently etched on his face. As though he would forever be disappointed by her.

"Hello, Zahra." He waved her to the opposite seat.

She didn't budge. She merely gripped the strap of her handbag until her hand ached. "Father."

"Stop looking at me as if you want to murder me in my sleep and sit."

"Call off your goon and I might consider it."

Her father leaned back in the seat. "Go get a drink, Bastian. Tell the bartender to put it on my tab."

With a nod, Bastian left and made his way to the bar. She waited until he was long gone before sliding in the booth across from him. She placed her handbag on the seat next to her and sat back, her hands in her lap, her senses on high alert.

"Would you like a drink?" he asked.

"I would not. I would like for you to get to the point of this little visit."

"Is it so wrong to want to see my daughter?"

"It is when you threaten her."

"It worked, didn't it?" A hint of a smile played on his lips.

She bristled, hating him even more than she already did. Hated he managed to manipulate her into coming. He likely didn't know she and Nemea had been corresponding weekly. He used it as bait.

"I'd appreciate it if you left Nemea out of your machinations, Father."

"I'm sure I don't know what you mean." He used his best innocent tone.

It took all her strength not to tell him to fuck off and then get out of there. Still, something kept her from leaving. Under the table, she clenched her hand into a tight fist, her nails digging into her palm. Heat flashed through her. Anger licked up her spine.

"What do you want?" Her voice was thin and tight.

"No small talk, then. You always did like to get right to the point of things." He sipped his drink and peered at her over the rim of his glass. "It's time you stop all this folly and come home."

"Folly? Is that what you think of my career?"

He slammed his glass against the table with a thud. "Galivanting around the human realm with a camera does not make a career."

"My bank account says differently," she snapped. "I've worked my ass off to build a prestigious portfolio but you wouldn't know anything about that, would you?"

"Oh, I know. I know you've been living a lie here. I know about the house in Phoenix and the apartment on Fifth Avenue. I know about your 'secret' messages to Nemea." He put secret in air quotes. He cut a glance to the handbag at her side. "I know about your penchant for high dollar handbags. I know a lot of things."

The blood drained from her head. "Have you been watching me? Having me followed?" She jerked a nod toward Bastian.

"Bastian is one of my best men. Or did you forget?"

She clenched her jaw. "I forget nothing. Least of all what you did to drive me away."

It was something she hadn't thought about in years. She didn't know why she thought of it now, why the sudden horrible memories came rushing to her in a flash of heated emotion. Her father had destroyed her life and taken away the one person she loved. She would never forgive him until the day she died.

"You know why I did it. That's also the reason why I'm here. It's time to come home, Zahra, and fulfill your obligations."

"My obligations? You mean that farce of a betrothal?"

"It's no farce. Marriage to Talal will forge a strong alliance for the Council."

"The Council." She huffed out a heated breath. "The Council can suck it."

"The Council is what helps to provide you with this life of yours so I would show a little more respect." He practically snarled the words.

"The Council has nothing to do with my life in the human realm."

"On the contrary, I've managed to keep them at bay with excuses while you enjoy a life of luxury masquerading as a human. They wanted to hunt you down and bring you back."

"I never asked you to cover for me." It was difficult to keep the ire out of her voice. She didn't believe for one second the Council would come after her.

"And yet you gave me no choice," he said. "I made a promise and so did you. The betrothal is an alliance between our families. I expect you to honor that."

"The only alliance you want with the Council is the one with Herrick and I want no part of that." Her hand tightened, making her muscles ache.

"You will return with me to the Hidden Lands. Even if that means I drag you there myself."

She stiffened at his hard tone. She refused to squirm under the piercing, unrelenting glint in his eyes yet fear spiked through her. He meant business and she knew it. She knew he would make good on his threat to take her out of the human realm because he was just that much of a hard ass. She shifted in her seat, trying to maintain her composure and keep her temper in check. She didn't want him to know he'd flustered her.

"I'm not going back. I have a wedding this weekend and I'm not leaving them without a photographer."

"You'll leave with me within the hour of your own accord or…" He lifted a brow, his lips in a hard, thin line.

"Or what? Threats, Father? Not very parental of you."

"If threats are what it takes to get you back home, then so be it."

White-hot anger went through her making the vein in the side of her head throb. She had to get it under control and quick. If only she had her dragon magic, she could incinerate him here, now.

Or would she? Would she really have the nerve to do that to her own father? He was a bastard, sure, but did he really deserve that kind of fate?

"Threats will get you nowhere and only reinforce what I already think about you."

"And what is that?" He clutched his glass, his nail beds turning white.

"That you're nothing but a bully and have been since I was a child."

His jaw clenched. She could see the tick of muscles as he ground his back teeth. "This arguing is pointless."

"You're right, it is. I don't have time for it. I have the rehearsal dinner tonight and the wedding tomorrow, so if you'll excuse me." She grabbed her handbag and started to slide to the edge of the booth.

"Wait. Please."

His softened tone stopped her. It had been a long time since she heard her father sound almost apologetic. Curiosity got the best of her and she paused, waiting for him to speak again.

"If this wedding photography is so important to you, then I will give you the weekend. Only if you promise you'll return to the Hidden Lands with me Monday."

She stared at him, searching his face for any deception or any hint of lies or threats. He seemed sincere and though she didn't want to return home and plan her own wedding, he was right in that she had obligations there. She'd never wanted to be betrothed to Talal but it had been a deal inked by their fathers and approved by the Council. There was no breaking it.

At last she sighed. "I will agree to return to the Hidden Lands with you, Father."

But what she didn't say was she had no intention of marrying Talal at all. She would find some way out of it.

"Good. Thank you." He paused, looking her over. For a moment, she thought he might smile but didn't. "How about that drink now?"

"The last time we had a drink together I was seven and had chocolate milk." And gods, that seemed like eons ago.

Her mother had just passed away leaving her father bereft. He didn't quite know what to do with her and her younger sister at that point. It was the last time they had been together as a family before the string of nannies came along. He'd hired them to care for them while he worked on the Council and was basically an absentee parent. She didn't know him.

A smile cracked through his rough exterior and, for a moment, she was seven again and he was her hero. The years since had been full of disappointment and bitterness, hatred and anger, rage and resentment. She knew how she got to that point with him, how she didn't want anything to do with him, but did he understand? Did he really get he destroyed her life and every shred of happiness? She doubted it because he was always working in the best interest of the Council. He was helping Herrick groom his son, Talal, for a place on the Council and, ultimately, marriage to her. He'd told her once it would help ensure the fire-drake bloodline.

"Then it's time you and I have adult beverages together."

She wanted to say yes but she didn't want to get that close to him. She didn't want to sit and have small talk with him about nothing and everything. And she certainly didn't want him knowing intimate details about her life. A life she worked hard to build for herself. She had plans to bring Nemea to the human realm soon, though she hadn't shared that with her sister. Nemea wasn't the rebellious daughter she was. Likely why their father favored her.

"I'd like to, really, but as I said, I have a previous engagement." She slipped the strap of her handbag over her shoulder and scooted out of the booth. "I'll see you Monday."

"We'll meet at the Empire State Building at dawn."

"Great."

Zahra turned to go but halted when she saw the familiar man standing a few feet away, his glittering gaze pinned on her. A strangled gasp erupted from her throat as her stomach dropped to her shoes. Her knees threatened to buckle. Sudden hot tears pricked the backs of her eyes. She had come face to face with a man she hadn't seen in years.

Jaxson Lane.

❧ 3 ❧

The last person Jaxson expected to see in Bar Inferno was Zahra. When he saw her unfold her tall, graceful body from the booth and stand, his heart stopped. She looked exactly the same as the last day he saw her. She flipped a lock of wavy rose-pink hair over her shoulder speaking to whoever remained in the booth. Then she turned, spotted him, and froze. Blood drained from her face. A face he could never forget.

Zahra's wild beauty was what attracted him to her. That face of hers was delicately carved with high cheekbones and heart-shaped full lips perfect for kissing. Her honey-colored eyes widened for a brief moment before she managed to get her emotions in check and regain her composure. Her surprise turned to disdain.

"Zahra." Her name came out on a breath and was the only thing he could think to say. He hadn't said it in so long it almost felt foreign on his tongue.

She said nothing as she brushed past him. Her hair swished behind her, her round hips swaying back and forth as she rushed out of the bar.

"Well, well. If it isn't Jaxson Lane."

He recognized that voice. Turning back to the booth, he saw her father, Fenwick Veritor, sitting there looking at him out of his smug face. A face he once punched. His knuckles tingled as he remembered how it good felt to break his nose and see blood spurting out of it.

"And Logan Blake. The Chief Magistrate himself. Isn't this cozy," he added.

Jaxson tensed and surged forward but Logan grabbed his arm and held him in place. What was Lord Fenwick doing in the human realm? He didn't belong here anymore than Lord Herrick did. Alarm bells rang in his head when he realized Zahra had been sitting with him.

"What are you doing in the human realm, Lord Fenwick?" Logan asked, his tone calm and even.

Jaxson recognized that tone. It was the all-business Logan when he was determined to get something done and didn't want anyone standing in his way. He moved to stand in front of Jaxson, placing himself like a shield between the two of them. A wise move since Logan knew their explosive history.

"Not that it's any of your business, but I have matters to tend to here."

Jaxson narrowed his gaze at the man. "Business with Zahra?"

He turned his dark glittering glare on him. "My daughter is none of your concern. I thought I made that quite clear to you when we last talked."

Anger burned deep inside him. His fingers curled into a fist. "It was clear. So was my fist in your face."

"Can I get you gentlemen another drink?"

Meg had suddenly appeared, perhaps sensing the discord between the three of them. She held a serving tray in one hand, her gaze flicking between them and a cautious look on her face. Meg didn't like trouble in the bar and went to great lengths to keep the peace.

"I was just leaving. If you'd be so kind as to close out my tab?" Fenwick said.

Meg was prepared for that. She handed him the check. "I'll take that as soon as you're ready."

But Fenwick was already tossing several large bills onto the table. "No change." He slid out of the booth, came to his full height. Jaxson had forgotten how tall he was, even next to Logan. "Good day, my lord."

And then he sauntered toward the door. One of the men at the bar joined him and together they exited. Only when they were out the door did Jaxson unclench his fist.

"Bastard," he muttered.

"Forget about Fenwick. Go find her, Jax," Logan said. "You can probably catch her before she gets too far away."

"Why bother? Her father got to her first."

Logan raked his hand through his dark hair and huffed out a breath. "Her father is in league with Herrick. They're trying to take down the Council together. They've had men tailing me for weeks."

Surprise flickered through him as he cut him a glance. "You didn't mention this before."

"I'm handling it." Logan glanced toward the door. "Rafe is back in the States in a few days to help me."

"He is?"

Logan merely nodded as Jaxson frowned, surprised he was leaving Andonia and his bride-to-be. Rafe's upcoming royal wedding to Mia, queen of Andonia, was splashed over every newspaper and tabloid everywhere. The former exiled knight had been named the Duke of Montmark prior to the nuptials.

"Did you know Fenwick was here?" He hadn't seen or heard from the man since that fateful day he left the realm. He had only returned for an occasional visit with his parents and to try to convince his father to let him take his mother to safety in the human realm.

"I suspected." He glanced around the bar. "The situation in the Hidden Lands is dire."

Alarm swept through him. His parents were still there. "How dire?"

"I don't expect the Dragon's Breath around the Whispering Mountains will last much longer. Herrick knows he can't save the Hidden Lands without the relics."

"Which you have," Jaxson pointed out.

He nodded. "All but the dragon scale. He sent his Drakana to try to steal them once. Likely they know Zahra is the third one and will go after her next. That's why you have to get to her before they do."

Jaxson glanced toward the door, his heart pumping hard as the fury surged through him. What would they do to her if they caught her?

"You no doubt remember what Herrick did to Mia's father."

He remembered. Herrick used drugs to make the king of Andonia shift into his dragon form and then ripped out his tooth by force. If it hadn't been for Rafe, that would have been Mia instead but he'd managed to keep her safe.

"Go," Logan urged.

Logan was right. He had to get to her before the Drakana, before Herrick.

He hurried toward the door.

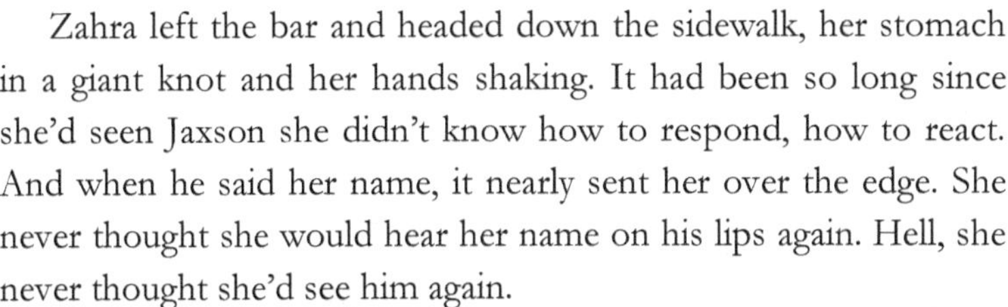

Zahra left the bar and headed down the sidewalk, her stomach in a giant knot and her hands shaking. It had been so long since she'd seen Jaxson she didn't know how to respond, how to react. And when he said her name, it nearly sent her over the edge. She never thought she would hear her name on his lips again. Hell, she never thought she'd see him again.

It had been a long time. So long she'd forgotten what he sounded like, smelled like. Never what he looked like, though. That handsome sun-kissed face had been burned into her mind, leaving an imprint so deep she would never forget those mesmerizing azure eyes, the scruff of beard on his hard, square jaw, the perfect angles of his face in profile. Nor would she forget his tall, broad shouldered, broad-chested form. Or the way the sun glinted bronze off his short-cropped brown hair.

Thinking about it now sent heat surging to her core. She had to stop right now. But, oh, gods, it was hard not to think about him.

She halted at the corner realizing she had no idea where she was. In her furor, she had walked from the bar not paying attention to her direction and ended up in a place she didn't recognize. Whenever she visited New York, she tended to stick close to her own neighborhood off Fifth Avenue.

She avoided Hell's Kitchen because she knew it was a frequent haven for shifters and vamps and other supernaturals. The streets were jam packed with cars, cabs and Ubers honking their way through intersections. Pedestrians crammed the sidewalks as they hustled from one place to the next, some entering the subway tunnels, others hailing cabs and all wanting nothing more than to get home.

When the pedestrian light changed, she stepped into the street. As soon as she did, she sensed someone behind her, closing in. She had been in enough situations like this to know it was typical behavior of the natives. She didn't like it and it put her on high alert. There was always the one chance it could be a purse snatcher. With slow movements, she stuck her hand into her bag and gripped the pepper spray, thumbing off the safety. When she reached the other side of the street, she glanced back over her shoulder.

Two men were behind her stepping into the crosswalk. She took a deep breath and realized they were not ordinary men. They were dragon-shifters and they didn't look friendly at all. She stepped up on the curb and turned left, eyeing the street ahead and looking for a place to duck into. The crowd thinned a bit here as she headed up the sidewalk toward the next intersection. She could hear their footsteps closing in on her and knew they had accelerated.

No one was going to save her here, so she had to take matters into her own hands. Gripping the pepper spray, she slowed her pace to allow them to catch up to her. Her acute hearing tuned into the quickened heavy steps.

As they neared, she spun and pressed the button. She managed to get one of them right in the eyes. He cried out, covered his face with his hands and fell to his knees. Before she could turn the pepper spray on the second one, though, he lunged for her. They collided in a violent crash. He knocked the small canister out of her hand as he wrapped his arms around her, pulling her to him. She screamed, trying to get help from someone, anyone, but passersby ignored her, choosing not to get involved.

The henchman released her almost as quickly as he grabbed her. The sudden absence of him holding her sent her stumbling. She got her balance and took off at a run, putting as much distance between her and the man as she could. For some reason, she glanced over her shoulder and came to a shuddering halt.

Jaxson had the man by the collar and punched him. He staggered backward, falling to the ground next to the one still trying to recover from the pepper spray. He stood over them saying something she couldn't hear. Then he picked up the small canister of spray and turned to face her.

Time stood still. Their eyes met. Her heart fluttered. Her stomach clenched. Her mouth went bone dry. When he headed toward her, prickling desire went through her. He held the pepper spray out to her.

"This is yours I believe."

She took it from him and stashed it back in her handbag. "Thanks."

"You all right?"

"Yes."

He looked back at the men still writhing on the ground trying to regain their footing. "We should get you out of here before they recover and call for reinforcements."

"You aren't going to say something silly like, 'come with me if you want to live,' are you?"

He didn't even crack a smile when he replied. "No."

"Good. Because I can take care of myself."

"Are you sure? Because you look lost to me."

She gritted her teeth to keep from lashing out at him. "I'm not lost. And anyway, how did you get here so fast?"

"Portal," was all he said, his tone quiet and succinct.

Oh, right. She'd forgotten he could do that.

"And you are lost," he added.

"No, I'm not."

"I know you're lying, Zahra."

Her name again. It sent tingles of joy through her which both delighted and annoyed her.

She had also forgotten he could sense when someone was lying. It made their relationship an interesting one. It was hard to keep things from him.

"Let me get you home," he said.

"I can find my own way," she snapped. "I don't need you protecting me."

"As you wish."

She turned on her heel and started back down the sidewalk. He fell in step behind her. She could sense him there, keeping a good distance away from her but following nonetheless. Annoyance went through her as she halted at the next corner, trying to decide which way to go. Jaxson paused right behind her, the scent of him wafting over her on the slight breeze. Her eyes fluttered closed and for a brief second, she inhaled his familiar smell.

"Fifth Avenue is to your right." His voice was dangerously close to her ear. So close, his warm breath trickled over her lobe.

Her eyes popped open, her head snapping to the side. She cut him a sideways glance as he moved to stand beside her.

"I know where I am."

"Liar."

Frustration edged through her. She clutched the strap of her handbag tighter until her hand cramped. "Leave me alone."

"I can't do that."

"Yes, you can. It's easy. Just turn and walk the other way."

"It's not that simple."

She pressed her lips together and clenched her jaw until her back teeth ached. "You are maddening."

"I know." He didn't even smile when he said it.

The light turned green. She stepped off the curb and started to cross the street when she saw a black sedan whiz around the corner. She sucked in a sharp breath as she tried to step back but then suddenly Jaxson was there. He snatched her by the arm and dragged her backward, pulling her into him. She crashed against him. His arm wrapped around her waist as he pulled her away from the curb to safety.

She didn't even have a chance to recover from that, her heart beating a wild tattoo, when another car pulled up to the sidewalk next to them. As it slowed to a stop, the widow rolled down. The next thing she knew she was looking down the barrel of a gun.

Jaxson spun her away from the gunman, his hand clamping on her wrist so tight his fingers dug into her flesh. She barely noticed. Her attention was focused on the gunman who pulled the trigger. A sharp, piercing pain lanced through her shoulder. With a quick glance down, she saw the tranquilizer dart sticking out. In that instance, it was as though all her muscles seized. She went stiff. Had Jaxson not been there to catch her, she would have crashed to the ground. He caught her in his arms, pulling her to him as he dragged her away from the curb.

Her vision clouded but, in her haze, she saw the men get out of the sedan and rush toward them, guns in hand. Jaxson clutched her hard against him, his body tense and rigid. He flung out one hand and drew a circle in the space in front of him. The air crackled and sparked as he opened a portal. Clutching her under the arms, he dragged her through it. But that was the last thing she remembered before she passed out.

✜ 4 ✜

Zahra came to sometime later, her eyes still sealed shut, her head throbbing, her limbs aching. Light pressed against her closed eyelids. It took some doing to pry them open. Her eyes watered against the brightness, making her blink furiously. When she was finally able to focus, she realized the light wasn't as bright as she first thought.

A groan escaped her lips. Her dry mouth felt as though it had been lined with cotton. The last thing she remembered was the dart sticking out of her shoulder. She reached up to feel for it but it was gone. She focused on the unfamiliar coffered ceiling trying to make sense of where she was. She was on a strange sofa in a strange place she didn't know.

Terror sliced through her as she snapped upright, her head objecting to the sudden movement. She groaned again and put her fingers to her head and rubbed.

"Easy."

She knew that voice. Jaxson. He'd been there when she was shot with the tranq gun. He'd caught her, held her against his big body and shielded her from those men. A glass of water appeared in her line of vision. She accepted it, grateful for it as she gave him a small nod. It hurt to move very much. He put distance between them as though he were afraid to stand too close to her.

She downed the water. The cold liquid soothed her parched throat.

"The effects of the tranq should fully wear off in a couple of hours."

"What happened?" Despite the water, her raspy voice croaked the words. "Who were those men?"

"Drakana." He stood at the window peering down into the street, his hands shoved deep into the pockets of his khaki cargo pants. He was nothing more than a silhouette against the sunlit windows.

"Drakana? What do they want?" She breathed out the words, unwilling to believe they were here. Her father's words came back to her in a rush. They wanted to hunt you down and bring you back.

His glittering blue gaze landed on her as he said, "You."

A laugh threatened to bubble up her throat. She swallowed it when she realized he wasn't kidding. His face was lined with a serious expression she had never seen. One that told her he wasn't fooling around. The beginnings of fear trickled through her. They wanted to hunt you down.

Could it be true her father had been trying to protect her all these years while she hid in the human realm? If so, it was the only kind thing he'd done for her since her mother died.

"Why? Where did you bring me?"

She placed the empty glass on the cocktail table in front of her and gave the room a cursory glance. The morning light filtered in from the windows. Dust motes danced in the beams. It was a small living room with bookshelves lining the opposite wall. She perched on the edge of a low sofa in dark blue leather. A cocktail table was in front of her. A blue leather club chair to her left. A white shag rug decorated the floor. Behind her, she could hear the hum of a refrigerator. To her left, a doorway leading to what she assumed was the bedroom and bathroom. This was the smallest apartment she'd ever seen.

"My place and the why is a long story."

"Your place." He had a place in the city? How long had he been here under her nose? "You live in New York?"

"Yes."

"How long have you been here?"

"A while."

She huffed out an irritated breath. She recognized the evasive answers and it unnerved her. If he told her more, then she would grill him for more information and she knew that would only make him clam up and keep his mouth shut. And, really, it didn't matter how long he'd lived in the city, did it? The fact was he was there and so was she. It was only a matter of time before their paths would cross. She'd photographed numerous New York weddings—

Oh, gods. The wedding. She launched to her feet and frantically searched the surroundings for her handbag.

"What time is it? How long have I been here?"

She glanced at her watch. It was nearly nine in the morning. She was due at the cathedral a half hour ago. She had missed the rehearsal dinner the previous night and now she was missing the pre-wedding.

"You passed out when the tranq dart hit you. I tried to wake you, but you were out cold. Whatever they put in that dart was enough to keep you out for several hours."

She swore under her breath. If she hurried, she would have time to fly by the apartment to grab her equipment. With any luck, she would make it to the cathedral before the wedding started.

"I have to go. Where's my purse?"

"You're not going anywhere." He ignored her question and moved to stand between her and the front door. "There may be more of them out there."

Panic skittered through her, her heart beating a wild, frenzied beat. She raked her hand through her tangled hair. "You don't understand. I have to be somewhere right now and I'm late."

But he stood firm. "I'm not letting you leave."

"For god's sake, Jaxson. You can't keep me here."

"No, but it's for your own safety."

She shoved him out of the way and searched again for her handbag. "Since when do you care about that? And where the hell is my bag?"

"Since always. And I hid it from you because I knew you'd try to bolt the second you woke up."

She halted, turned to gape at him. Anger roiled through her. She only wished she could shoot daggers from her eyes. Her hands curled into tight fists.

"I have to get out of here. You don't understand."

"I'm sorry, Zahra. I can't let you leave until I know it's safe out there."

Gods, he said her name again. It sent a little thrill through her to hear it. Even so, she couldn't allow that to deter her.

Her lips peeled back from her teeth in a savage snarl. "You son of a bitch. I'm getting out of this apartment one way or another. I have to be somewhere in the next thirty minutes or—"

She clamped her mouth shut. Anything she had to offer sounded ridiculous. It was her career that was at stake here, nothing more. Deflated, her shoulders sagged. What did it matter if she didn't show up? It wasn't like she would ever work again in the human realm. After all, she was destined to become a councilor's wife in the Hidden Lands.

"Or what?" He folded his powerful forearms over his chest.

Slowly, her hands uncurled. "Nothing. It doesn't matter."

But it did matter. It mattered to her. It mattered to her client. She made a business contract. She promised she would be there to enshrine the couple's happy day forever in photographs. She never shirked a job and she didn't want to start now.

She stomped to the nearby windows and looked out. They were several floors up. High enough to make those down on the street look small and inconsequential. Like her life. Cars rushed through intersections, honking. Somewhere in the distance she could hear the peal of first responders' sirens. She recognized this area as the Upper West Side, not far from Hell's Kitchen.

All this time, Jaxson was here, right on the other side of Central Park from her. How long had he been here? Since the day he left her without saying goodbye?

"It seems to matter a great deal to you," he said, his tone soft and almost caring. "I don't want to keep you here against your will, but I don't want to see anything happen to you, either. They'll find you again and you might not be so lucky next time. Especially if I'm not with you."

"Are you my bodyguard now?" She shook her head. "I don't need your hero shit."

"Zee, please."

She snapped her head in his direction and inhaled sharply through her nose. Zee. Her sister had been the only other one to call her that. But he was the only one who had said it with affection and reverence.

Your heart is mine, Zee. I'm not giving it back and no one else can claim it.

Why did she remember that now? He'd said it to her how long ago? It seemed like eons. As soon as he said it, he snapped his mouth shut and clenched his jaw. She could see the tick of muscles under the scruff of beard even in the half light.

"Do not call me that." Her words were stilted. "Only one person gets to call me that and it isn't you."

They glared at each other a long, quiet moment. Then he stalked into the bedroom and came back out with her handbag. He tossed it on the sofa.

"You want to leave so bad, then go. Get out."

Her emotions raged through her as she made for the sofa, snatched her purse and headed to the door. She didn't look back as she flung it open and then slammed it closed so hard the walls rattled.

She hated him. She hated everything about him. How dare he speak to her that way?

It didn't matter. Nothing mattered. All she had left was her last job as a photographer. If she hurried, she could make it.

As soon as the door slammed and she was gone, Jaxson knew it was a mistake to let her go. He heaved a heated breath and leaned against the closed door, banging the back of his head on the steel door. Once. Twice. He was an idiot. He stared at the sofa she vacated and berated himself for mishandling the situation.

After he dragged her through the portal, he gently laid her on the cushions and then stepped back, standing in the center of the living room watching her sleep. Her angelic face had never looked more beautiful. How many countless hours had he spent watching her sleep? How many times had he traced the soft lines of her face as she slumbered?

He thought of everything he would say to her when she finally woke. He'd tell her immediately about the curse and the dragon relics needed to break it. He intended to talk to her about giving up a dragon scale, returning with him and Logan to the Hidden Lands to perform the blood ritual. In his mind, she would be ready and willing to help. Instead, he'd let his anger over her stubbornness get the best of him. He'd kicked her out like garbage.

And to make matters worse, he'd called her Zee. The nickname had come out of nowhere, pulled from the dregs of his mind and memory. Her face had paled, her lips had thinned, and she looked about ready to murder him.

"For fucks sake," he muttered.

He knew what he had to do. He had to go after her.

He stormed to the bedroom, flung open the closet door. He keyed the passcode into his weapons safe and pulled open the door. It was loaded with knives, guns, and ammo. Since the whole thing started with the Council of Five, he'd been slowly arming himself. He couldn't exactly walk down the streets of Manhattan armed to the teeth, but he grabbed one of his sharpest folding knives and stuck it in his pocket. On a whim, he grabbed the Beretta handgun that was small enough to fit into his pocket.

All he had to do now was find her.

He stalked to the middle of the living room, inhaling the what was left of her essence. That faint signature scent of applewood and lavender. His eyes drifted closed. He reached for that tendril of connection trying to find it. Trying to find her. It had been so long since he'd tried, he didn't know if he could find her again. He had buried it deep inside him, hoping to never resurrect it. He preferred to lose himself in the sweet scent and bodies of other women and gained a reputation as a man who had commitment issues in the process. He knew they were all distractions and nothing more.

There.

The mating between two dragons was different for everyone. No two were alike. When some mated for life, they did it with calm reverence worshipping each other with every breath, every kiss, every caress. With others, it was a wild, passionate, intense mating so powerful, it threatened to tear them both apart. The kind of mating they could not touch each other enough, they could not bear to be parted because of the extreme pain it would cause them.

Zahra and Jaxson did not have the reverent, sweet mating. No. Theirs was of the fervent, obsessive, passionate kind. Perhaps because they had been so young when the mating fever took hold and refused to release them both. They could not get enough of each other and used every possible moment alone to love each other.

Thinking of it now made him painfully hard. He groaned, trying to shove those memories away and concentrate on what he was truly after—the bond between them. After sifting through memory after memory, he finally found the first glimmer of it in the deep, dark recesses of his psyche. She was, in fact, still there. Lingering like a glowing ember.

Jaxson grasped it, pulling it to the forefront of his mind and connecting to her frantic thoughts. She was so panic-stricken about something she didn't know he was there. She bit the tip off her thumbnail as she dashed from a cab and into a posh apartment on Fifth Avenue. She was like a whirlwind through the apartment gathering equipment and then leaving moments later. She had one place on her mind she had to go.

St. Patrick's Cathedral.

$$\backsim 5 \backsim$$

Panic pumped through every vein in her body as Zahra ran from the cab into her apartment on Fifth Avenue. Thankfully, she had all her camera equipment in one place and could grab and go. She kicked off her kitten heels and slipped on her comfy shoes, then paused for a quick glance in the mirror. She ran her hands through her tangled hair, combing through the knots. She swept it into a pony tail. It would have to do. She hoped the bride would forgive her disheveled rumpled attire.

She hailed another cab and begged the driver to hurry to St. Patrick's with promises of a large tip if he could get her there in ten minutes or less. She knew it was asking a lot but he seemed happy to take her cash and drive like a madman.

When they arrived, she tossed bills over the front seat and got out, her camera bag on one shoulder, her handbag on the other. She ran up the steps and hurried inside. Then paused to take a breath. Sweat tricked down her back and misted the nape of her neck. She wished she had the forethought to sweep her hair into a ponytail. She smoothed her sweating palm down the front of her jeans.

The cathedral was a bustle of activity. The florist was busy setting up an elaborate archway covered in flowers. Giant urns with gorgeous flowers flanked either side of the alter. Two women walked up and down the aisle putting lengths of tulle on each pew and tying them with ribbons, bows, and more flowers. A tall man arranged a red runner down the length of the aisle. And every single one of them ignored her.

After several inquiries, she at last found the bride's room and hurried through the back of the church. She could hear the female voices inside. One in particular of the anxious bride. Zahra took a deep breath and knocked. The door flew open a second later. She was faced with a wild-eyed, seething half-dressed bride.

"You! Where have you been? You missed the rehearsal dinner and today you're late. How dare you ruin my day."

Zahra wanted to shrink into oblivion. Instead, she squared her shoulders and looked her in the eye. "I'm so sorry, Kristen. I was struck with a horrible migraine last night and passed out. I didn't wake up until an hour ago."

That was, at least, partially true.

Kristen pressed her lips together and took in her appearance, looking at her from head to toe with disdain.

"Look at the poor dear, Kristen, honey. She looks a fright." This from the bride's mother. Zahra recalled her from the portrait session. "Come in, darling. It's perfectly all right. Are you feeling better? Would you like a glass of water?"

She brushed by the bride and took her by the hand leading her inside. The bride was on her cell phone telling the groom Zahra had finally arrived and perhaps the day wasn't so ruined after all.

"No, thank you, ma'am. I'm ready to get to work," Zahra replied.

"You should be for what I'm paying you," Kristen snapped.

And Zahra wanted to remind her that her daddy was paying her bill, not her. But she kept her cool and her mouth shut as she unzipped her camera bag, snapped on the lens and got to work, somewhat relieved this was the last sanctimonious, high and mighty bride she would ever have to photograph.

Jaxson stood in front of the Atlas statue and kept a watchful eye on St. Patrick's Cathedral across the street. For the life of him, he couldn't figure out what Zahra was doing there. A string of black limos and other cars pulled up to the curb. Beautiful, finely dressed people got out of the cars and headed into the church. A wedding?

Another limo pulled up. Several men dressed in tuxedos got out of the car. They all had boutonnières on their lapels. Jaxson was certain this was the groom and groomsmen who had arrived. This was definitely a wedding. But whose?

He could not stop the burn of jealousy even if he wanted to. Clenching his fist, he crossed the street and headed up the steps, pausing inside the doors. Every row was full and looked like a who's who of New York's high society dressed in couture and looking as though they sucked on a lemon. Pachebel's Canon in D played from the speakers as the men walked down the aisle and took their position at the altar.

The bridesmaids entered from the other side door. The first one made her way down the aisle, smiling a broad red-lipped smile in her pale pink dress. Two more followed. Then the flower girl tossing white petals on the red carpet. The photographer followed them down the aisle, snapping pictures as they went.

His heart thudded hard in his chest when he saw the bride, resplendent in her puffy gown. A twinkling tiara held her veil in place, covering her face as she stood, alone, waiting for her cue.

Everyone stood. When the wedding song started, she took her first step. Jaxson could stand it no longer. He charged toward her, intending to stop her when a glimpse of the photographer caught his eye. He recognized that pink hair swept high into a ponytail.

He froze. Zahra was a wedding photographer? He watched her work, mesmerized by how she managed to capture the bride's walk down the aisle while being unobtrusive at the same time. She skittered to the edge of the church and hurried up the aisle, then pointed her camera at the alter as the bride met the groom. All the while snapping away.

It was incredible. Jaxson took the last pew at the back of the church and sat, alone, and became a spectator in a wedding to which he wasn't even invited. But he wasn't interested in the bride and groom. He was more interested in Zahra and how she managed to work around the couple taking pictures and making sure she captured everything from the vows to the first kiss as husband and wife.

A sharp pain stabbed his chest. He pressed his hand there, rubbing it and willing it to go away. He and Zahra would never marry, despite their mating bond. They would forever be parted because she was promised to another. The betrothal was the one thing standing between them, keeping them apart, and the very reason why he had to get out of the Hidden Lands and as far from her as possible. If he had stayed…hell, he should have stayed. He should have stayed and initiated matrim-duella, the right to fight for her hand in marriage. He could have fought her betrothed and won.

Could have but didn't. He'd left because he promised his mother there would be no bloodshed. That he would honor the betrothal, that he would forget Zahra. That it was better for everyone if he did. What his mother didn't know was he and Zahra had already mated, bonding for life.

But that wasn't the only reason. Zahra's father had threatened him and his family if he didn't leave her. While his life didn't matter so much, he wouldn't put his parents at risk.

So, he left. He couldn't stay in the Hidden Lands and watch her marry another. The very thought of it made him sick to his stomach even now. And when he thought this bride was Zahra, he could have murdered the man standing at the altar waiting to pledge forever.

"Jaxson? What the hell are you doing here?"

Zahra's rough whisper-shout broke him out of his thoughts. He looked up at her, focused on her face lined with annoyance and a hint of curiosity. He had no idea what to say to her so instead he sat there, mute, staring at her like a lovesick teenager.

She scowled. "Stay here. I'll be back."

She hurried to the end of the aisle. He couldn't take his eyes off her round bottom in jeans hugging her long legs and curves. He hadn't really paid attention to what she wore before because he'd been so focused on her face. Her white linen shirt was wrinkled and untucked giving her a sexy, just rolled out of bed appearance. She changed from low heeled shoes to sneakers, her feet silent on the tile floor through the church keeping her mind focused on the task at hand.

The bridal party disappeared out the doors and down the front steps. Zahra followed. He got to his feet and watched the wedding guests file out. A few cut him a scowling glance, eyeing his attire.

And that's when he noticed two men who didn't belong. They stuck out as much as he did. He caught a glimpse of the starburst in the inside wrist of one of them and knew they were Drakana. They both were dressed in black pants, boots, shirt. One had a dagger sheathed at his side. A dagger with a black hilt. If his suspicion was right, it was an obsidian blade. One gave the other a go-ahead nod as they followed the rest of the guests outside. Clearly, they had a plan and were about to engage.

Fear prickled the back of his neck as he followed them out of the church. They headed for Zahra who was unaware of their presence while she took candid shots of the wedding party. He had to act before they attacked her. Likely they wanted her alive and wouldn't hurt her. Even so he had to intervene. Neither had spotted him so at least he had that to his advantage.

He slipped the folding knife from his pocket and flicked it open. Before he could act, the one with the dagger at his waist wielded it and pointed it to Zahra's back. Obsidian blade. Gods, how he hated to be right.

She stiffened and straightened, turning her head to look at him over her shoulder. Even from this distance, he could see fire flashing in her honey colored eyes. As her assailant spoke in her ear, her face drained of color. Zahra lowered her camera giving the Drakana room to wrap an arm around her shoulders and place the knife to her throat.

The bride shrieked. The Drakana barked at her to shut up. He gripped Zahra against him, backing away and pulling her along while the second one waved a gun at the wedding party and guests who threatened to intervene.

Jaxson swore under his breath. This was not going well at all.

He hung back, watching the man back away dragging her with him. A black sedan pulled up to the curb and halted, tires screeching. The second man was at the back door, holding it open giving the first one room to shove Zahra inside the back of the car. He followed, slamming the door behind him as the second man got in the passenger side. And then the car was gone while he stood there and hesitated.

He had to find her and quickly before something happened to her. Before Herrick got his hands on her. In the distance, he could hear the cacophony of noise from the wedding party and guests, their cries of despair and shock as they watched her being kidnapped off the street in broad daylight.

Jaxson melted back away from the crowd, forcing his mind to concentrate so he could tap into that connection between them and find her. It didn't take as long this time for him to locate her. When he did, he sensed her terror and an underlying hint of rage. He sent one clear thought to her, hoping she would hear it.

Hang on, Zee. I'm coming.

The man shoved Zahra roughly into the back of the car and then climbed in after her. Before he even slammed his door shut, she tried the handle on the opposite door. But they had already thought of that and made sure the child locks were on. There was no escape.

"Get us out of here!" the man in the backseat with her barked.

The car peeled out from the curb and entered traffic to a chorus of honks. The driver made the block then headed north on Madison Avenue.

She didn't miss the starburst on the inside of her kidnapper's wrist. He kept the obsidian blade on her as a threat to keep her in line. He was Drakana and so were the two in the front seat. All she had on her was her camera. She'd left all her other belongings back at the cathedral. If she'd had her handbag, she could have at least tried to pepper spray them. These were different goons from the ones that went after her in Hell's Kitchen.

It took a lot of self-control to keep the terror from taking over. Under the surface of her fear, rage bubbled there. Then a thought occurred to her.

Jaxson.

He had been at the church. Had he known something was about to happen to her? Is that why he was there? He must have followed her. With her dragon magic gone, she doubted she could mindspeak to him anymore. Their connection had been broken after he'd ripped out her heart and destroyed it.

Her heart thudded hard in her chest, vibrating through her. She clutched the door handle, her nails digging into the hard material, and gave a sideways glance to the man sitting next to her. All she could do was pray he would find her and the men would pay with their lives.

They arrived at a building ten minutes from the cathedral, the car coming to a halt at the front. The man in the passenger seat was out first. The one sharing the backseat clamped a hand around her wrist and pushed open the door. He dragged her from the car, then pushed her in front of him. He placed the blade at her lower back again. She could feel the prick of the point through her shirt.

He dragged her to the building through the gold-trimmed revolving door and shoved her toward the elevators, the doorman ignoring them. She suspected he, too, was Drakana. They got off on the twentieth floor and entered the corner apartment with windows wrapping around the dining and living rooms giving a panoramic view of the city. The whitewashed walls were unadorned as were the windows. Furniture was sparse. Only a sofa and a chair. He jerked her toward the sofa and pushed her down into the cushions with a warning look that said not to move.

"Who are you?" She used her best authoritative voice.

"You'll find out soon enough." The one who put the blade to

her throat took out a cell phone and dialed. "We're at the safe house."

He ended the call after a brief moment of silence, then took up his post at the windows. The second man was stationed at the door in case she tried to run. It was the only exit she could see, but then, Jaxson didn't need a door to enter. All he needed was a portal.

"You'll die for this," she told the man at the window.

He scoffed at her. "Not likely."

A shift in the air around her made her senses go on high alert. It crackled and sparked. She knew that sound. She stiffened and watched as a hole erupted in the space near her and then, suddenly, Jaxson was there. He stepped through and wasted no time. He pulled a gun and shot the man at the window first, then spun and killed the one at the door before he had time to react. And then it was just the two of them.

He stashed the small handgun back in the deep pocket of his cargo pants and met her gaze. Her heart fluttered when she saw the fierce warrior look on his face. He hadn't even broken a sweat stepping through the portal and killing the men.

"Are you hurt?" he asked.

"No."

"Good." He held a hand down to her. "Let's get out of here before they realize what's happened."

She didn't even hesitate to slip her hand in his. His warm, strong fingers closed over hers as he pulled her up from the sofa. He created another portal and together they stepped through.

$$\approx 6 \approx$$

The cold from the portal pierced through her, freezing the air in her lungs. A breath shuddered out of her in a fog and seconds later they were on the other side back at his tiny apartment. He released her hand as soon as they were through. The portal closed behind them.

She removed the camera from around her neck and placed it on the cocktail table. Then she sank to the sofa, wedging herself into the soft cushions, and watched him prowl the room checking the locks on the doors, the windows. He disappeared into the bedroom and returned a moment later, as though making sure there was no one lying in wait for their return. When he was finished, he moved to stand across from her. Their eyes locked as he stood there, arms crossed over his chest. He wore a gray three-button Henley with the sleeves pushed to the elbows, khaki cargo pants, black boots, and a look of shear annoyance on his face.

Zahra had forgotten so many things about him. The way he stood as though he owned the world with feet shoulder-width apart. How he walked like he was pissed off at everyone even when he wasn't. The fine hairs on his forearms. The visible veins on the backs of his hands. And those brilliant blue eyes that were like azure jewels winking in the sunlight.

She bit her lower lip, remembering the way his mind used to brush hers. It had been so long since she'd felt that, she'd forgotten what it was like. His voice had been a warm comfort there. Like curling up with your favorite fleece blanket on a cold winter's night wearing your favorite pajamas and sipping Earl Grey. A crackling fire the only light in the darkness.

"Stop," he said. The words came out terse and harsh.

Her brows knit. "Stop what?"

"That memory. You're projecting it."

Oh, gods, that was a memory. A memory of a night they'd shared. The night they'd mated. She'd pulled on his oversized t-shirt and pajama bottoms and wrapped herself in a plaid fleece lined blanket. He brought her a cup of steaming tea and they sat together, in companionable silence, in front of the fire while snow fell outside, muffling any sounds except for that of the fire. Her body had throbbed desire for him even when he wasn't touching her.

She hadn't meant to project the memory, if in fact that's what she as doing. She didn't know how she could since she hadn't the magic to do it. And if she wasn't projecting the memory, that meant he was still in her head. Annoyance flared bright.

"I wasn't, so get out of my head," she snapped.

As soon as she said it, the warm feeling disappeared. It confirmed what she knew—he was in her head and pulled abruptly away. Which meant he somehow still had a connection to her. Why, then, didn't she still have that connection to him?

"Those men were Drakana," he said.

He didn't want to admit he'd been in her head, so he changed the subject.

"Yes," she agreed. "And the doorman of that building was also Drakana."

"How do you know?"

"The kidnapper kept the obsidian blade on me as we entered and he ignored us. I merely assumed that's what he was."

He looked thoughtful. "Likely. Do you believe me now the threat is real?"

She considered. It hadn't really crossed her mind until then. She assumed the men on the street in Hell's Kitchen were typical thugs. But now with her semi-successful abduction attempt at the cathedral...she swallowed the bile that rose to her throat. They wanted to hunt you down.

Her father's words haunted her. Had he sent them after her?

"I guess I have to believe you but I don't know what this is all about." She waited but he offered no other information. "Do you?"

"It's complicated."

Frustration edged through her. She leaned her head back on the cushion and closed her eyes, trying to maintain her cool. She didn't know if she should ask for more information or wait for him to volunteer. Either way, she didn't think she'd get the full story.

Her stomach growled a gnawing sound that reminded her she hadn't eaten since yesterday. Fatigue smacked into her, throbbing to her very core. It was only then she realized how horribly hungry and tired she was. She hadn't fully recovered from the tranq gun, nor had she taken care of her own needs. She'd left Jaxson's place and went straight for hers and then to the wedding.

"I'll get us some food and then we can talk."

She cracked her eyes open and watched him through slits as he moved like a prowling feline to the bedroom. When he returned, he had changed from the Henley into a black t-shirt that hugged every muscle he had. Through the material, she could see the fine outline of his shoulders, collarbones and, above the scooped neckline, the hollow of his throat.

Heat pulsed through her as she looked at it and a sudden memory burst into her mind. A memory of her dipping her tongue there, sampling the salty sweet taste of his heated skin.

"Stop." The word edged out through clenched teeth. His hands fisted at his sides.

She blinked, clearing the memory from her foggy, tired mind. He must have seen it, too, which meant he was once again in her head.

"Get out and stay out of my head." She practically growled the words.

He huffed out a breath. "I can tell you're tired—"

"In my head again?"

His jaw clenched, the muscles ticking along the edge. When he spoke, the words edged out through his thinned lips. "You have dark circles under your eyes."

"Oh." Her cheeks flushed with her embarrassment.

"You can take a shower if you want. The bathroom is through there." He pointed to the bedroom. "I'll get us some lunch."

"I don't have clothes."

"I'll bring you some."

She stared at him, stunned. "How?"

He rolled his eyes. "There's these places called stores. You might have heard of them." Then his gaze raked up and down her. "I think I remember your size."

Desire flashed through her, wild and furious. She didn't want him to think of her size or anything else but at the same time…he remembered her size? Instead of basking in that, she lashed back. "I don't need your dripping sarcasm."

"And I don't need your pompous attitude."

Pompous? Was she?

"You carry a three-thousand-dollar purse, Zahra."

She sucked in a sharp breath and snapped upright. "And I earned every penny to pay for it."

She didn't miss his quick and cutting glance to her camera sitting on the cocktail table.

"I'll be back." He turned on the toe of his boot and was gone.

Herrick arrived at the apartment doubling as the safe house for his Drakana and the place he deemed as his headquarters in the human realm. He'd bought the building and stationed his men inside it as the doorman and other workers from security to maintenance. He unlocked the door and tried to open it but something heavy was wedged against it. He gave it a mighty shove. When he finally got it open, he saw the obstruction—one of his men, dead.

He stepped over the dead man and into the apartment. His second man was dead by the window. Both of them shot in the head.

The fury rose up fast and hot inside him as he surveyed the scene. Who could have infiltrated the apartment, killed his men, and taken the woman? All without breaking down the door? The place looked virtually undisturbed.

Herrick left the apartment and went back down to the lobby. He flagged down one of his security men.

"Call someone and have the mess in apartment 20B cleaned up, will you? Also, I want to see video surveillance of everyone who entered and exited this building in the last two hours."

"Yes, sir."

His man radioed for a cleanup crew without question. Likely he understood why Herrick was asking. Then he followed him from the lobby to the security room and waited while he pulled up the video surveillance. He saw where his men brought the woman through the front revolving door, but she hadn't left between the time his man called to alert him they were at the safe house and Herrick's arrival. Nor had anyone else arrived.

"She never left through the front door, did she?" he asked. It took a lot of control to tamp down his anger.

"No, sir," he agreed.

For the second time, she had managed to slip out of his grasp. He needed the girl. As one of the last fire-drakes, he needed a scale from her dragon form. Since Fenwick wasn't willing to force her return as they discussed, he would take the girl by force and get what he needed. Then he could marry her off to his son and begin the creation of his legacy.

How was it possible she was able to leave the apartment without being seen on the security cameras? It had to be one of Logan's men but which one? Possibly the same one who thwarted the attempt to apprehend the girl in Hell's Kitchen. The same one who helped Rafe and Logan at the warehouse in Brooklyn.

He already had his hands full with trying to recover the Blood

Stone and the cold-drake dragon tooth Logan managed to steal from him. He had yet to find out where Logan was hiding the relics. He had his best men watching and waiting for the right moment to infiltrate the Chief Magistrate's home, but the place was like a fortress. He had installed new security measures that made it difficult for his men to get past.

"Will there be anything else, sir?"

He didn't know who the man was helping Zahra, but he intended to find out and make him pay for stealing the girl out from under him.

"Was a portal opened?" he asked.

The man gave him a blank look as though he didn't understand what he asked. Herrick huffed out a sharp breath.

"A portal can be opened by a few of shifters who have that magic. Do you know if a portal was opened?"

"I don't know, sir."

"Well, find out. And stop wasting my time with your dumb looks."

The man gave him a sour look but turned back to the console and picked up his cell phone. Presumably to call someone who could help him find out if a portal had been opened. Herrick's phone buzzed in his pocket. Fenwick was on his caller ID.

"Fenwick."

"Are you tracking my daughter?" His tone was edged with frustration. Herrick could only imagine the vein pulsing at the side of his neck.

"I think I've waited long enough for you to make good on your promise to bring her home, Fenwick. You've left me no other choice."

"I told you we would return after the weekend. You couldn't give me two days?"

"Someone is helping her," he said, ignoring his question. "Do you happen to know who?"

Silence pressed against his ear. Finally, he said, "I have an idea."

"Good. Then I still have a use for you. Meet me at the

apartment building and we'll discuss."

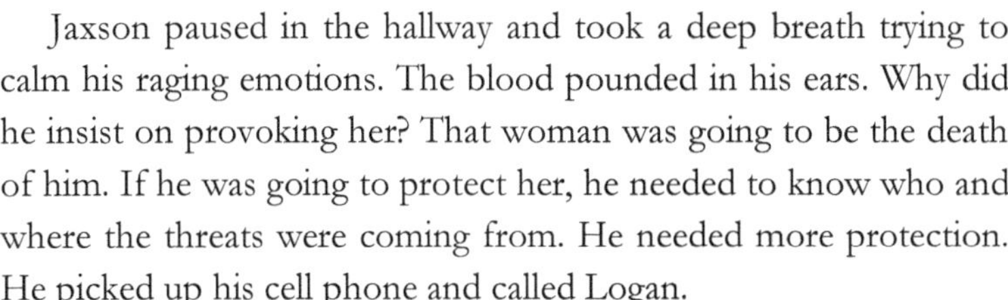

Jaxson paused in the hallway and took a deep breath trying to calm his raging emotions. The blood pounded in his ears. Why did he insist on provoking her? That woman was going to be the death of him. If he was going to protect her, he needed to know who and where the threats were coming from. He needed more protection. He picked up his cell phone and called Logan.

"I hope you're calling to give me a progress report," Logan said by way of answering.

"By progress report if you mean there have been two attempts to kidnap her, then sure." He headed down the hallway to the elevator and punched the button.

"Two?" There was a wariness in Logan's voice.

"Once on the street in Hell's Kitchen yesterday. Once today at St. Patrick's Cathedral."

"Where is she now? Is she all right?"

"She's at my place but it's not safe, Logan. I can't hide her there. It's only a matter of time before the Drakana track her. I had to use a portal."

"I'll talk to Rafe. Maybe he has some ideas."

Rafe owned real estate all over New York City plus a place in the Hamptons and a cabin in the mountains. He'd been in the human realm a long time and had amassed a hefty portfolio. He was a wealthy man now engaged to the ruler of Andonia.

Then, as an afterthought, Logan added, "I can't leave Bree and the baby. Herrick's men have been watching the place for days."

Cold tendrils of fear crept up Jaxson's spine. "He's watching you?"

"Don't worry about me. Worry about Zahra."

"I assume Herrick's men are after her, too, aren't they?" Jaxson asked.

"Yes." Logan's voice sounded tired. "He's wasting no time

trying to get to her before we do. Have you talked to her yet?"

Jaxson stepped out of the elevator and stalked toward the building exit. "Not yet. There hasn't been time. I'm out to pick up food and clothes for her."

"We don't have much time—"

"I know that, Logan, but she doesn't have any idea what's happening or why. She may know what she is, but I don't think she realizes how important she is. It's not going to be easy explaining that to her."

A beat of silence passed, then Logan said, "I know this isn't easy for you and I hate putting you in this position. But you're the only one who can do this, Jax."

"I know." He heaved a sigh. "I'll find a way to tell her. I've managed to get her away from the Drakana twice. Maybe she trusts me a little now."

"Good luck."

Jaxson hit end and headed out of the building towards Hell's Kitchen.

❧ 7 ❧

With Jaxson out of the apartment, Zahra took the opportunity to rummage through the fridge. All he had was half a block of moldy cheese, one egg, a few condiments. She slammed the door, the half-empty jars ratting, and then took to the cabinets. A can of expired tuna and a box of stale saltines resided among plastic dishes.

What did the man eat?

She padded to the bedroom and glanced around. The mismatched décor was simple and suitable for a bachelor. The unmade bed was in the center with a what looked like a TV tray table beside it doubling for a bedside table. A well-worn dog-eared paperback of To Kill A Mockingbird was open and upside down next to a cheap-looking lamp.

The closet door stood open. Amidst the hanging clothes, she could see a large safe with a dial. Curiosity got the better of her. She approached, noticed the door was ajar, and nudged it open. Inside was a small arsenal of weapons. Knives in all shapes and sizes, a handgun or two, ammo. Surprise flickered through her. She had never known him to own any type of weapon before. But then, she didn't know him well anymore, did she?

She made her way to the bathroom where she could see only the bare necessities. Toothbrush, tooth paste, shampoo, hand soap. She found a clean towel and pulled it from the cabinet over the toilet. Then she went back into his bedroom and searched through the dresser drawers looking for something clean and comfortable to wear when she halted. Tucked neatly under a pair of black socks was a picture she hadn't seen in years.

Her. Him. That night in his father's country cabin in the early onset of winter. The first heavy snows had trapped them there for a few days. Together. Alone. They were young and stupid and so incredibly hot for each. She had snapped the picture as a self-portrait with an old camera she always carried around with her. He had one arm around her, holding her close, his lips pressed against her cheek. His hair was longer then. A stray stand had fallen over his forehead. Her smile was brilliant, genuine. And the joy on her face was unmistakable even though she wasn't looking at the camera. She'd been looking at their entwined fingers. It had been one of the first pictures she'd ever taken.

That had been so long ago.

The picture had faded. She flipped it over. The handwriting—hers—on the back was also faded but she could still make out what it said. Us. Forever.

Her heart lodged in her throat. Hot tears stung the backs of her eyes. He had kept this picture all this time. For all these years. That had to mean something. Even if he did leave her without saying goodbye. Even if he did break her heart into a million pieces.

She tucked the photo back underneath the socks and moved onto the next drawer. There she found a pair of men's pajama pants and white t-shirt. She snagged them out of the drawer and padded back to the bathroom hoping at hot shower would wash away the swarm of feelings she couldn't begin to name.

Jaxson returned to his apartment carrying an oversized shopping bag with clothes and shoes for her. He'd also stopped by the cathedral and managed to talk his way into getting her handbag and camera backpack she left behind. He didn't want to acknowledge the guilt sweeping through him when made the dig to her about her purse. She had looked so indignant and offended. He'd tucked the oversized bag in with the clothes and slung the backpack over his shoulder. In his other hand, he cradled a bag of take-out from Bar Inferno.

He stuck his key in the lock and pushed open the door and immediately halted. Zahra sat on the sofa cross-legged staring at nothing. Her damp hair hung over one shoulder. Damp circles dotted the white shirt she'd managed to steal from his dresser. He hadn't really expected her to take him up on his offer of a shower but she had. Even from this distance he could smell the faint hint of his soap lingering on her skin.

She didn't move as he shut the door and made his way toward her. He dropped the shopping bag and the backpack on the floor in front of her and then went to the kitchen to divvy up the food. Her gaze followed him the whole way, then she leaned forward to inspect what he'd brought her.

A soft gasp escaped her. She lifted the handbag and held it up for him to see.

"My backpack and handbag. How did you get these? I left them at the church."

"I have my ways," he said.

He didn't want to tell her about the barrage of questions he got from the priest on duty at the cathedral about her abduction. He'd mentioned the bride had been so upset about it she had broken down shortly after and it took a lot of consoling to calm her down. Jaxson assured the priest Zahra was shaken but quite safe now. The relief on his face was evident.

"Thank you." She dropped it on the sofa next to her, then poked around in the bag some more. "And thanks for the clothes."

"Hopefully I got the sizes right."

She held a shirt in the softest cotton he could find and looked at the label. Then her fantastic gaze met his. He thought he could see the beat of her pulse in the long column of her neck.

"You did." She inhaled slowly. Exhaled just as slowly.

"Hungry?"

"Famished." To punctuate her point, her stomach rumbled again. She rose from the cushions and made her way to the kitchen, pausing in the doorway to watch him.

He opened the take-out containers. One with a burger dripping with cheese and a side of fries. The other with a cobb salad.

"When did you take up photography professionally?"

He knew he'd promise her they'd talk when he returned. His question was an effort to keep the conversation off the topic of the Drakana and Herrick for as long as possible.

"It was never a conscious decision to do it professionally," she said. "I sort of fell into it."

"Lady's choice." He waved toward the food, then grabbed a plastic fork and handed it to her.

She took the salad and headed back into the living room. She sat on the floor, placing the container on the low table in front of her, and stretched her long legs out.

"I'd like to see your pictures some time." He grabbed the burger and followed her lead. He sat on the edge of the sofa with the take-out container in his lap.

She snorted. "Sure, you would."

"I really would." He thought of the picture of the two of them he'd tucked away his sock drawer. He hadn't looked at it in a long time. Somehow, he'd managed to keep it all these years. Even when she wasn't trying, she was an accomplished photographer.

Us. Forever.

The words she'd written on the back floated through his mind for the first time in ages.

She shoved aside the half-eaten salad and reached for her camera. Climbing to her feet, she moved to sit next to him on the sofa as she flicked it on. She thumbed through the pictures she took earlier that day. All he could see was a flash of color. The images flipped past in quick succession on the tiny LCD screen. Then she halted on one and turned the camera around for him to see.

It was the smiling bride, holding her bouquet while one of the bridesmaids adjusted her veil. The woman looked absolutely radiant.

"One of my bridezillas." She snickered. "She was a beautiful bride but very demanding."

He said nothing as she turned the camera back toward her and thumbed through more pictures.

"I have a fairly large portfolio now and mostly do weddings. Some lifestyle photographs. Portrait sittings and such. But my true love is landscape. It doesn't pay the bills, though."

She turned the camera around to him again. His breath pooled in his lungs. He hadn't expected to see a picture of his homeland. The Hidden Lands. But there it was. The Crystal Lake, sunlight sparkling along the clear waters. Lush green trees dotted the shorelines, the sun slanting through the limbs. Overhead, a brilliant blue sky scattered with puffy clouds.

"That's beautiful," he said.

"I've traveled a lot of places taking pictures, but the one place I love to photograph the most is home. I guess I never downloaded these. I can't even remember when I took it."

She turned the camera back around looking at the picture with such longing he could tell it had been a while since she'd been back.

"How long has it been?" he asked.

"Since what?" She turned her head, met his gaze.

"Since you've been home. To the Hidden Lands."

A faint smile tugged at the corner of her mouth. "Is it that obvious?"

It was to him because it had been awhile since he'd been home. And he missed it like he missed her. There was a gaping hole deep in his chest, in his psyche, dark and aching and full of longing and loneliness.

"My father wants me to come home." She clicked the camera off and put it on the table. Then she moved back to the floor and took up her fork again.

There was something in the way she said it that indicated she wasn't all that keen on returning home to the Hidden Lands. Did she know about the curse? Did she understand if she returned with her father, the very atmosphere they breathed would likely kill them?

"And you don't want to go?"

"My life is here." She fiddled with her salad, pushing lettuce around in the container. She wouldn't meet his gaze. "I've been here a long time. I have friends here. Work. I don't exactly want to give all that up."

He sensed there was something else, something she wasn't telling him. She tugged her lower lip through her teeth and stabbed a tomato. Finally, she gave up and tossed the utensil down. She huffed out a breath and at last looked up at him.

"You haven't touched your food."

He'd been holding the container of now cold food, forgotten. He placed it on the table next to hers. "Guess I'm not that hungry."

She gave it a brief glance, then stole a fry. "So, what's the story?"

"What do you mean?"

She gave him a look of disdain. "Don't play dumb with me. You said we'd talk when you got back. Start talking. Why are those Drakana after me?"

Zahra was never one to mince words. He'd always liked that about her. Until now. When he was faced with telling her the truth and making her understand the dire situation in the Hidden Lands.

"Because you are something they want."

A pale pink eyebrow lifted. "And what is that?"

"A fire-drake."

She rolled her eyes. "Duh. I've been one all my life."

"Then I'll clarify. A fire-drake of the Rindhara bloodline."

Silence. She stilled. He wasn't even sure if she breathed. She stared at him with her wide honey-colored eyes for a full ten seconds before she shook free of the shock and reached for another fry. If he hadn't been watching her closely, he wouldn't have seen the imperceptible shake of her hand.

"That's ridiculous. The Rindhara died out ages ago."

"No." His voice was flat.

Her gaze flickered back to his face as she held the fry halfway to her mouth. "Yes."

"No, they didn't and you're living proof."

"My father would have told me that. He never mentioned it. Not once. Not ever."

"Perhaps your father doesn't want you to know the truth."

"Perhaps my father doesn't know the truth at all," she retorted.

He sighed. "It is the truth, Zahra."

"How do you know?"

He could see her ire rising as frustration raked through her. He wasn't getting through to her. She wasn't listening and didn't want to listen. How could he even answer that question? He knew because Logan told him because of something he'd read in his father's journals. Journals Jaxson had never seen. Not that he thought Logan would lie about such a thing—he wouldn't. But he had no tangible proof to give her.

"You don't know, do you?" She flung the uneaten fry into the salad. "You're trying to scare me into staying here and doubt my heritage."

"Why would I do that, Zahra?"

"I have no idea. You're the mastermind here. Did you follow me into that bar in Hell's Kitchen, too? Is that how you knew I was there?" She launched to her feet. She took a step, turned, took another, then huffed out a breath. "Gods, I can't even get away from you in this tiny apartment."

"I did not follow you." Somehow, he managed to keep his voice calm despite the agitation raking through him. "I didn't know you were there. I didn't even know you were in New York City."

"Sure, okay."

"For fucks sake, Zahra." He launched to his feet.

The words exploded from him before he could stop them. Before his brain could tell his mouth to hold his tongue. The outburst made her halt, take a step back from him. Her eyes went wide as surprise etched across her face. She clutched her elbows, crossing her arms over her chest as if a cold breeze had stung her exposed skin. Gooseflesh prickled her arms.

Jaxson raked a hand through his hair. "Everything I've told you has been the truth. I have no reason to lie to you."

"No, I suppose you don't. Especially since we haven't spoken to each other in, what, nearly a decade?"

He stared at her, silent. Had it really been that long? He'd never allowed himself to dwell on the expanse of time that had passed since the last time he saw her. Now that she'd voiced it, he couldn't quite believe it. From the day he left her, remorse and guilt had been etched upon his heart, his very soul. He'd lost her then. He never thought they would speak to each other again, much less stand mere feet apart in the same room.

She scoffed. "Don't look so surprised, Jax. Or didn't you know it'd been that long?"

"I knew." But his voice cracked a little when he spoke.

She said nothing more as she stalked by him. She snatched up the bag of clothes and her handbag as she went by. The slamming of the bedroom door followed. He sank to the sofa, dropping his head back on the cushions and expelling a hot breath.

He hadn't a clue what to do next.

❧ 8 ❧

As if in answer, someone knocked on the apartment door. Jaxson's eyes flew to the closed door. Caution and suspicion pounded through him as he got to his feet and went to the door to look out the peephole. The tension subsided as he opened it to Rafe.

"Rafe?" Jaxson held the door open for him.

He gave him a nod of greeting as he entered the apartment. Jaxson closed the door behind him.

"Logan said you needed help."

He halted in the middle of the living room and glanced around, as if surveying it for every entrance and exit. His gaze paused on the camera sitting on the table and the discarded food for two.

"Where is she?"

He knew instantly who he was talking about. "In the bedroom not talking to me."

"Because she knows the truth?" He turned to look at him. There was a sense of hope etched on his face. Rafe wanted to return to the Hidden Lands as much as Logan did.

"Because she hates my guts."

Rafe cracked a rare smile. "I doubt she hates your guts." He paused, glanced at the closed door. "Logan told me about her…and you."

"I'm surprised he didn't write a memo and email it to the entire Council."

Jaxson couldn't stop the flicker of annoyance moving through him. He stepped around Rafe and into the kitchen. He opened a cabinet and pulled down two highball glasses and a bottle of bourbon that was half empty.

"He's trying to help you and so am I," Rafe's voice was rough. "I went through something similar not so long ago."

Ah, yes, with his cold-drake princess. He poured two fingers neat in each glass and headed back to the living room. He handed one to Rafe.

"I smelled her on you before." Rafe took the glass but didn't drink.

That stopped him cold. His fingers tightened. "When?"

"At the cabin. I knew you had a mate even then. I just didn't know who she was until Logan told me. You're right about it not being safe here for her or you. Herrick has his Drakana all over the city."

"So, what do you suggest? Go into hiding? That didn't work so well for you or your princess."

"It did for a while."

He gave him a coy grin. They both new what happened when he and Mia hid out in the cabin. Jaxson had been there because he'd been stabbed by an obsidian blade. Rafe was the only one who had the antidote to the poison. Rafe reached into his pocket and pulled out a set of keys. He held them out to him.

"Not that you need a getaway car since you can open portals."

"Portals draw unwanted attention not to mention opening and closing them drain my power. I'm only good for a few in a short period of time." Jaxson took the keys, glancing down at the BMW emblem on the fob. There was another key that looked like a house key. "Why do I need a getaway car?"

"Take her to my cabin in the Adirondacks. Try not to destroy it like Logan did my place in the Hamptons, eh?"

"You have a place in the Adirondacks, too?"

Rafe's response was a mere silent nod as if it was common knowledge. Jaxson wasn't surprised. Not really. He never realized how many different places Rafe owned all over the city and state.

"Are you sure?" He clutched the keys in his fist, the cold metal biting into his skin.

"I'm sure. Logan and I will buy you some time here in the city while you get her out of here."

Heat flickered through him as he thought about being alone with Zahra in a cabin in the mountains. They were barely getting along here in the apartment. He couldn't imagine being stuck with her indefinitely in an isolated place like that. They may end up at each other's throats even more than they were now.

"I'm not even sure she'll agree to come with me."

"Convince her," Rafe said.

He almost laughed. "As if it's that easy. You don't know her."

"I know enough. She's a fire-drake. She's a royal. And if she's anything like Mia, she's stubborn and opinionated."

Rafe was definitely the voice of experience. He'd had his hands full with Mia. But something he said caught Jaxson off guard. When Logan mentioned she was Rindhara nobility, it hadn't occurred to him it was an ancient royal bloodline.

"What do you mean she's a royal?"

"I thought you knew?"

He shook his head. "I know she's of the Rindhara bloodline."

"Right. Royal. Like the Gildhara."

A cold prickling sensation went through Jaxson as the blood whooshed from his head in a rush. The Rindhara royal clan, along with the Gildhara, had once ruled part of the Hidden Lands eons ago. Most of them had died out.

"Logan didn't tell me that."

"Likely he assumed you knew," Rafe said. "I need to get back. Mia doesn't like when I'm away from her for very long."

"She came with you?"

He flashed a grin. "Did you hear about it in the news? It was all over the local morning shows. And I don't like being parted from her for very long, either. Not in her condition."

"What condition is that?"

"She's pregnant."

The news surprised Jaxson. His brows went up. "You two work

fast."

"It hasn't been formally announced yet. We're waiting until after the wedding."

Jaxson could see how happy he was to know they were expecting their first child. "Congratulations are in order then."

He remembered the glass he held then and lifted it. They clinked and both downed the bourbon in one gulp. Rafe placed it on the cocktail table and headed to the door.

"Don't linger here. It's only a matter of time before Herrick discovers you're hiding her."

"We'll leave as soon as possible," he promised.

Rafe gave him a satisfied nod. He opened the door and was gone.

As soon as the door closed behind him, the bedroom door popped open. Zahra stood in the doorway with her arms crossed over her chest.

"If you think I'm leaving the city with you, you're crazy."

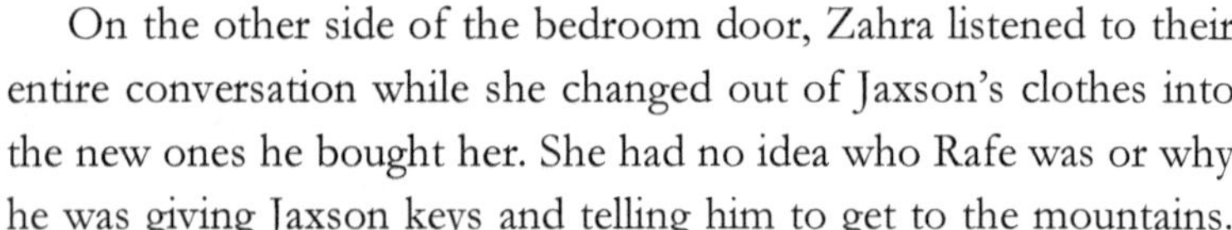

On the other side of the bedroom door, Zahra listened to their entire conversation while she changed out of Jaxson's clothes into the new ones he bought her. She had no idea who Rafe was or why he was giving Jaxson keys and telling him to get to the mountains. Nor did she particularly care.

But what had piqued her interest was when he mentioned she was of the royal Rindhara bloodline. More new information. How did this person know Logan? Clearly, the new Chief Magistrate trusted him enough to share with him who and what she was. That didn't mean she trusted him.

And the very idea of going into hiding with Jaxson, of all people, nearly sent her into an apoplexy. She couldn't—wouldn't—be alone with him and nothing he could do or say would change her mind.

Jaxson stood with his back against the apartment door. As the sun dipped toward the horizon, the shadows in the room deepened. Even so, she could see the consternation on his face. His lips had thinned, his jaw had clenched, and she could tell there was an acid retort he wanted to say but didn't.

"I'd tell you to be reasonable, but that ship has sailed."

She willed a snappy comeback into her mind but nothing came. Instead, she watched him stalk to the kitchen and pour another drink. She eyed the half bottle of bourbon and wondered how she'd missed it in her search of his kitchen cabinets earlier. She hated bourbon but she would down a gulp if only to feel the burn to the tips of her toes.

Jaxson must have sensed her need for the liquor. He pulled down another glass from the cabinet and poured her one. He slid the glass to the edge of the kitchen counter.

"What? No acid retort?" he asked.

She padded to the kitchen and snatched the drink. Holding it in her hand, she could smell the oaky scent wafting up to her.

"Tell me why I should go with you."

"I thought that was fairly clear with the two attempted abductions." He took a sip.

Zahra had chalked those up to being nothing but coincidental. But maybe there was more to it than she thought. They were Drakana after all. And her father had insisted she return with him to the Hidden Lands. She was supposed to meet him at the Empire State Building in a little over twenty-four hours.

"But why do they want me? And I want the truth, Jax."

At the mention of his nickname, his hand tightened around the glass, the nailbeds turning white.

"I already told you. Because of who and what you are."

"That's not an answer and you know it."

He slammed the glass on the counter sloshing the amber liquid. "What else do you want?"

"I want to know why. There has to be some reason besides who I am. Why do they want me? What is it about me that's so bloody special? And what does Lord Herrick have to do with this?"

His face drained of color. He snatched up his glass and turned away from her. She could see the tense muscles in his back rippling under the shirt. He downed the drink and banged the empty glass against the counter again. So hard, in fact, it cracked.

"Lord Herrick is leading a rebellion against Logan to take over the Council of Five and the Hidden Lands."

The hair on the nape of her neck lifted. Her heart kicked into high gear and rammed against her chest. She stared, unblinking, at Jaxson while a million things whirled through her mind. Was that why her father wanted her to return to the Hidden Lands with him and marry Talal? Was her father in league with Herrick and this rebellion of his? If he was, why? What did he hope to gain? He already had a permanent seat on the Council. At least until his death at which point his seat would then pass down to his male heir, which he didn't have. Yet.

But married to Talal and the birth of a child could follow soon after that. Talal would inherit his father's seat while their son, should they have one, would inherit hers. Her stomach clenched.

"You didn't know, did you?" His voice softened.

"No." The word came out on a faint whisper.

"He leads the Drakana. This past winter, he and his men launched an attack on the country of Andonia. He tried to take over the obsidian glass forges so he could start making weapons."

She'd heard about that in the news but didn't give it much of her attention. She had been busy with her business. There was also something about a missing princess…Princess Mia.

Wait. Rafe was marrying Princess Mia, now queen, of Andonia.

Understanding dawned. It still didn't explain how Jaxson was involved.

"There's more but I'm not sure you're ready to hear it now."

"Tell me," she demanded.

"The only thing that's standing between him and the Council is Logan. Herrick would sooner see him dead than as Chief Magistrate," he said.

"Why the sudden hatred?"

"He doesn't think the clans should be leaving the Hidden Lands."

Her head snapped at that. She'd heard nothing of the sort. "Since when?"

"Since the air has turned toxic."

She was stunned into silence. If the air was toxic, why, then, would her father even want to return? She was missing some crucial bit of information Jaxson wasn't sharing with her. Either he didn't know it or he didn't want to tell her.

"I don't understand," she said, her voice still faint.

"I didn't either until recently. Then Logan explained it to me." He paused, as if choosing his next words with care.

"Explain what?"

"The Hidden Lands are dying, Zahra."

❧ 9 ❧

Zahra stared at him, not fully comprehending. "What do you mean? The Hidden Lands are dying?"

In all her communications with her sister, she had made no mention of it.

He shoved his hands deep into his pockets and walked to the wall of windows, his back to her. "How long has it been since you've been home?"

"I don't see what that has to do with—"

"How long?" He turned to face her.

Bewildered, she searched her memory as she calculated how long it truly had been since she went home. She couldn't remember the last time and avoided it like the plague. Mostly because she didn't want to deal with her father or the farce of a betrothal. A betrothal that was soon to come to fruition. She had left the Hidden Lands shortly after Jaxson broke her heart. She pressed her lips together in a thin line.

"That long, huh?" he said.

"And you?" She lifted her chin a little higher.

"I left last year when Logan came through a portal to fight for his right to lead the Council of Five. I haven't returned."

Her brows crinkled. She didn't know about any of that. All she knew was Logan was appointed Chief Magistrate and now led the Council. Her father made no mention of it to her when they had their last discussion. She removed herself far from the goings-on of the Council and politics.

"You didn't know about that, either, did you?"

She shook her head.

"That's a story for another day. Our homeland is cursed, Zahra. The air is turning toxic. It's wiped out a few clans. That's why others are migrating here. But there are a few who are determined to remain behind."

Like her father. And Herrick and his son Talal.

Holy Gods. Her knees weakened and threatened to buckle. She stumbled back to the sofa and collapsed into the cushions. She rubbed the tight skin at her temples at the onset of a headache.

"What happens to those left behind?"

"They become ill. It doesn't affect everyone the same way."

"What kind of illness?"

Nemean mentioned nothing of being ill, either.

"It's like they're slowly being poisoned. For some, it takes years until the illness kills them. Others, only months." His mouth was set in a grim line.

She thought of her sister who seemed to be happy and healthy back in the Hidden Lands. If the air in the Hidden Lands was toxic, there was no way she would go back there. But then, she couldn't leave her baby sister there, either.

She thought of her father who was here in the human realm, waiting for her to meet him at the Empire State Building at dawn on Monday. She had no interest in marrying someone she wasn't in love with. Before she could ask more questions, he continued.

"There is a way to break the curse." He paused, his hands still in his pockets as he looked at her with that piercing azure gaze.

She didn't like that look. It made her stomach flip. "Are you going to share this with me?"

He sucked in a deep breath through his nose then blew it out through his mouth. "I'm not sure you're going to like it."

"Just tell me," she snapped. Frustration edged through her.

"Logan found a way to do it through his father's journals, but it requires three relics—the Blood Stone, a tooth from a cold-drake and..." He paused and visibly swallowed.

"And?" she demanded.

"And a scale from a fire-drake."

The blood drained from her head so fast, she saw dark pinpricks dancing in her vision. She dropped her face into her hands, trying to alleviate the lightheaded feeling.

"And that fire-drake is me, I suppose." Her words were muffled against her palms. Her head snapped up. "Find someone else."

"There is no one else, Zahra. You have the ancient bloodline of the Rindhara. Without you, the curse can't be broken."

"There is someone else. My father—"

"Is not so willing to cooperate," he said, matter of fact.

She cut him a glance, those pinpricks once again dancing in her vision. She suspected her father didn't want to cooperate because he was already working with someone else. Someone like Herrick. Cold dread settled in the pit of her stomach. And Nemea was out of the question. She wouldn't volunteer her for that.

"How am I supposed to give you a scale? Shift into my true form and let you yank one out?"

He didn't like the way she phrased it. A dark glower creased his face. "You'll have to shift, yes, but—"

"Well, I won't do it."

The panic nearly seized her as it bubbled up into her throat. How was she supposed to tell him she couldn't shift? She didn't have any of her dragon magic anymore. Not since…she shut off that part of her mind. She would not think of it. Not now. He had been able to sense her thoughts before. She didn't want him to sense that.

He said nothing as he looked at her, his hands still deep in his pockets. "That's why the Drakana want you. Why Herrick wants you. He wants to use you to break the curse first so he can be the hero of the realm. Using that as leverage, he then intends to fight Logan for control of the Council."

And why her father was determined to get her back to the Hidden Lands and marry her off and, no doubt, produce an heir.

"Without you, we can never go home."

She never wanted to go home in the first place. Now, between

Jaxson and her father, they were forcing her to make a decision she didn't want to make.

"Just be quiet, all right?" She shot to her feet. "I don't want to hear any more about the Hidden Lands or Herrick or any of it."

She snatched up her bags and stormed away to the bedroom, slamming the door behind her. As she leaned against it, she closed her eyes and tried to calm her wildly beating heart. Even if she wanted to help him, she couldn't. She'd lost her ability to shift.

What was she going to do? She couldn't return with her father because he would expect her to marry Talal.

Either way, she was screwed.

Jaxson watched her storm away and heaved a sigh. That didn't go well at all. He had hoped he could get through to her. Instead, she shut down and refused to listen any more. When Logan said he was met with resistance from her, he thought it was because she didn't want anything to do with him. Now, he wasn't so sure. Her angry reaction made him wonder if there was more to it than simply refusing to help. Perhaps there was a reason why she didn't want to help them.

When he told her he left last year, that was only partially true. He had been in and out of the Hidden Lands numerous times before then. When Logan was set to fight Archer, he left and hadn't returned. His mission to help Logan had become more important than returning home. That and stopping Herrick and his Drakana.

If Zahra refused to help, then he wasn't sure how they would ever break the curse.

He walked to his closed bedroom door and paused outside it, straining his ears to listen. He could hear nothing. He gave a faint knock.

"Zahra, will you open the door?" Silence. "I know you don't trust me or even like me anymore. I can live with that. But what

I'm telling you is the truth. Do you really want to see our realm die?"

"Go away," came her muffed words.

He wanted to yell at her, but that wouldn't do any good. He wanted to tell her she was being unreasonable, but he doubted she'd listen. He wanted to fling open the door and kiss some sense into her, but he didn't think she'd be all that receptive.

Trying something different, he said, "Logan told me he came to see you. He said you didn't want to talk to him." Silence again. He took a deep breath and plowed on. "He said, Zahra, he could smell you on me."

Saying the words to her aloud sent a ripple of emotion through him. Everything from fear she would reject him again to desire. His inner dragon had been quiet since he'd made contact with Zahra again. He didn't understand why. But there was one thing he did understand—Logan was right. They were still a bonded pair.

The door cracked open. She pushed it wide, her eyes downcast as though she was afraid to meet his gaze.

"He said that?" Her voice was a whisper.

"He did."

Her lashes fluttered upward and, at last, her gaze met his. That beautiful honey-brown gaze that was so clear, he could almost see into her soul. As they looked at each other, his inner dragon stirred. It emitted a contented sigh as though it finally realized she was here with him.

"He did come see me," she said. "I didn't want to hear what he had to say. I slammed the door in his face." Color stained high in her cheeks as she blushed.

He knew. Logan told him. He held his breath, waiting to see what her next move was while he waited. He didn't want to move for fear it would scare her away. This was the closest they'd managed to get to each other since Bar Inferno.

"I shouldn't have done that. We were all friends once."

He could see the memories playing behind her eyes. He had them, too. Memories of the three of them, almost inseparable, in the Hidden Lands as they hit those certain coming-of-age milestones together. First Flight. Ka daeko. And, for her, kah daeka.

"We can be again," he said.

At that, he could see the pulse in her throat quicken. "I'm not so sure about that."

"I am."

"I want to believe we can, Jax, but I…need time."

She had extended the proverbial olive branch. If time was what she needed, he would give her all the time in the world if that meant she'd come back to him.

"You'll get no pressure from me." And he meant that. He didn't want to lose her again. But if she truly wanted to sever the mating bond, he would find a way to do it. "You have my word."

She chewed on her lower lip and nodded. "Thank you. Now, tell me about this place we're going."

❧ 10 ❧

She must have been insane to agree to leave the city with him. The last place she wanted to go was the Adirondacks. She hated being in a place where there wasn't a Starbucks on every corner. It wasn't civilized and she'd gotten used to civilization in her time here in the human realm. Zahra only agreed because Jaxson said it was the safest place for them.

Besides, she didn't want to return with her father to the Hidden Lands. If she wasn't in the city at dawn tomorrow morning, then she couldn't very well do that. It was hard to assuage the traitorous feelings running rampant through her. She had, after all, promised her father she would be there. The thought of returning and marrying Talal made her stomach cramp to the point she wanted to hurl.

"I don't get it. Why don't you just open a portal and take us there?" She pulled on the seatbelt.

"Because portals take a lot of energy, even for me." He tossed the duffle he'd packed in the backseat.

"And Rafe owns this place in the Adirondacks?" she asked as Jaxson slid behind the wheel of the BMW. She tucked her handbag under her legs. She'd decided to leave her camera bag behind in his place for safekeeping.

"Yes. And this car."

"And who is he exactly?"

"He was the Exiled Knight."

"Was?" she asked.

"Was," he agreed. "No longer."

"How is that possible?"

"Logan released him from exile, that's how."

"I thought the Exiled Knight was a myth."

She glanced over her cuticles trying to sound bored as they pulled out of the parking garage and into traffic. In truth, the subject had always fascinated her. She knew all about the Exiled Knight. He had been a legendary knight banished to the human realm for all eternity. Everyone knew the story. She never imagined he was actually a real dragon-shifter.

"Not a myth. He's lived here long enough to amass wealth and property all over the state."

"I assumed that since we're in his BMW. I need to swing by my apartment before we leave."

"I don't think that's a good idea. It's too dangerous."

"I need my things, Jax."

"The Drakana are still hunting you. They won't stop hunting you."

"I'm aware of that but a five-minute stop at the apartment isn't going to attract any attention."

His hands tightened on the wheel, his knuckles turning white. She didn't miss the scowl on his face, either. "The Drakana could be watching your place."

"Then it's a good thing my bodyguard came with me."

He glared at her, unappreciative of her flippant tone. She flashed a smile.

"It won't take me long. I just need to pick up some clothes and toiletries. I can pack a bag in a flash. Five minutes. That's all I need."

"Five minutes it's all you'll get. Got it?"

She huffed and rolled her eyes. "Yes, Dad."

He scowled again at her jab.

They made their way around Central Park to Fifth Avenue. She directed him to park at the curb and wait for her, but he ignored that command and put the car in park.

"I'll be back before you know it." She gathered her purse and pushed open the door.

"I'm not letting you go up there alone." He opened the door and got out.

"You're in a no parking zone."

He gave her a dark look across the top of the car that told her he wasn't taking no for an answer. She shrugged.

"Okay, but if you get a parking ticket, I warned you."

"Parking tickets are the least of my worries."

He grabbed the oversized duffle bag from the backseat. She knew the bag was stuffed full of weapons. They entered through the revolving door. As they walked through the lobby, she was aware of a few people scattered throughout, which wasn't unusual at this time of day. But there were two in particular that stuck out. Trying to ignore the warning bells in her head, she led him to the elevator and punched the button. As they waited for the elevator, two more men arrived, flanking them. Next to her, Jaxson stiffened and she immediately sensed the tension in his body.

She cut a glance to the man on her right. He was tall, broad-shouldered with dark hair. Her gaze drifted down to his wrists, but she couldn't see if there was a starburst there or not. The hairs on the back of her neck stood on end as she realized Jaxson was right. These men were here for her and nothing else. These men must be Drakana. She didn't have to see the starburst on the inside of his wrist to know it was true.

The elevator dinged and the doors whooshed open. She stepped inside, her nerves jangling. Jaxson followed on her heels then turned immediately and blocked the door with his free hand. One of the men tried to push his way into the elevator.

"Sorry, this one is full," Jaxson said.

But there were two of them and only one of him. Together, they surged forward and shoved Jaxson inside the elevator. She stumbled to the back corner, trying to avoid a collision with him. One of the men punched the button to the top floor as the doors closed and they started to ascend.

Jaxson squared off with the first one while the second one

made eye contact with her. She didn't like the way he looked at her, as though she were nothing but a piece of meat. She cowered in the corner, clutching her handbag close to her body. She had no weapons.

The duffle Jaxson carried thumped against the floor. He and the first Drakana squared off in the tight space, fists up. Jaxson threw a punch, grazing the guy's cheek. The second man reached for her, grabbed her by the upper arm and jerked her into him. She slammed against his chest. He wrapped an arm around her and pressed the tip of a blade against her ribs.

"Stand down," the man holding her said. "Or I'll stab her."

Jaxson cut him a glance, realizing she was held captive. He dropped his fists and met her gaze.

"Don't listen to him, Jax," she said.

He jabbed the point of the blade into her side. She could feel it pricking through the thin material of her shirt. The other Drakana snatched up the discarded duffle. Jaxson never broke her gaze. She could see his mind working behind those dazzling blue eyes and knew he was coming up with a plan to get them out of there. Whatever he was doing, she wished like hell he'd do it faster.

"You won't kill her," Jaxson said. "You need her alive."

"I can take her in as damaged goods and still get what we need," the Drakana replied.

The elevator dinged and came to a halt. The doors opened. The first Drakana ripped a gun out of the duffle. He waved Jaxson out of the elevator with it while the second dragged her into the hallway. This wasn't her floor but it didn't matter. She'd abandoned the idea of getting to her place and packing a bag. Now it was about survival and escape. And then later he would likely say I told you so.

Her mind raced as the man dragged her down the hallway, the second one and Jaxson following. Then she heard a thwak as flesh met flesh. She turned her head, trying to see behind her, but the man still had hold of her and kept the blade pressed against her side. He made her keep moving.

Another smack followed by several grunts and then a loud thump, as if a large body fell to the ground. The next thing she heard was the gunshot and the Drakana holding her let her go with a shout. He reached for his shoulder and slumped toward the wall. Zahra spun around to see Jaxson holding the gun, the other Drakana on the floor behind him unconscious. And the duffle bag sat at his feet.

"Drop the blade and get away from her," he snarled.

She had never heard him sound more menacing. Something like desire uncoiled deep inside her as she kept her gaze focused solely on him. The rage etched along the lines of his face would be terrifying to anyone but her because she knew him more intimately than anyone.

The Drakana tossed the blade to the floor. He stumbled away from her. She bent and picked it up, wrapping her fingers around the onyx hilt. As she suspected, the blade was obsidian. Rainbows of light danced along the knife-edge. Jaxson waved her toward him.

As she hurried to him, he snatched up the duffle and backed toward the elevator, stepping deftly over the unconscious Drakana.

"Get to the elevator," he said to her under his breath.

He kept the gun pointed on the two Drakana as she hurried to the doors and punched the button. A second later, it dinged. They entered and the door whooshed closed. Before she could push the button to her floor, he stabbed the first floor with his index finger. Then he turned his dark look on her. It was almost enough to make her shrink away.

"But I—" she started.

"No. We're getting out of here. No more stops."

She opened her mouth to protest.

"I mean it, Zahra."

Even though he didn't voice it, his face and eyes conveyed the annoyance and the I told you so look which made her cringe.

He held out his hand for the blade. "I'll take that."

She handed it over. He dropped to the floor, unzipped the duffle and stuck it inside. All she was left holding was that of her handbag.

She should have apologized and admitted he was right. Instead, she pressed her lips closed and said nothing else as they descended in silence. Once the elevator stopped, they hurried out of the building and into the balmy evening air in time to see a cop leaving a ticket on the windshield of the BMW twenty yards up the street.

He growled deep in his throat, making his whole body vibrate next to her. She bit back her own I told you so because she was too focused on how that throaty growl sounded. Her traitorous mind remembered that was the way he sounded when they were naked, together.

It was a memory that flashed through her mind with such clarity, it surprised her. She sucked in a gasp. His head snapped in her direction as he swallowed hard, his throat working with the movement. And she knew, in that instant, he somehow saw it, too. He took in a deep breath, blew it out.

"Lavender," he said.

She flushed, her cheeks so hot she feared they burned bright red. It was her favorite scent. She'd dug out the small bottle from the bottom of her purse and spritzed it on her wrists when she was hiding in the bedroom. She cleared her throat.

"I tried to warn you," she said, nodding to the departing cop.

"Hopefully, Rafe isn't too mad when I tell him I got a parking ticket. Let's go." He motioned toward the car a few feet away.

Zahra took one step toward it as the car exploded in a ball of fiery flame. Jaxson reacted by slamming into her from behind. He wrapped his body around hers and dragged her toward the building as debris rained down around them. He crushed her against the wall, shielding her from the heat and the flames. For a moment, she forgot they were in danger as she reveled in the way his body felt crushing against her.

"Are you hurt?" He was so close to her, his warm breath brushed along her cheek. The unexpected sensation made the hairs on the back of her neck stand on end.

"I'm fine," she managed to say.

When he moved away from her and pulled away his warmth, it left her feeling cold. She glanced down the street at the destroyed car.

"So much for that parking ticket," she said. "Now what?"

"Now we find another way to get there."

"Why don't you just open a portal?"

He shook his head. "No portals. They attract too much attention."

"It appears we have already attracted attention."

Her gaze was pinned on the two men moving down the sidewalk toward them. Jaxson swore under his breath.

"He's certainly determined, isn't he?" she said.

He took her by the hand. "Come on."

Spinning around, they headed in the opposite direction of the men. Not that it did much good. Ahead of them were more Drakana. These men openly carried weapons and she realized then they were willing to kill him to get to her. Fear tingled through her. Fear that Jaxson would be killed because of her.

If only she had her dragon magic, she could actually do something besides stand there like a helpless waif.

"Maybe you should rethink that portal idea," she urged.

He didn't reply as he wrapped an arm around her waist, pulled her to him with a snap, and waved his hand in a circle before them. The portal opened and a second later they stepped through.

They ended up in a place she didn't recognize. It appeared to be another apartment building. Without wasting time, Jaxson dragged her down the corridor to an apartment at the end of the hall. As they passed closed doors, she realized they were on the twentieth floor.

A quick knock on the door and a second later it opened. Rafe stood on the other side.

"What are you two doing here?"

"We ran into some trouble." Jaxson pushed his way inside as Rafe closed the door.

He looked as though he had just rolled out of bed. His button-down shirt was open and untucked from his jeans. He was barefoot. His hair stood on end.

Zahra did her best to ignore the way he looked and focused instead on her surroundings. The large contemporary apartment was furnished with lavish décor. Floor-to-ceiling windows with opaque shades blocked out the bright flashing lights of Times Square lighting up the night. Beyond the windows, a jungle of skyscrapers. Classic black and white furnishings filled the room— two white sofas, a white shag rug and black accents.

"You arrived here on foot, didn't you?" Rafe's tone was flat as if he already suspected something happened to his car.

"Sorry about the car," Jaxson said with a nod.

A woman with long silver hair emerged from the bedroom. "Jaxson, what a surprise. We weren't expecting you."

This woman had to be the princess. When her rumpled appearance matched that of Rafe's, she knew they interrupted their sexy time. The heat of embarrassment flashed through her.

"No, we weren't." Rafe gave Jaxson a pointed, annoyed look.

"We need a place to lay low until we can get out of the city."

"You were supposed to already be out of it." Rafe's brow lifted as he glanced from Jaxson to her.

"We were delayed," Jaxson said.

She waited for him to blame her for that delay because of her insistence she stop for her things. But he didn't. It endeared him to her.

"You can use the spare bedroom." Rafe motioned to a closed door down the hallway. "I'll order dinner."

At the sound of dinner, her stomach rumbled. In all the excitement, she'd forgotten about her half-eaten salad at Jaxson's place. Jaxson gave him a nod of thanks, took her by the hand and led her to the room where he shut the door behind them and leaned against it.

"I guess we arrived at a bad time," he muttered.

When she glanced his way and saw his sheepish grin, she could not stop the laugh that bubbled up her throat.

❧ 11 ❧

To hear Zahra's bubbled laughter nearly knocked him to his knees. That melodious laugh of hers was something he had missed and he didn't even know it until he heard it again. She sucked in a breath, smiling at him as if he'd told the funniest joke ever.

"What's so funny?" He didn't mean to sound gruff or annoyed, but it came out that way.

Her smile faltered. "Nothing. I guess I'm tired."

She padded to the bed and dropped her handbag on the floor. She plopped down on the edge, leaning back on the heels of her hands. She dropped her head back, looking up at the ceiling. The site of the expanse of her throat did not do him any good. Seeing it made a memory flash through his mind of planting long, slow kisses along the length to her shoulder, then down, down, down to other parts of her he hadn't seen or thought of in years.

There was an unmistakable tightness in his groin as he hardened. He angled his body away from her so she wouldn't see. He ran his hand through his hair trying to make the boner go away. Zahra could always illicit that reaction out of him, though.

"We'll stay here for a while. Maybe you should get some sleep."

"And what are you going to do? Stay up all night?"

"Yes," he said without hesitation.

She rolled her eyes. "You have to be as tired as I am."

And then she patted the bed next to her in invitation.

He stared at her hand for a long, silent moment. His eyes met hers. Those tawny, lion-like eyes that seemed to glow in the evening shadows. There wasn't a hint of seduction or malicious intent on her face. The invitation was a sincere one.

"It's been a long day," he agreed with a nod, "but I don't think that's a good idea."

"Why? Don't you trust yourself around me?" She smirked, the corners of her mouth lifting ever so slightly.

"Aren't you a funny girl." He said it deadpan.

"You used to think so."

"Not being with you for the last decade, I'll have to get back to you on that."

She frowned at the reminder of their separation.

"Sorry. I shouldn't have said that."

"No, you should have. Because it's the truth, isn't it?" She clutched her elbows. "I never thought I'd see you again. Then, that day in Bar Inferno, there you were."

"That was Friday," he reminded her.

"Was it? It seems so long ago."

He couldn't agree more. It seemed as though a lifetime had passed since he was in the cathedral, envisioning her as the bride behind the veil. In that moment, he realized how much he had regretted leaving her and how much he wished he could go back and do everything over again. His relief was palpable when he discovered she was not the bride at all.

"I'm supposed to meet my father at the Empire State Building Monday at dawn." Her voice warbled a bit when she said it, as though the thought of doing so pained her. "He wants me to return to the Hidden Lands with him to fulfill my promise."

She wouldn't look at him. He knew what that promise was. It was that betrothal neither one of them wanted to mention. He waited while she kept her face turned up to the ceiling, looking at it as if it was the most interesting thing in the world.

"I don't want to go, especially now that I know the Hidden Lands are toxic."

His palms broke into a cold sweat. "What will you do?"

Zahra dropped her head and met his gaze. There was a hard set to the line of her jaw as she looked at him, determination and stubbornness lining her face. "I'm going to the Adirondacks with you."

His mouth went dry. He could hear the truth in her words. "Is that what you truly want?"

"I think it's pretty clear to both of us I don't want to return to the Hidden Lands to marry someone I don't love." Her voice was soft as she spoke. "My absence will stall the marriage ceremony. They'll have no choice but to release me from my vow."

"You and I both know what will never happen. Once a marriage contract is sealed, there is no breaking it."

It was why he left the Hidden Lands. He had no hope of ever getting her back, so why stay? He had no intention of seeing her marry someone else.

"I refuse to believe there isn't a way to break it," she said.

"There's only one person who has the power to break a marriage contract."

She gave him a quizzical look. "Who is that?"

"The Chief Magistrate."

"Logan." A breath fluttered out between her lips.

He sensed her delight. Logan had been their childhood friend. If there was a way to break it, he would find it.

"I'm not going back there," she said again.

"So, you're using me to run away from that problem."

For a moment, fire flashed in her eyes until she realized he teased her. Then she smiled. "I suppose I am."

He walked to the edge of the bed and sat next to her. In an unexpected move, she placed her head on his shoulder. Surprise flickered through him at the small gesture. He wasn't about to say anything that would make her stop leaning on him.

"Logan has his father's journals and Rafe knows about the Old Ways. I could ask them to look into it," he suggested.

"It?"

"Breaking the betrothal."

She stilled. He didn't even hear her breathing. She lifted her head from his shoulder. He turned to look at her. Their faces were merely a breath apart.

"You would do that for me?"

He would do anything for her. Hell, he'd die for her. The words flickered through his mind, but instead he said, "If you'd like."

She dragged her lower lip through her teeth. "I'll think about it."

Then her gaze drifted down his lips. He wanted to kiss her. To see if it was as still spectacular as it was all those years ago when they were young, and stupid, and hot for each other. So hot for each other they would find any excuse to be alone, to spend stolen hours in each other's arms.

Zahra tipped her head to one side. An invitation? Or was she testing his resolve? He remained where he was, waiting for her to make the first move. She leaned in closer to him, her lips a breath away from his.

A knock on the door made them spring apart as if they were two teenagers caught by a parent. Jaxson got up from the bed and stomped to the door, flinging it open. He tried to act as casual as he could, but it was hard to slow down the furious pound of his heart. Rafe stood on the other side holding a bag with grease stains along the bottom and the logo for Bar Inferno emblazoned on the side.

"Don't make a mess, eh?" He shoved the bag at Jaxson.

Jaxson closed the door. He turned, holding up the bag. "Cheeseburger and fries?"

Her stomach rumbled so loud in response, she blushed. "Yes, please."

She dropped to her knees on the floor next to the bed. He did the same and placed the bag between them. They made a makeshift table with napkins spread along the carpet. Jaxson dug out the takeout boxes with the aromatic food permeating the small bedroom. She immediately dug into one of the burgers. She was definitely a girl with a healthy appetite.

There was something intimate and yet awkward about them

sharing a meal together on the floor. It brought back more memories of them together in that cabin when they mated. Jaxson's stomach was in knots and he suddenly lost his appetite. He pushed up from the floor.

"You want a drink?"

"Sure."

He left the room and found Rafe in the kitchen pouring a whiskey. While it wasn't his alcohol of choice, it would do.

"How's it going in there?" Rafe nodded toward the bedroom door.

"Give me one of those, will you?"

He lifted an eyebrow in amusement. "That good, huh?" He handed over the highball. "You can't stay here forever. The Drakana will find you."

"I know. They already tracked us to her place. That's where we were when we had an issue with the car."

"What sort of issue?"

"They blew it up. That kind of issue."

Rafe seemed unfazed by the destruction of his car. "You and Logan are the reason why I can't have nice things."

His friend said it in jest, but it made Jaxson wince. Logan had shifted into dragon form in his house in the Hamptons and destroyed it. The cabin in the mountains west of the city had been destroyed when they were ambushed and Princess Mia was kidnapped. Now the car.

"Sorry about the car."

"Eh. Forget about it. You better get back in there. And take this. You might need it." Rafe shoved the whiskey bottle at him.

He took it and headed back to the bedroom. He could hear Rafe snickering as he walked away.

By all the gods, Zahra had nearly kissed him. What was she thinking? Had she lost her mind?

Oh, she knew what she was thinking. She was thinking how delightful those lips of his looked. How much she wanted to taste them again. How much she wanted to remember what kissing him felt like once again. It had been so long since their last kiss.

She should have never invited him to sit next to her in the first place. That was an invitation to disaster, to heartache, to disappointment. And yet she did it anyway. And when he finally sat next to her, what did she do? She rested her head on his shoulder. Because she needed to feel the safety and security, the warm comfort of someone. And not anyone. Jaxson.

When he left, she forced her the erratic beat of her heart to calm. But it was impossible to make it stop. She was a bundle of nervous energy with no place to direct it. So, she finished her cheeseburger and her fries, completely wrecking her diet. She'd sworn off all that bad food years ago when she decided to work out and eat healthy.

She knew what she needed—she needed to meditate to get her mind back in the right place. And by right place that would be off Jaxson and his sexy lips. She dug around in her handbag for her smartphone and opened the app that played her calming music. She shoved aside the empty takeout container, crossed her legs, placed her palms flat on her knees and closed her eyes. She breathed in deep, exhaled, breathed in, exhaled. Everything was starting to feel right again when the door flung open. She knew Jaxson stood there staring at her. She didn't have to open her eyes to know that.

"What are you doing?" he asked.

"Meditating."

"I brought whiskey."

Her eyes popped open. She stopped the calming music and stuck the phone in her front pocket. Then she held out her hand for a glass. "Screw meditating."

Chuckling, he gave her the glass full of the amber liquid. She swirled it, wondering how she could pretend to like it when all she really wanted was to feel numb.

"You should know Rafe has exceptional taste in whiskey," Jaxson said.

"Does he?" She downed the drink, letting it burn down to her gut. And then the strangest thing happened. Her eardrums warmed as if she were standing inside a sauna.

Jaxson refilled her glass, then his. They clinked in a toast and then drank again.

Never in her wildest dreams would she have thought she'd be doing shots of whiskey with the man who used to be her lover while sitting amid takeout trash on the floor of a swanky apartment.

It was the best time she'd had in a long while.

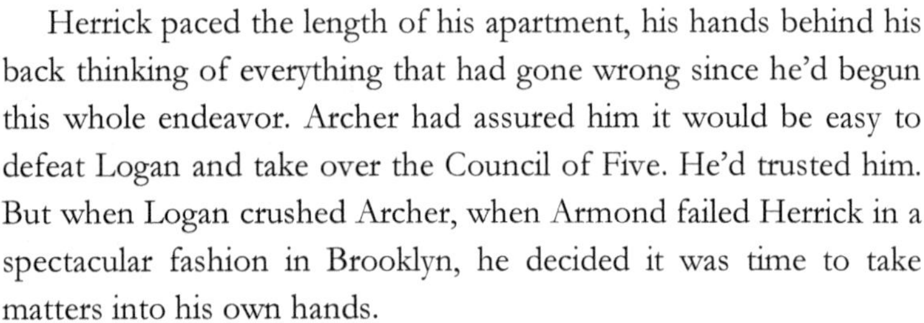

Herrick paced the length of his apartment, his hands behind his back thinking of everything that had gone wrong since he'd begun this whole endeavor. Archer had assured him it would be easy to defeat Logan and take over the Council of Five. He'd trusted him. But when Logan crushed Archer, when Armond failed Herrick in a spectacular fashion in Brooklyn, he decided it was time to take matters into his own hands.

Killing Logan's parents had been the first step in that. He'd relished doing the job himself. He hadn't counted on old Eli Blake to have the forethought to use a portal and Dragon's Breath to send his son through to the human realm. It had been his last act of defiance.

He'd lost the Blood Stone to Logan when he defeated Archer and took over the Council. Herrick had made it his mission to destroy him.

The building he'd purchased had once been apartments. He didn't need much, but he needed to be out of the human's prying eyes. He'd recruited Armond's Drakana forces to continue their work with him, promising the leaders large payouts and plots of land in the Hidden Lands when he took it over. Even Armond couldn't complete the job Herrick hired him to do. Now, not only did Logan have his hands on the Blood Stone, but the cold-drake dragon tooth.

If Herrick and his men weren't able to get the fire-drake scale before Logan, all would be lost. If Logan had all three relics, then he was sure to break the curse on the Hidden Lands first. Herrick was doing everything in his power to thwart those efforts.

He stood at the window, hands behind his back, staring out at everything and nothing. For all his planning, nothing had gone right. Archer was dead. Armond was dead. All he had left was his son Talal, and his fellow councilmember, Fenwick, and he hadn't managed to retrieve his daughter to return to the Hidden Lands.

Frustration edged through him. When he discovered it was Nyles' son, Jaxson, helping her elude them, it took every ounce of self-control not to return to the Hidden Lands and kill the man. He would be dead soon enough, anyway.

He heard the door to the apartment open and close and then heavy footsteps. The scuff of his feet told Herrick he'd stopped in the doorway.

"I did what you asked," Talal said. "I tracked his portal magic and found them."

"Where are they?" His voice was calm, quiet.

"Hiding out in the dragon knight's apartment."

"Send a group to retrieve her. Orders are to kill whoever gets in the way. I am your bride alive and unharmed." He turned his head, looked at his son over his shoulder. "Understood?"

He nodded. "Yes."

He dismissed him with a nod of his head. Then he picked up his phone and called Fenwick. When he answered on the first ring, he said, "We found them."

❦ 12 ❧

Zahra laid on the floor and peered up at the wavering ceiling. She was highly tipsy bordering on the edge of a drunken stupor.

Jaxson sat on the floor with his back against the wall opposite the bed. Somehow, he managed to stay upright, though she wasn't sure how he did it. Why wasn't he drunk out of his mind? She was, at least, coherent enough to remember the last time she was shit-faced. That was when Jaxson left her. She'd gone on a three-day bender, drowning her sorrows in the bottom of a vodka bottle.

That had been the most painful part of her life. She could live with the horrible betrothal—she was certain she could find a way out of that. She could live with the thought of her father hating her guts for defying him. She could even live with never returning to the Hidden Lands.

She could not live with the thought of leaving her sister behind. Her mind had been working on a way to get her out of the Hidden Lands since Jaxson told her they were dying. She hadn't yet come up with a way to do that.

She glanced at him leaning against the wall, his eyes closed. It had been hard to take when he abandoned her. She thought she would hate him forever, that she would never forgive him. Now, she wasn't so sure.

"Why did you leave me, Jax?" In her state of mind, she could not stop the words from spilling out of her head onto her tongue.

Silence was her response. She managed to roll her head to the side and look at him through bleary eyes. He held the bottle in one hand, balanced on his thigh and peered at her intently, those azure eyes piercing her. His face was lined with an expression she couldn't read. He always did have a good poker face.

"You know why," he said at last.

An answer that wasn't an answer. She scowled. "Tell me the truth. I deserve to know it, don't I?"

"You do." He paused to take a swig from the bottle, stalling. He heaved a sigh. "Your father told me about the betrothal."

"That's why you left?" Her brows drew together in question.

"Partly."

Hearing it was more painful than she expected. Hot tears threatened. Her stomach clenched, threatening to heave all the alcohol and food she'd ingested. "Why didn't you stay and fight for me?"

Gods, she sounded pathetic even to her own ears.

"I tried, Zee. I told him you deserved to choose for yourself but he wouldn't hear it. He told me to stay away from you or he'd make sure my father would lose his seat on the Council. And if I still insisted on trying to see you…" He paused, took another swig. "He'd kill me. He'd kill my parents."

Her father had been the one to divide them for all eternity? He threatened Jaxson and his family and for what? To make sure she married someone she didn't even like for political reasons? She and her father had never seen eye to eye, but now matters were worse. Her hatred and disgust for him increased tenfold.

"So, I left but not before letting him know exactly what I thought about that," Jaxson said.

Her breath caught. "What did you do?"

"I punched him. Broke his nose." He lifted his hand, flex his fingers into a fist and then relaxed them.

By the gods, he punched her father? If only she had been there to see that. She would have cheered him on. She would have liked to see blood spurt from his nose.

"I should have come back for you. I should have fought harder to get you back. But I didn't. I'll regret that for the rest of my life."

She could hear the guilt and the regret in his voice. She understood why he didn't. Her father was a powerful figure on the Council of Five. Jaxson was loyal to his family and would never do anything to jeopardize his father's position. Aside from that, they had been young. So young and hot for each other all they wanted was to be together.

"Oh, Jax." Her voice broke.

She rolled to her side and got up on her hands and knees, then crawled toward him. The impulsive need to touch him, to feel him next to her was too great even in her inebriated state. Of that she was certain. She moved between his legs and nestled her body on his lap, wrapping her arms around his neck and tucking her head under his chin. His body stiffened against her and then gradually relaxed. He still held the near-empty bottle in one hand, but he wrapped his arm around her with his free one.

"That was a long time ago," she said.

"It was," he agreed.

"My father told me you left because you didn't want me anymore. I was heartbroken."

"I never stopped wanting you."

Her eyes drifted closed at the sincerity in his voice. She whispered, "I never stopped wanting you, either."

It was an admission she hadn't allowed herself to think of or voice since that fateful day that altered the course of her life. If he had stayed, if they had married to make their mating official, how different would things be for both of them? Instead, they'd spent the last years separated, cold silence between them.

He set the bottle aside. His hand swept through her hair, fisting the long locks and tugging her head back. She looked up at him, saw the heart-rending tenderness there in his face and nearly came undone. She knew, without a doubt, he was going to kiss her. Just as she knew, without a doubt, she was going to let him.

Oh, gods, she wanted that. She wanted his mouth on hers, tasting her. Teasing her. Reminding her of all the things they once were to each other. There was hesitation and doubt in his eyes. She lifted her hand, pressed it against his scruffy cheek.

"Kiss me. I want you to. I want to remember what that's like."

It was all the invitation he needed. His head dipped low. Tentatively, he brushed his mouth against hers. A zing of desire punched through her. Every hair follicle tingled. Every inch of exposed skin erupted in gooseflesh. A breathy moan escaped through her lips before she could stop it. The next thing she knew, he crushed his mouth against hers.

The kiss was fierce and hot. She opened her lips as his tongue dove in, their tongues bumping together for the first time in forever. She tasted the hint of the smoky flavor of whiskey. She decided she could learn to like the drink if she could sip it from his mouth forevermore. He was gentle at first and then more and more demanding, kissing her with pent-up reckless abandon. She kissed him right back with the same pent-up reckless abandon.

It reminded her much of their early days when they were determined to rip each other's clothes off and fuck like it was the last time they would ever see each other. It was the way their coupling always was—sizzling, hard, needy, intense. Her orgasms would always be a violent vibration that shattered her. Even thinking it now sent warm heat cascading through her, pooling between her legs.

Her hand slid from his roughened cheek to around his neck as she pulled him, close, closer still, to allow their bodies to collide. She could feel the rapid beat of his heart thrumming through him into her.

Her pushed her to the floor, his hot mouth moving to her neck. He kissed a searing line from her earlobe down. His tongue dipped into the hollow of her throat making her moan and wiggle underneath him.

"That." His heated breath trickled over her kiss-dampened skin. "It's my favorite part to lick."

Her hands fisted in his short hair as she clutched him. "That part? Are you sure?"

"Correction. Second favorite part to lick." He punctuated that with another taste of her skin.

"Jax, I..." Her voice hitched, the treat of tears once again as she was overcome with emotion. She swallowed hard, regaining her composure. She could only think of one thing she needed, wanted. "I need you. Here. Now."

She ground her hips against his, the desperate need to have him inside her nearly too much for her to bear. One hand slid under her shirt and cupped her breast over the material of her bra while he continued the onslaught of her neck with his mouth. His other hand fumbled with the button on his jeans. She was trying to decide how to get out of her clothes while still holding on to him, because she didn't want to let him go.

A sharp knock on the door made them both freeze.

"We have company," came Rafe's voice through the door. "Drakana."

Jaxson swore the dirtiest, vilest curse she'd ever heard. It turned her on even more. He sucked her earlobe between his teeth and gave one last nip. "We'll finish this later."

When he moved away from her and stood, she felt cold and unsatisfied. He helped her to her feet. "I'm going to hold you to that, mister."

Jaxson flung open the bedroom door and hurried out. She followed, hot on his heels. Rafe was already armed and ready.

"They won't stop hunting her. I'll hold them off while you two get out of here," Rafe said, his eyes pinned on the door.

"If I use a portal, they'll be able to trace the magic," Jaxson said.

"Not if I help cover your tracks." This from Mia who emerged from the master suite.

"How do you plan to do that?" Jaxson reached for Zahra's hand, lacing their fingers. He gave a gentle tug and pulled her closer.

"Like this."

The Queen of Andonia lifted her hands, palms flat to the ceiling. Snowflakes appeared to dance above her hands. Then she blew out a shallow breath that crystallized in the air before her.

Zahra could see the sparkling magic dancing in the queen's breath.

"Dragon's Breath?" she asked, surprised.

"When did you learn to do that?" Jaxson asked.

"Only recently." She smiled, looking well-pleased. "When I discovered I was pregnant."

"It's a defense mechanism." Zahra didn't hide the amazement and wonder in her voice. "To help you protect the life of your unborn child."

A pang of longing went through her that she could not deny. With her magic gone, would she ever be able to do the same should she become with child? Even so, only a few dragon-shifters, male or female, were gifted with Dragon's Breath. She knew Logan's father had the gift as well as the first dragon-shifter, Ienir the Great, who used it to hide the Whispering Mountains.

"Use the portal to get to the mountains. You and I both know it's the quickest way to get you to safety," Rafe said. "Stay there until Logan and I can figure out what our next move is."

Zahra didn't miss the pointed look he gave her. She knew their next move was dependent upon her giving up one of her dragon scales. She hadn't forgotten but she hadn't changed her mind either.

"All right," Jaxson said, relenting at last. He released her hand to retrieve the duffle bag full of weapons.

"The cabin is fully stocked. You should be safe there for a while," Rafe said.

He gave a nod of understanding. With his free hand, he began to make a circular motion in the air to open a portal. Meanwhile, the queen used her Dragon's Breath to conceal the area around them. Light sparkled and the opening appeared. Together, they stepped through the portal.

❧ 13 ❧

Talal returned a short time later to the apartment building. Herrick knew immediately they had failed to capture the girl. His anger throbbed just under the surface.

"And your excuse this time?" Herrick demanded.

"The dragon knight and his woman were there. She used Dragon's Breath to hide their escape," his son said.

Presuming Jaxson used a portal to escape, there would be no way to track the magic due to the Dragon's Breath. He swore under his breath.

"There was no chance to even try to capture her. The dragon knight has some sort of alarms on his place."

Fools. They were all fools.

"Let me think."

Herrick rubbed his forehead, pinching it between thumb and forefinger. They had failed numerous times, and now the girl was gone. It didn't help his son was an idiot. It would take someone with a lot of power to trace her whereabouts. There was only one person who could find her. One person who could bring her to him.

Her father.

They stepped into the wilderness as darkness set in. Zahra moved closer to him as he got out his smartphone and used it as a flashlight.

"Stay close." He headed through the trees, his feet crunching on the bracken as he made his way out.

"I thought you knew where this place was?" She couldn't resist the opportunity to give him some grief about missing the mark. He never missed.

"I've never been here," he replied. "I tried to get close based on Rafe's description and directions."

"Do you think we'll truly be safe here?"

He halted, turned toward her. The light from the smartphone illuminated his face, making his azure eyes appear to glow in the dark. "Do you want the truth?"

Her heart thunked against her chest. She didn't like the sound of that. "Yes."

"For a while, yes. But Rafe was right. Herrick and his men will never stop hunting you."

They wanted to hunt you down and bring you back.

Cold fear crept into her gut. "He's that determined?"

"To win against Logan? Yes. If he gets to you first..." He paused, dropped the duffel to the ground and then brushed the back of his hand against her cheek. "He'll do whatever he needs to do to get a scale from your dragon self."

Her stomach clenched. "What does that mean?"

He reached for the duffle, picked it up. "He used drugs to shift Mia's father into his dragon form and steal his tooth. The trauma killed him."

Oh, gods. She had no idea. Her mouth went dry.

"I won't allow that to happen to you," he added. "Now, come on. Let's find this cabin, okay?"

She nodded. "Okay."

They continued through the trees, walking along in silence. It gave Zahra time to think about what he'd said and worry. She should tell him she no longer had the ability to shift or do any of her dragon magic, but she didn't know how. How would he take the news when she told him it wasn't that she wouldn't help them, it was that she couldn't? Would he hate her? Would he never speak to her again?

And now that they kissed, what did that mean for their relationship? Were they back together? Would they try to find a way to reconcile completely?

It was too much to think about. So, she wouldn't. She shoved it down into the dark recesses of her mind to think about later. As they emerged from the trees, the cabin came into view. It was small with a wrap-around porch. It was hard to see too many details in the dark.

"Here it is," Jaxson said.

They climbed the porch steps. He dropped the duffle again to dig into his pocket for the key. A second later, he had the front door pushed open and stood aside to let her in first. She stood in the dark, staring at the shapes of furniture as a sense of familiarity went through her. Her stomach knotted and all she could think about was the night they mated. It was a cabin much like this one in a time not so long ago.

Jaxson flipped on a light switch, flooding the small room in pale yellow light. The place was rustic, with a fireplace on one side. The living area hosted wood and leather furniture. Beyond that, a small kitchen fully furnished with all the best appliances. A hallway was off the living area which she assumed led to the bedrooms.

Jaxson stood next to her. She sensed the tension coming off him in waves. Likely feeling much like she did as he remembered the time they shared in a place not so dissimilar. He closed and locked the door behind them.

"We should get some sleep."

He said nothing else as he disappeared down the hallway, leaving her alone in the middle of the living room.

"That's it? That's all you have to say?" She charged down the hall after him. He ducked into a room to the left.

He chunked the duffle on the floor next to the bed covered with a red and white quilt. "It's been a long day. I'm sure you're tired."

She stood in the doorway trying to read his expression. He had put on his poker face again. "I am but—"

"We'll figure out our next move in the morning." He moved to the door, his hand on the knob. He started to swing it closed. "Good night."

She stepped back as he closed it with a snap, shutting her out. Emotionally and physically. Her heart went into her throat. Hot tears pricked the backs of her eyes. Confused, she turned on her heel and stepped into the room across the hall.

Did nothing they shared at Rafe's mean anything to him? Or perhaps it meant more to her than him. He could have been saying all that to make her sympathetic. She didn't know if the story he told her about her father was true. There was one way to find out.

She'd managed to keep her cell phone on her throughout the ordeal. She pulled it out of her pocket. The screen showed she had thirty-nine missed calls. She ignored all the texts and missed calls when she tried meditating. Now she scrolled through the call list. Some were from potential clients, a few acquaintances and the bulk of them from her father. No doubt calling to make sure she was still going to be at the appointed meeting time and place to return to the Hidden Lands.

She wasn't sure what made her do it, but on impulse she called him back. He answered on the first ring. "Zahra, where are you? I've been trying to reach you."

"I'm fine," she said, ignoring his question. "I need you to answer something for me. And I need the truth."

There was a long pause. "What is it?"

"You said Jaxson left me because he didn't want me anymore. Is that true?"

"Why are you asking me about something that happened years ago?"

She could hear the annoyance in his voice but she ignored it and plowed on. "Because I need to know." Another long pause. She checked the phone to make sure they were still connected. "Dad?"

"No, it wasn't true. I told him to leave you."

Her hand tightened on the phone. "You threatened him and his family, didn't you?"

"I told him you were betrothed to Talal and to give you up," he said.

"Don't lie to me!" Those hot tears were back. This time, she could not stop them from falling. "You threatened him and his family. You told him to leave me."

"I told him I would never allow him to marry you."

Her breath hitched. "Why?"

"Because he's not good enough for you. He'll never be good enough for you."

"Don't I get to decide that?"

"No." His voice was hard, cold. "You are my daughter. The eldest daughter of a Councilman and you will do what I say and marry whom I wish."

Oh, how she hated him. "I will not."

"You do not have a choice, Zahra."

"I've always had a choice. I'm glad Jaxson broke your nose."

The heavy silence on the other end made her question if he was still there. "He told you that?"

"He did."

"Zahra, if you don't return to the Hidden Lands and fulfill your promise, you will force me to make unpleasant decisions. I'd rather you cooperate."

She didn't know what he meant by that nor did she care.

"To make things easier for you?" she scoffed. "I'm not ever coming back."

She hung up before he could reply. She flung the phone to the floor, then crumpled into a ball on the bed and wept.

She awoke in the middle of the night, still curled into a ball. It had been some time since she cried until she fell asleep. In fact, the last time had been when she discovered Jaxson had left the Hidden Lands without telling her goodbye. Shortly after that, she went on a three-day drinking binge.

Now, she knew the truth. Her father was the one who came between them, the one who made sure she would never see Jaxson again.

Her father had to know from their phone call she wouldn't be showing up at the Empire State Building for their scheduled meeting. There was no way she was going back to him, to the Hidden Lands, to Talal. She would find a way to break that betrothal. She would find a way to get her sister out.

She pushed to a sitting position on the bed. Her head throbbed from the intense emotions pounding through her. Her eyes felt puffy and dry. She probably looked like a mess. She had nothing with her. She'd left her handbag behind at Rafe's. She slid to the edge of the bed and got to her feet, running her hands through her tangled hair.

Thankfully, the small bedroom had an even smaller en-suite bathroom. She padded into the room and flipped on the light. The sight of her pale, tear-streaked face and red-rimmed eyes in the mirror was somewhat terrifying. Gods, her worst fears were realized. She really did look like hell.

And she had a bit of a hangover from drinking whiskey with Jaxson. She splashed lukewarm water on her face and then cleaned away the runs of mascara. The thought of a shower was too inviting, so she shed her clothes and stepped in under the hot spray. She washed her long hair, scrubbed her scalp and her body until her skin was bright pink.

Once she was out of the shower and wrapped in a thick, plush towel, she went through the drawers until she found a bottle of ibuprofen and downed two. She leaned against the edge of the countertop and stared, hard, at her face in the mirror.

Gone were the tear-streaks and all remnants of make-up. Her face was all natural and clean. Her damp hair hung over her shoulder, the ends dripping against the terrycloth. She was here, in a cabin, alone with the man she'd loved since she was fourteen. How could she stand here and ignore that?

She opened the towel and stared at her naked figure in the mirror, inspecting it with a critical eye. She hadn't changed much since the last time they'd been together. In fact, her body had changed very little. Was Jaxson's the same?

With her heart throbbing a wicked beat, she wrapped the towel back around her and tucked the end between her breasts. She could stay here, hiding in the bathroom, or she could march across the hall, fling open his bedroom door, and demand to know why he pushed her away.

She could guess, but she wanted to hear it directly from him.

Throwing caution to the wind, and steeling her nerves, she turned on her bare heel and left her bedroom behind. She made it across the hall and hesitated a moment with her hand hovering over the knob of his bedroom door.

She could do this. She would do this. She loved him and he loved her and it was time to put the past behind them once and for all and start living again, start loving again.

Zahra shoved open the door, ready to fire off her prepared speech when she stopped cold. All thoughts of a proper scolding left her head.

Moonlight drifted in through the blinds, making a slanted pattern across the bed and the half-naked form on it. Jaxson had shed everything except his underwear. He laid flat on his back, one arm over his head, the other across his middle.

Her heart leapt into her throat at the sight of his long, lean, muscular form. He no longer had the body of a boy, but that of a man. A very hot and sexy man. A man who must have spent hours in the gym to hone his abs and pecks and upper thighs.

She backed toward the door and put her hand on the knob. She started to close it behind her when his voice stopped her.

"Where do you think you're going, missy?"

Her breath hitched in her throat as he came up on one elbow and eyed her standing there in nothing but a towel. He didn't smile. He didn't say anything else. He just looked at her.

She didn't know what her next move should be. She was frozen there, watching him look at her. Those eyes mesmerized her, fascinated her, captivated her. As they always had from the first time she realized what it felt like to want someone so bad it hurt.

The same way she felt now.

"Well?" he prompted.

She swallowed, her mouth so dry she couldn't even form words.

Jaxson sat up, swinging his legs off the side of the bed. He reached for his discarded pants.

"No, don't," she heard herself say.

He stopped, gave her a quizzical look. Even in the pale light of the room, she could see his features clearly.

"Don't?" he asked.

"Don't," she repeated, her voice soft and breathy.

She was either about to embarrass herself to the point she wished to die, or she was about to get everything she ever wanted.

Him.

Zahra reached for the end of the towel tucked between her breasts. She tugged it out, slowly, and then let the material drop to the floor.

He didn't move. He didn't react. He sat there looking at her. She watched him with an intense fire burning in her gut, the red-hot desire scorching through her and the heat pooling between her legs.

She knew she was tempting him back into her arms. It took everything she had to stand there and let him look at her, let his gaze drift over her from head to toe, pausing only a brief moment at the apex of her thighs, then back up again to her breasts. His gaze lingered there a long moment before finally coming back up and resting on her face.

Heat burned her cheeks with his scrutiny.

But she shoved aside the mortification, the fear of rejection, the anxious apprehension and remained standing there, naked and hopeful.

Jaxson got to his feet slowly, methodically, his eyes still on hers as he shed his remaining piece of clothing. Her chest heaved with her erratic breathing. Desperation to look at him the way he had her clawed through her until finally she could no longer resist.

No, this was certainly not the body of the boy she remembered. He was a man and he was definitely glad to see her.

"Are you going to tell me we shouldn't?" she asked.

"Is that what you want? You want me to deny you when you're standing there tempting a starving man?"

He was starving for her. She bit her bottom lip. No, that bloody wasn't what she wanted. She didn't want to deny him. "Why did you shut me out earlier?"

"You want to talk about that now?"

"Why?" she demanded.

"Because you belong to another." He didn't bother to hide the disappointment and the pain.

"I belong to only one man." She took a tentative step toward him, closing the gap with unhurried steps. The thought of brushing against him, flesh to flesh, sent a tingling sensation through her.

"And who is that?" His voice was dark and breathy and full of hope.

She halted in front of him, reached for him, and placed her palms on his chest. A flicker of satisfaction went through her when she realized his heart was beating as hard as hers.

"You, Jax. It's always been you."

His big, warm hands landed on her hips. "And the betrothal?"

"I don't love him. I never loved him. And I don't want him. I will refuse to marry him despite my father's wishes."

"Are you sure that's what you want?"

"The only thing I've ever been sure about is how much I want you. That's never changed."

His eyes searched hers for any hint of deception. He wouldn't find any. Everything she said was true and sincere. Why else would she stand here, exposed and naked, in front of him? She meant everything she said, too. He was all she wanted, needed.

He fingered her damp hair, then traced the outline of her collarbone. "I'm sorry about earlier."

"Why'd you do it?" she whispered.

"Because we'd both been drinking. I didn't want our first time together to be because of alcohol."

"It's not our first time together," she corrected.

"Since you require me to be succinct, first time since the last time we were together."

She knew what he meant but she couldn't resist the urge to needle him a little. A smile played at the corner of her mouth. "I'm sober now. Are you?"

"I am." His response was deep, throaty, sexy. "Are you sure about this, Zee? We're different people now."

"The only thing that's changed is that we're older. Everything else is merely details."

He cupped her breast, his thumb grazing one taut nipple. It nearly made her come undone. Why wouldn't he toss her to the bed and have his way with her? The want of him drove her crazy.

"Details we can worry about later," she added and stepped closer to him.

She slipped her arms around his waist. His heated skin pressed into her, the hard length of his erection pushed against her upper thigh. He fisted his hands in her damp hair, tugging her head back like he had before. His hot, wet mouth landed on her throat.

The moan escaped her before she could stop it. It shuddered out between her lips. Both hands cupped her breasts as he kissed his way down, bending at the waist to suck one hard pebble between his lips. She arched her back to give him more access, shoving her hips into his to convey her urgency.

It had been so long since she had been with him, she wondered what it would be like. Would they still have the same fiery passion for each other as they once did. There was only one way to find out.

His mouth broke from her and he straightened. He turned her in his arms and pressed his hard body against her back. His arms slipped around her waist as he walked her toward the bed, halting in front of it. He pressed his hand in the middle of her back and pushed her forward.

She complied, her breath shuddering in and out of her lips as he pushed inside of her from behind.

All thoughts flew from her mind as she braced her upper body on the mattress. Her mind was nothing but a whirlwind of emotion. He pounded against her, his hands on her hips so tight his fingers dug into her flesh. She bit her lip hard to keep from crying out even though all she wanted to do was scream with pleasure. It reminded her of the first few times they had been together when they were much younger and less experienced.

But she didn't want this to be how they ended this first round of lovemaking. She gave him a hard shove backward with her hips and moved away from him before he had a chance to regroup. She spun toward him, falling against him and kissing him hard. Their mouths crashed against each other in wild abandoned. She wrapped her arms around him and pulled him to her, falling backward onto the bed.

She wrapped her legs around his waist, her heated inner core desperately searching for his hardened length. He plunged deep inside her, making her gasp. His mouth was on her neck as he moved inside her. Her orgasm came swift and hot and vibrated through her until she could no longer stand it. She dug her fingernails into his back. He groaned and pushed against her again in one hard final thrust before he came inside her.

When he stilled, he kissed her cheek. One hand tangled in his soft hair, the other pressed against his back. As she thought about the pleasure he'd given her, the way he'd made her come hard and fast, she realized there was still no hint of her dragon magic.

Was it forever lost to her? Was their mating bond severed completely because they had been apart so long and for so many years? She should tell him, but she didn't want to ruin the magic of the moment. She inhaled the scent of him, and memorized the way his hard body felt against hers. She would never forget it.

"Well…" His heated breath was on the side of her neck. "I hope you enjoyed that as much as I did."

He started to pull away, but she clutched him hard, keeping him in place inside her. It had been like it once was. She remembered everything about the way he felt, the way he touched her, the way he made her want to come undone at the seams every time he looked at her.

"You okay?" he asked.

"Yes." Her voice was a roughened whisper and full of unexpected emotion.

How could she tell him she loved him with everything she had? How could she tell him she'd lost her dragon magic and they would never feel that mating bond again?

"Are you sure?"

Curse him and his lie detector. She squeezed him and cleared her mind of all the negative fearful thoughts. "I'm sure." She could only think of one thing that would wipe away the fear at least for a little while. She flicked her tongue over his earlobe and whispered, "Let's do that again."

He happily complied.

⬯ 14 ⬭

Jaxson held Zahra in his arms all night. He couldn't get enough of touching her, kissing her, or making love to her. It had been far too long since the last time he'd had her this close to him and he didn't want it to end. He didn't want to forget anything about their night together.

He never expected her to come back to him after shutting her out. He wouldn't blame her if she never spoke to him again. He'd been a dick to her and he knew it. What he told her was true, though, he didn't want their first time together again to be tainted by alcohol. He wanted to remember, to feel everything from the first moment he saw her naked to when he finally put his mouth on her.

His only regret was not undressing her, slowly, methodically. But there would be plenty of other opportunities for that later. He hoped. He certainly didn't want this to be the last time they were together.

He ran his fingers through her now dry hair, the long strands whispered across his skin, cascading down in a waterfall of pink. He loved her hair most. The way it fell in waves down her back or over her shoulders. He couldn't get enough of it. He couldn't get enough of her.

Deep down, his inner dragon purred contentment. But even so, something was off. Something didn't feel quite right. He couldn't figure out what it was, or why he felt that way. He tried to sense the mating bond but it was nothing but a weak pulse deep down. It wasn't as bright or strong has it once had been. It was almost as though it was thinning, threatening to break.

"Do you remember that cabin in the Hidden Lands?" she asked, her voice quiet in the darkness.

Did he? He never forgot it. "I remember."

"Do you know if it's still there?"

It had been where they're illicit love affair began, where they forged their mating bond. Where they sealed their love for each other. He hadn't been back to it since that night.

"I don't know."

She rolled on top of him. She folded her hands on his chest and propped her chin there. "Would you ever want to go back?"

His hands whispered through her hair, brushing back the locks from her face. "Are you asking me out on a date?"

A smile quirked the corner of her mouth. "Do you think we should date after tonight? I mean, I'm still naked on top of you."

"I wouldn't want it any other way," he said.

"Are you sure?"

"Why wouldn't I be?"

"Because you may have someone you like more than me."

He stared at her, mute, for a long moment. Someone he liked more than her? Never. No other woman compared to her. No other woman was perfect like her. "Not likely."

She tipped her head to one side, a questioning look on her face. "Have you been with other women?"

He lifted a brow, staring down at her. "Is that where the line of questioning is going? How many women I've slept with?"

"There have been others?"

"Have you slept with other men?" he countered.

She tugged the bottom of her lip between her teeth. "This isn't about me right now."

He laughed. "I'm a man who has needs, Zee. What do you think?"

She rolled off him and stared up at the ceiling. "I think it means you've been with other women."

"Are you going to ask me how many next?" When she didn't

reply, he said, "Does it really matter? It doesn't to me. Should it to you?"

"I suppose not."

The last woman he'd had a dalliance with was Freya, Princess Mia's assistant. She'd helped him heal after he was stabbed with the obsidian blade. While he liked her well enough, and she was good in bed, she wasn't Zahra. Freya knew, deep down, there was no future for the two of them and accepted it. Their time together had been nothing more than a physical attraction they both gave into. When she departed to return to Andonia, their parting had been amicable.

She huffed out a breath and rolled to her side, propping up on an elbow and looking at him. He'd always loved her tawny eyes, too. They were so lucid and clear. Almost as though he could see to the depths of her soul. A soul that was full of beauty.

She traced the lines of his chest down his abs until her finger bumped across the mark left by the obsidian blade. She lifted enough to peer down at the silvery scar.

"What happened here?"

"I had a run-in with an obsidian blade."

"Those are poison." Her gaze flickered back up to his. He could see the worry and concern there.

"They are, but I survived thanks to Rafe. He had the antidote."

"He's a man of many hidden talents, then. When did it happen?" She traced the jagged scar with the tip of her finger.

"A few months ago. I was helping protect Princess Mia from the Drakana." He could see the question flicker in her eyes and knew she'd have more. "We've been in this fight a while now."

"We?"

"Me, Logan, Rafe. Logan mostly. He's been trying to keep the Council from imploding but Herrick isn't making things easy for him."

"Herrick." She scoffed his name as if it vexed her completely. "I never did like him."

"No one does except for your father."

At that, she scowled. "He's not very happy with me at the moment."

"If you're running away from him, I can see why."

"I told him off."

Surprise flashed through him. "You did? When?"

"I called him to find out if the story you told me was true." She paused, tracing a lazy circle on his abdomen. "It was."

"You didn't believe me?"

"I wanted to make sure."

"And you're sure now?" he asked.

"Yes." She scooted closer, her curves pressing against the hard planes of his body. "I'm sure."

"We won't be safe here for long, you know."

Worry flickered through her eyes. "I suspected. Then what happens?"

"Then we fight for the Hidden Lands."

She chewed on the inside of her lower lip. "But you still need one of my scales."

"Ideally, yes."

She nodded understanding but he could see something troubled her. Something she wasn't willing to tell him. A secret, perhaps. He didn't want to pry, not yet. Whatever was bothering her, he hoped she would volunteer the information sooner rather than later.

"How does having all these relics help break the curse?" she asked.

"Only Logan knows the answer to that."

Her brows drew together. "He's the only one who knows?"

"He has his father's journals. His father looked for a way to break the curse for years. He left fragments of information throughout those books. Logan's slowly been putting the pieces together. He thinks by using the Blood Stone, the cold-drake tooth and the fire-drake scale, there is a way to break the curse for good."

"Sounds farfetched."

"It does to me, too," he agreed.

"But?" she prompted.

"But I trust Logan."

She gave a nod and then flopped back on the bed. He watched her as her mind worked while she stared up at the ceiling. There was definitely something going on in that head of hers.

"What do you suppose there is to eat around here? I'm famished," she said.

The sun morning sun pressed through the closed blinds of the little cabin when they finally untangled from each other and the bed sheets.

She had no idea things were going to be so complicated. Eating was a way of distracting her from her thoughts. But distracting her wasn't going to be enough. She needed to figure out why she lost her dragon magic and a way to get it back before she had to come clean to Jaxson. She needed to tell him the truth.

The problem was she didn't want to admit to him the truth. She wanted to figure it out before she had to tell him. Eventually, he was going to ask her if she was willing to help them break the curse. He'd managed to suck her in his undertow and drag her through the current and, like an idiot, she'd let him sweep her along.

Who was she kidding? She had no intention of returning to the Hidden Lands with her father. Hiding out in a cabin in the Adirondacks with Jaxson was the perfect excuse. An excuse, she feared, would not be viable for long.

Yes, she was definitely going to have to tell him.

But she would worry about that later. Right now, she was more interested in finding clothes and food. Jaxson was already in the kitchen making noise while she was busy pawing through the dresser drawers in her room. She found an oversized t-shirt and sweatpants. Finally dressed, she made her way into the kitchen.

Jaxson was busy cooking bacon in one pan. He had a stack of eggs ready to crack and cook in another.

"Wow, Rafe was right. This place is stocked."

"Almost as though he was expecting to use it." Jaxson gave her a thin-lipped expression.

She flushed. "Do you think he and Mia were planning to come up here?"

"Perhaps."

"And we interrupted their romantic getaway," she guessed.

"Likely."

She ran her hand down her face. "Well, that makes me feel bad."

"I wouldn't let it bother you. Rafe has other places. I'm sure he can find another romantic getaway for him and his bride."

"It seems unlikely he'd end up marrying a princess. I mean, he was the exiled knight, after all." She plopped down on the barstool across from him and watched him cook. "And I didn't know you could cook."

"This really isn't cooking. It's breakfast. Breakfast is easy." He waved the greasy spatula over the bacon. "You're right. Rafe was the exiled knight, but Logan changed all that for him."

"Oh? How?"

He told her how Princess Mia came to New York under the guise of an ambassadorial visit when in reality she was here searching for her missing family jewels. Jewels that included the Blood Stone. She and Rafe met quite by accident and, upon seeing the princess's life was in peril, took it upon himself to protect her from the Drakana.

"When Herrick and his men managed to capture her parents—"

"You mean the king and queen of Andonia?" she interrupted.

He nodded. "Yes. When they were captured, Rafe, Logan, and I intervened. But it was too late for the king. Herrick had already managed to rip the tooth from him."

The thought made her stomach turned into a knot. "He's a monster."

"He is." He paused flipping bacon and gave her a pointed look. "And he'll do the same to you."

"No, he won't."

"How do you know for sure?"

"Because I have you." She gave him a smile. "You're my bodyguard."

He stilled, clutching the spatula in one had while the bacon sizzled in the pan in front of him. "I won't let them take you."

The hard look in his eyes, the way he said, she knew he meant it. "I believe that."

"But we can talk more about that later. Let's eat."

She watched him plate the food, then hand her one. He took the stool next to her and dug into the eggs with alacrity. She fiddled with a piece of bacon, thinking about the loss of her magic. Not telling him niggled at her. Everything inside her told her she should tell him the truth.

"What's wrong? Bacon too crisp?" he asked around a mouthful.

"No." She broke it in half and nibbled on the end.

"Then what is it? I thought you said you were starving."

"I was. Am."

"What's bothering you, Zee?"

Zee. Why did he insist on calling her that? Didn't he know it made her weak in the knees? Made her want to tell him everything? She wasn't ready to tell him about her dragon magic. Not yet. So, instead, she deflected.

"I found the picture of us in your sock drawer."

He stopped eating long enough to inhale a shaky breath. He was silent a moment and then started shoveling eggs into his mouth again, hurrying to finish. When he was, he slid off the stool and walked back into the kitchen to rinse his plate.

"You have nothing to say to that?" she asked.

"What do you want me to say?"

Infuriating man. "You kept it. All these years."

The plate clinked in the bottom of the sink. "I did."

"Why?"

"Why do you think?"

It irked her he answered her question with a question. Couldn't he just admit the truth? "That's why I'm asking you."

"It was the only thing I kept from us. I wanted to remember that day."

Her heart tripped as heat washed over her. That day in the cabin, he meant. That day they become one, when their magic fused and they mated. For life. But was it for life? She tried to tap into her dragon magic but found it barely an ember.

"I'm glad you kept it." Her voice was strained when she spoke.

"Of course, I did. You took it." He slid his dishes into the dishwasher. "I'm going to shower."

He didn't wait for her response as he left.

$$\approx 15 \approx$$

As he padded to the bathroom, Jaxson was certain Zahra was hiding something from him. He hadn't figured it out yet, but he would. And though she hadn't outright lied to him, there was something deep down she concealed from him, something she didn't want him to know.

Everything she'd said to him had been the truth. With his dragon magic, he could sense when someone was lying, so he knew she wasn't. But when he first mentioned he needed her help, that they needed one of her dragon scales, it had sent her into near panic. Even now, when the subject was brought up, he could tell she was uneasy.

Could her reluctance have something to do with her ability to shift?

In the bathroom, he turned on the shower, then stripped. As he stood there, leaning against the vanity, the reached out a tentative touch with his magic to find their mating bond. It was, as before, nothing but a faint glimmer. And even though he had sensed her thoughts earlier, he had seen memories flickering through her mind, he could not mindspeak to her. He'd tried but she didn't hear him and likely couldn't mindspeak back.

How could their mating bond be so weak, though? When dragons mated, it was for life. The bond would remain there no matter how much time or distance separated them.

Unless…unless their lengthy separation did something to erode the mating bond.

The only person he could think to ask would be his father. He made a mental note to call him after his shower.

As he stepped under the hot spray, he heard the vibration of his phone still in his jeans pocket. He started to ignore it, but something niggled at the back of his mind not to. He reached for his pants, grabbing the phone while dripping all over the floor.

Oddly, it was his father calling.

"Dad? Everything okay?"

"Jax…I've been trying to reach you. Where have you been?"

"I've been busy trying to keep Zahra out of the hands of the Drakana."

There was a long pause, then, "You found Zahra?"

"Yes, it's a long story. I'll explain after. What's wrong?"

"It's your mother. I think…" Another pause as his father's voice wavered. "I think you should come home."

"Home? To the Hidden Lands?"

"Yes. I don't think she'll live much longer, Jax."

His hand tightened on the phone. He knew his mother was sick, knew she was likely dying from the poison in air in the Hidden Lands. But he hadn't set foot there in nearly a year.

"She'll want to see you," his father added. "She's been asking for you."

But Jaxson knew, as his father did, that if he used a portal of his own creation, it would be like a homing beacon to Herrick and his cronies. How was he going to get back there without them following?

"You can bring Zahra with you. In fact, I recommended you do so. She'll want to see her, too, when she knows you've found her."

"How will she know that?"

"Because I intend to tell her. Get here as soon as you can, son."

He hung up before he could reply. Jaxson tossed the phone on the vanity counter and stared at it, his heart in his throat. His mother was the one that had given Logan Zahra's address and phone number. How had she gotten it? And why had she never shared it with him before?

A sense of urgency pounded through him. He needed to get

back home. But how without drawing undue attention?

Unless Mia and her Dragon's Breath could help. He snatched up the phone and dialed.

"Rafe, I need a favor. A big one."

It was settled. He was going home and taking Zahra with him. He wasn't going to hide out here while his mother died. Maybe if he got Zahra back to the Hidden Lands, she could see how dire the situation truly was there. Then, she'd want to help.

After he talked to Rafe and told him about his mother, Rafe offered Mia's Dragon's Breath. They both agreed Jaxson using a portal to get them there would garner too much attention, especially if Herrick was trying to track him that way. He'd made Rafe promise he wouldn't tell Logan he was returning to the Hidden Lands.

"Why?" Rafe asked. "He'll want to know. He'll be ready to meet you there to try to break the curse."

"I'm not ready yet. Zahra isn't ready yet," Jaxson replied.

"She hasn't agreed to help?"

"No, but she will."

He was sure of it. She had to help.

Rafe told him he and Mia would drive up from Manhattan. He and Zahra would have to bide their time for the next five hours. That would give him plenty of time to convince Zahra to come home with him. He suspected she would resist the idea, especially since she was trying to avoid it in the first place. He would have to make sure that she understood it was for no other reason than to see his mother before she passed.

After he dressed, he made his way back to the living area. Zahra had cleaned up the breakfast dishes and was busy tidying the kitchen when he entered. She had braided her long, pink hair. The plait hung over one shoulder while she worked. He paused to watch her, thinking how domestic she looked and wishing the circumstances of their situation was different.

"We need to talk," he said.

She stopped cleaning. "That sounds serious."

"It is serious. It's about my mother."

Her face drained of color. "Your mother?"

"She's dying."

Her face creased with sadness. "Oh, Jax. I'm sorry."

"My father called. He wants me to come home. She wants to see me."

"Then you should go."

"I'm not leaving you here alone." He took a step toward her. "I want you to come with me."

"That's kind of you to ask, but shouldn't you be alone with your family? It's a private moment between you and your parents. I'll get in the way," she said.

He shook his head before she finished. "No, Zahra. She wants you to come with me."

She swallowed hard and shifted from one foot to the other, clearly uncomfortable. "She knows we're together?"

"She will when my father tells her."

She looked even more uncomfortable. "He knows we're together?"

"He does now. I told him." He reached for her hand. "I won't leave you here alone so Herrick can get his hands on you. Come with me."

He searched her eyes, saw the indecision flash deep there until finally she nodded.

"All right. I'll come with you. Do they live in the city?"

"No." He held her hand, tight, and pulled her closer. "The Hidden Lands."

She sucked in a sharp breath. He could tell she wanted to protest, to change her mind and tell him she wasn't going back there with him.

"I know you don't want to go back there," he said, quickly. "But you'll be with me. Herrick, Talal, and his men won't be able to touch you."

"I don't know about that." She tried to tug her hand away, but he held fast.

"I do. You have my word."

There was a hard glint in her eyes. When she spoke, her tone was hard, cold. "What side of the Council is Lord Nyles on, Jax?"

"What do you mean?"

"You know what I mean. Who does he side with? I know where my father's loyalties are, but where are your father's?"

"Is this a test?" he asked. If it was, he wasn't a fan.

"Answer the question."

"What are you afraid of, Zahra?"

She pressed her lips together in a thin line of aggravation. "I'm not afraid of anything. Now answer the question."

That was a lie. If he had to guess, he'd say she was afraid of returning to the Hidden Lands. He decided not to press the issue, at least not yet, and answer her question.

"My father wants to break the curse as much as Logan does. He doesn't want to control the Hidden Lands like Herrick. He wants the realm to return to what it once was and he wants to see the dragon-shifters return."

"Is that what you want?"

"Logan earned his title as Chief Magistrate. I want him to keep it."

"And defeat Herrick?"

"Defeat Herrick and all his Drakana, yes."

"And break the curse?"

"Yes."

"And break my betrothal to Talal?"

He could see the flutter of her pulse in her throat. "That and I want you safe."

She swallowed hard again but remained silent.

"Does that satisfy you?" he asked.

She nodded.

"Good. I know why you don't want to go back there. Thank

you for coming with me."

She gave him a nod. "How are we getting back? You said opening a portal was too dangerous."

"It is too dangerous, so I asked Rafe and Mia for help. They'll be here in a few hours."

"You're using her Dragon's Breath to hide us again, aren't you?"

"It's the only way to leave here without having Herrick follow us right away."

She didn't look convinced. "He'll find us, though, won't he?"

Jaxson kissed her forehead. "Maybe. But we'll worry about that when the time comes." He fingered her braid. "Now, how about we find a way to kill time until they arrive?"

They found several ways to kill time until Rafe and Mia arrived. She and Jaxson were finally dressed when they arrived at the cabin. Zahra wished she and Jaxson could have spent more quality time there together. Maybe she would have had the nerve to tell him the truth about her magic and that she could no longer sense their mating bond.

"Thanks for coming," Jaxson said.

"Are you sure about this?" Rafe asked.

"I have to go."

Rafe nodded understanding. He looked at Mia who readied the Dragon's Breath. "Then let's get started."

Zahra's heart thumped hard in her chest as she moved closer to Jaxson. She watched as Mia created the Dragon's Breath with ease. It misted around them, spreading through the room like a fog. Jaxson used his magic to open a portal.

A portal to home.

She hadn't stepped foot back there in years. She wasn't sure what to expect, how to act, what to think. Her body vibrated with nervous energy from both fear and excitement. Through the portal, she could see to the other side. It was a room she hadn't seen in a very long time.

"Be careful," Rafe said.

Jaxson nodded as he reached for Zahra's hand.

Her heart was in her throat as they stepped through the portal. A blast of cold air hit her, punching through to the marrow of her bones. It was the pass-through between realms, the in-between. Jaxson held onto her hand as they took another step and made it to the other side.

Looking back, they could see Mia and Rafe still in the cabin in the human realm. He lifted his hand in a wave. Jaxson gave a wave back and then the circle of fiery light was gone.

They stood together in the living room of the house he grew up in. It smelled and looked just the same as it had years and years ago. Nothing had changed. The heavy paneling on the walls was the same. The dark draperies at the windows the same. The oak furniture with well-worn cushions the same. The wood-planked floor with a family heirloom rug in warm colors of brown, red and gold was the same.

A sense of calm washed over her. The last time she had been in this room was shortly before they ran off to the cabin together. It had been the dead of winter. So cold outside, the blustery wind pierced exposed skin with sharp icy needles. They hadn't intended to spend the entire weekend together in that cabin, but the weather had other ideas. It kept them there, together, alone.

She'd spent more time the last two days living in the past than she had since she left the Hidden Lands. Now here she was, back in the realm of her birth, her childhood. She pushed away the thoughts and tried to focus on the present.

"Your parent's house looks how I remembered." She hadn't mean to sound so wistful.

"My mother was the decorator, but since her illness, she's mostly been bedridden."

His mother was bedridden? She didn't know that. She'd been so out of touch with everything involving the Hidden Lands, it had never occurred to her to check in on the people she still loved to see if they were all right. Well, with the exception of her sister, Nemea. But Nemea hadn't mentioned anything about the toxic air or that the realm was cursed. She didn't even know about that until Jaxson told her.

She regretted that now. She should have been a better person. She should have come back to make sure all was well here with those who had meant the most to her. When Jaxson left, there was no reason to stay.

She'd only kept in touch with her sister via text and phone. Now that she was back, perhaps there was a chance she could get her away from their horrid father.

The front door opened in a whoosh of air. She caught a glimpse of the outside before the door closed. All she saw was a bright pink evening sky. It was dusk in this realm.

Lord Nyles Lane startled when he saw the two of them standing there, his hand still on the knob. His hair, now peppered with silvery strands, looked wind-blown. He had crinkles around his eyes and laugh lines etched in his cheeks. She couldn't help but notice how much older he looked than the last time she'd seen him.

His shoulders drooped as though he was relieved to see his son standing there. He moved from the door and embraced him in a hug.

"I'm glad you came, son."

"Me, too. Dad, you remember Zahra." He motioned toward her then.

Lord Nyles turned his pale green gaze on her. His light-colored eyes used to frighten her when she was a child but no longer. He smiled when he saw her and embraced her as though she were his long-lost daughter. She hugged him back. She had forgotten how good it was to hug someone like that. Her father had never offered her that type of affection.

"Lord Nyles, it's good to see you." Her voice wobbled with the threat of tears but she managed to control it.

"We've known each other a long time, Zahra. Please call me Nyles." He patted her shoulder.

But Zahra knew it wasn't proper to call an elder and a Councilman by anything other than his title. She nodded even though she knew she wouldn't do it.

"Where is she?" Jaxson asked.

"Resting." Nyles nodded toward the second floor. "She'll want to see you both right away."

Jaxson glanced at her and she gave him an encouraging nod. "I'm with you."

"I'll make tea while you go up." Nyles shuffled off to the kitchen at the back of the house.

Jaxson reached for her hand, squeezing her fingers in his. It was then she sensed the fear and apprehension through him. She tried to tap into his mind, to see if she could sense how he was feeling, but she couldn't sense anything. She moved closer to him, to give him comfort.

"I'll be with you every step," she said.

Together, they ascended the stairs. She didn't miss the creak of the third step, the one that was always the tell-tale sign of someone going up or down. She recalled one particular night where she tried to sneak up the stairs with him to his bedroom and that damn step gave them away. His father sent her home with a good scolding and turned his disappointment on Jaxson. They were forbidden to see each other for weeks after that.

But they always found a way to find each other.

At the top of the steps, Jaxson paused to take a deep breath.

"I should warn you. She's been ill for a while. I don't know what state she'll be in, but the last time I saw her, she didn't look well," he said.

"It's all right, Jaxson. I can handle it."

He went down the hall to the first door on the right and gave a light knock. He didn't wait for an answer when he pushed open the door and paused in the opening.

Lady Isabella sat curled up in an oversized chair on the other side of the bed next to the window. Her legs were tucked underneath her and her thin body was wrapped in a thick shawl. She rested her head against the back of the chair, her eyes closed and her face in repose. Her skin was pale, not the normal warm tone matching that of Jaxson. And she was thin. She looked much older than her actual age. Her hair had turned white. She had one long braid over her shoulder.

The sight of her looking so frail and weak caught Zahra off guard. This was not the vibrant, vivacious woman she recalled from her youth. She had been so tall, regal, with dark brown hair and eyes the same color as Jaxson—a striking azure. It pained her to see Jaxson's mother looking like that. Even though he'd tried to warn her, nothing could prepare her for that.

Jaxson left her standing in the doorway as he went to her side. He kneeled beside the chair so she could look down at him. He placed his hand over hers and held it there for a long, silent moment. Until at last her eyes fluttered open and focused on his face. It took a moment before recognition set in and then she smiled, the light coming into her eyes. She pressed a bony hand against his cheek.

"My boy," she whispered. "You came home."

"I came home." He put his hand against hers. "I'm home, Mother."

"I'm so glad." Her eyes drifted closed again. Her hand dropped back into her lap as she drifted back to sleep.

Jaxson rose to his full height, gazing down at her with a look of sadness. It shredded Zahra's heart. She had lost her own mother when she was a girl, so she knew full well the pain of losing a parent.

"She doesn't have a lot of energy these days." Lord Nyles' voice behind her startled her.

Jaxson remained where he was, staring down at her.

"I should have let you take her away from this place like you asked," his father said. "Now, I fear it's too late."

"It doesn't matter now."

He turned away from her and headed out of the room. Zahra stepped aside to let him exit. He brushed by her and disappeared down the hall. She could hear a door open and close and assumed he went to his old childhood bedroom.

"What do you mean take her away from here?" she asked.

"Jaxson wanted to take her to the human realm when he left. I should have let him. Maybe she wouldn't be as sick as she is." His gaze flickered back to his wife. "Maybe she would have a better quality of life. Maybe she'd have a fighting chance to live."

"Is there nothing that can be done?"

"No." There was a note of finality in his voice. "Come, dear. Let's have some tea while he broods. He'll come out eventually." He reached for the door and closed it. Then he wrapped an arm around her shoulders and led her back to the stairs. "Besides, I want to know what you've been up to all these years."

As the went down the stairs, Zahra could not get the sight of Lady Isabella out of her head. There had to be something they could do, some bit of magic or cure for whatever was poisoning her.

She followed Nyles to the kitchen, which was just as she remembered. White washed cabinets, stainless appliances, an island in the center, butcher block countertops. She had spent many evening meals in the small eat-in nook off to one side. He motioned to the large wooden table to have a seat while he poured two cups of steaming tea. She recognized the scent of bergamot immediately. A feeling of comfort went through her as she sat at the table, eyeing the nicks and scratches of the well-worn top. He brought over the cups on a tray along with a sugar bowl and creamer. He took the seat opposite her. She watched as he dropped two teaspoons of sugar in his cup and stirred with a delicate silver spoon. He hadn't changed. He still liked his black tea exactly the same way.

Zahra took her steaming mug, letting it warm her face as she inhaled the heady scent. It was her favorite tea. He hadn't forgotten that about her.

"How long has she been like that?" Zahra asked, staring down into the black liquid.

"A few months. She appears to be getting worse. That's why I wanted Jaxson to come home." He sipped his tea.

She held the mug, the porcelain warming her fingers which had suddenly turned cold. "Are you sure nothing can be done?"

"I've explored every option. There is nothing to be done. It's the toxic air poisoning her, killing her."

She met his gaze then, as something occurred to her. She looked him over. He didn't appear to have any of the signs of illness. "Why hasn't it affected you?"

"That is the biggest mystery of all, my dear. The air doesn't seem to bother me. In fact, there are several others who have yet to be affected by the toxic air. I have no symptoms whatsoever."

She wondered, then, about her sister. Perhaps Nemea didn't mention it because she wasn't sick. She prayed to the gods that was the truth. If she could get away, she intended to go to her sister and make sure she was all right. But right now, Jaxson needed her here.

Then she thought of Logan, the Blood Stone, and the other relics he had or needed to break the curse. If the curse was broken, would it somehow reverse the illness? Would there be a way to use the Blood Stone and the other relics to heal Isabella? She made a mental note to talk to Jaxson about it and to urge him to ask Logan. She refused to believe there was no way to save her.

"There are others?" Zahra asked.

"Most have migrated to the human realm. Only a few clans remain here," Nyles said. "I do think there are others who are as ill as my wife."

"But you don't know for sure?"

"I couldn't say, no. I rarely leave the house because I fear something will happen to her while I'm gone. I would never forgive myself if she passed while I was out."

He ran his finger around the rim of the cup. She could see both the terror and sadness of losing his wife deep in his eyes and it pained her.

"I'm so sorry." She didn't have any words of comfort for him and didn't know what else to say.

He forced a half smile. "Let's talk about something else. What have you been doing all these years?"

"I have my own photography business."

Even as she said it, though, she realized her business was pretty much in ruins. She never uploaded the photos for her last client and her camera was still at Jaxson's, abandoned. She hadn't even thought about it until now. Her highbrow, high-class client was probably smearing her name all over social media for her lack of response.

"You always were great at taking pictures."

As he said it, he rose from the table. He shuffled over to a cork board hanging on the far wall and unpinned something. When he returned, he handed her the black and white photograph. It was of Nyles and Isabella. She barely remembered taking that picture, it had been so long ago. But there they were, smiling and looking young and healthy and happy. Everywhere Zahra went when she was a teen, she carried a camera. She took pictures of anything and everything. Every subject willing to pose for her while she learned the settings on her camera, how to take the best pictures, the best angles, the best lighting. She had a million pictures of her sister as well as Jaxson.

"You took that on our anniversary."

"Your twenty-fifth. I remember."

They'd had a small gathering of their closest friends, which included the Council of Five and their families. Logan's father, Eli, had been Chief Magistrate at the time. The other members, Archer, Herrick, her father and Nyles had all been friends once.

"What happened to the Council, Nyles?" She handed back the picture.

He held it between his hands as he sat again. "I'm not sure. One day, we were all fine and then the next, Archer turned on Eli. He started saying horrible things about him, dragging his reputation through the mud, trying to destroy his family."

"Why?" She finally took a sip of her tea, which was now lukewarm.

"When word about the toxic air and the curse got out, Archer demanded answers. Eli didn't have any. So, Archer decided he was not fit to lead. But none of us knew at the time Eli was gathering information and trying to find a way to break the curse."

Jaxson had mentioned Logan had his father's journals. He must have written everything down in secret. But why keep it a secret? Unless he thought the situation was hopeless and irreversible.

"Why wouldn't he share that with the Council?"

"Herrick and Archer couldn't be trusted. Once Archer turned on him, he was determined to destroy him and take over as Chief Magistrate. He and Herrick decided they would be able to find a way to break the curse without Eli's help. And…" He paused, giving her a sad look. "I'm afraid your father couldn't be trusted either."

Zahra resisted the urge to snort. She didn't need to hear that to know she couldn't trust her father. He had spent every moment he could trying to keep her away from Jaxson. She never understood why but now things were becoming clearer.

"My father and I had a falling out," she said. "There is no love lost there between us."

"I didn't want to say anything to you, my dear, but since you seem to understand…" He paused again, looking pained at the thought of talking to her about her father.

"I understand more than you know. My father made a marriage contract between me and Talal to keep me away from Jaxson," she said.

"I know about the betrothal," he said with a nod. "I tried to talk him out of it. I knew how inseparable you and Jaxson were. I tried to warn him that forcing the two of you apart would only make matters worse."

It warmed her to hear Nyles tried to fight for the two of them. She smiled at him across the table. "You did that?"

"Keeping two young lovers—two mates—apart is never a good

idea."

She flushed so hot the roots of her hair tingled. "You know about that?"

He gave her a small smile that reached his twinkling eyes. "I did and so did my wife. When Herrick and your father made the betrothal between you and Talal, it nearly destroyed Jaxson."

A sharp pain went through her. It had nearly destroyed her, too.

"After you two mated, Fenwick came to me and demanded I do something about it. I refused."

This was news to her. Surprise flashed through her as she stared at him in shock. "What did he want you to do?"

Nyles shifted in his seat, looking uneasy. "I fear I've already said too much."

She reached across the table and rested her hand on his forearm. "Please tell me."

"The Ancients once had a way to break a mating bond by severing the ties between the two lovers."

Her heart throbbed hard. Blood whooshed to her head, making dark pinpricks dance in her vision. Her stomach cramped. When she spoke, her voice was weak and raspy. "How is it done?"

"A potion, I'm told. One that will erase the bond by eradicating the dragon magic in the drinker."

It couldn't be true, could it? As he said the words, she stared at him as though she were sitting in some other dimension, some other world. As though it was happening to someone else. She thought back to her final days in the Hidden Lands. They had been nothing but a blur of hazy memory she'd locked away forever. She never wanted to think about that time again. Until now.

After Jaxson left and she had been distraught over him leaving, her father had come to comfort her. Or so she thought. He had given her a mug of her favorite tea, to soothe her, he'd said. He must have slipped the potion into that drink then. He had killed her dragon magic and severed the bond she'd had with Jaxson. But in doing so, he also killed her way to shift into her dragon form. Even if she wanted to help Jaxson, there was no way she could.

That son of a bitch. She had more reason than ever to hate him.

Nyles patted her hand still on his forearm. "I never told my son."

Oh, gods. He'd never mentioned it to Jaxson. And now the burden of telling him was on her. She didn't know if she could.

"Is there any way to get it back?" she asked, her voice sounding far away and hollow.

"I don't know." He slowly shook his head. "Perhaps it was unwise of me to tell you but I thought you should know. If there is, in fact, a way to reverse it. If it's not too late." He got to his feet.

"Thank you."

It was all she could say as he walked away, leaving her alone. Zahra dropped her head in her hands and wept.

✶ 16 ✶

Zahra remained at the dining table long after Nyles left. Her tea had gone cold. She sat alone, listless, and stared around the empty room trying to decide what she should do next. All this time, she thought her dragon magic was merely dormant, that she could still shift, that their mating bond was somehow still there…but it wasn't. It was gone. She was nothing anymore.

"Are you all right?"

Jaxson's voice startled her. She hadn't heard him come in and wondered how long he stood in the kitchen doorway watching her.

"Yes." She shoved back from the table. "I'm just tired."

"Have you been crying?"

He could always sense her distress, even when she tried to mask it. Heat from her intense emotions throbbed through her cheeks. Her eyes were gritty and dry. She knew she couldn't hide it from him, so she admitted it. She pushed back from the table and got to her feet, ready to bolt.

"Yes."

"Why?" He moved deeper into the room, coming toward her.

Jaxson was the last person she wanted to see right now. She needed to be alone. No, she needed to see her sister, to make sure she was all right. She hadn't seen her in person in years. Suddenly, it was the only thing that mattered.

Jaxson wasn't going to let it go, though. He was never one to back down so easily.

"Seeing your mother that way…"

She shook her head, biting her lip, trying to keep the tears from

134

rising again. Part of her anguish did have to do with that, too. Isabella had once been so kind to her. She hated to see her that way.

"I know," was all he said.

He stood next to her now and reached up to finger the end of her long pink braid. "I need to call Logan, tell him we're here and safe."

"You mean for the time being."

"I can't worry about Herrick or anything but my mother right now."

"I understand."

"But you must be tired." He took her hand, lacing their fingers.

"I am."

"Come on."

Without waiting for her response, he led her from the kitchen and up the stairs to his childhood bedroom. Her heart beat a wicked beat at the thought of stepping foot in that room.

"The last time we were in there together," she said, "your father busted us."

"I don't think he'll mind this time." He gave her a wink and a quick smile as he pushed open the door.

Everything about his room was exactly the same as she remembered. Being here, back in this place, had given her a surprising amount of comfort. Even so, she could only think of her little sister back in their father's house. If her father was willing to destroy her, then what would he do to Nemea? Worry gnawed through her.

Jaxson led her to the bed and sat on the edge. She perched on the mattress next to him. His arm went around her shoulders as he pulled her to him. His presence was as warm and comfortable as a heated blanket on a cold winter's night.

"What's bothering you?" he asked, his voice gentle.

"Nothing."

"That's a lie. Try again."

She mentally kicked herself. She knew better. "I'm worried

about…things."

"Like what?"

"Your mother. My sister." Us. Me.

"Your sister?"

"My father is not a nice man, Jaxson. You know this. I left her behind. I shouldn't have. I should have found a way to bring her through to the human realm with me instead of leaving her here, alone, with that monster." She hadn't realized how much she was afraid for her sister until she voiced it. "I need to get to her."

"I don't think he'll hurt her."

She had her doubts, knowing what Nyles told her. If he had told her the truth. She didn't see why he would have a reason to lie. If her father would stoop to the lowest of the low to sever all ties she had with Jaxson, then what would he do to Nemea?

She had to tell him the truth. She had to let him know she had no magic and their mating bond was, quite possibly, broken. She turned toward him, taking his hands in hers and looking him in those spectacular azure eyes.

"Jax, there's something I need to tell you."

But she hesitated, unsure how to proceed.

"What is it?"

She took a deep breath. The only way she was going to get through it, was if she spilled her guts as fast as she could. She opened her mouth to tell him everything when the door to his room burst open. Nyles stood there, his eyes bright and wild.

"She's asking for you, son."

Jaxson jumped to his feet and hurried out of the bedroom. Zahra forgot everything she was supposed to tell him and followed him to the master bedroom. Lady Isabella was on the bed now, the blankets covering her. She leaned back in a mountain of pillows. Her eyes open and she looked more alert than she had earlier. When she saw Jaxson enter, she lifted a frail hand toward him. He hurried toward her, perched on the edge of the bed and gently took her hand in his.

"Mother."

"I thought it was a dream. But it wasn't." Her voice was stronger than it was before.

"No, Mother. I'm here."

"And the girl? Is she?" Isabella asked.

Jaxson looked back at Zahra. With her heart in her throat, she approached the bed. "I'm here, my lady."

A smile cracked on her aged face. "My lady. I haven't been called that in ages. Come here, child." She patted the other side of the bed next to her.

Zahra complied, sitting across from Jaxson.

"It's good to see you, too." Despite her illness, she looked her over with a critical eye. She reached for her braid, ran a finger down it. "Your hair is longer. Your face is prettier than I remember."

Zahra flushed at the compliment. She glanced down, a sudden shyness overtaking her.

"I'm glad Logan was able to track you down," Isabella said. Despite her frail voice, she managed to sound smug.

Zahra's head snapped back up. "You sent Logan to find me? How did you know where I was?"

"I may be old and ill, child, but I'm still resourceful and have ways of finding things out."

Zahra wasn't sure if she was being truthful or not. The fact she sent Logan to find her meant something to her. Nyles came bustling into the room with the tea tray. He paused in the doorway, looking at the two of them sitting on either side of her.

"I brought tea."

Isabella scoffed. "Tea. All he ever wants me to drink is tea," she said to Zahra, then, to her husband, "Bring me a bourbon."

"Mother, a bourbon?"

Zahra couldn't stifle the giggle that escaped her.

"What's gotten in you, Bella? This is the most you've spoken in weeks," Nyles said.

"I'm tired of my present company. I have new people to chat with." She smiled again at Zahra and then Jaxson.

Nyles placed the tray on the nearby dresser and poured a cup. He handed it to Isabella but she waved it away.

"It's not tea I want. Be gone, both of you. Leave me here with the lovely girl. Jax, dear, bring me that bourbon."

"You'll tire yourself out," Nyles warned.

"I'll be the judge of that. Now, shoo. Both of you."

Jaxson rose, reluctantly, and headed toward the door. Nyles shuffled after him. He paused only a moment before pulling it closed. As soon as they were gone, Isabella leaned heavily into the pillows and closed her eyes. Her breathing was raspy. She looked exhausted, as if the interaction had taken a lot out of her. Zahra scooted closer, taking her hand and holding it. She didn't know what to say, if anything, so she remained quiet.

"Sweet girl." Now she sounded like the frail woman from earlier, when it took every ounce of energy to speak to Jaxson. "Glad you came."

"Can I get you anything?"

"No." Her head rolled from side to side. "My son loves you, I'm sure you know this." Her eyes fluttered open as she pinned Zahra with her bright blue gaze.

Zahra's heart did a quick thud against her chest. She knew Jaxson loved her, yes, but that was a long time ago. "He did once."

"He still does." She closed her eyes again and blew out a shuddering breath. "I only have a surge of energy every now and then. I'm afraid my husband is right that I tire easily."

"I should let you rest." Zahra started to rise, but Isabella gripped her hand tighter.

"Not before I have my say." Another breath shuddered out of her as though it was a labor even to breathe. "Marry him, child."

She stared at her for a long, mute moment, trying to comprehend what Lady Isabella said to her. "I don't understand."

"I'm dying. I want to see my son happy and married. Marry him."

"But I…Jaxson hasn't asked me."

"He will." She reached for her wedding band and slipped it off her finger. She held it up for Zahra to see. It was a diamond and sapphire band. Simple. Elegant. Perfect. "I plan to give him this for you."

Emotion clotted her throat. She bit her lip with the sudden rise of hot tears. All these years she hadn't shed one. Now, it seemed, she couldn't stop.

"I don't know what to say," Zahra finally said.

"When he asks," her eyes closed again, "say yes. Now, send me my son."

Jaxson paced the length of the hallway outside his mother's room, his hands behind his back. His father wandered off downstairs, but he refused to leave and resorted to pacing when Zahra didn't come out right away. He tried to listen at the door, but he heard nothing on the other side. His mother was a master at keeping her voice down. What could they be talking about? Why would his mother want to talk to her alone?

After long, painful moments, Zahra finally opened the door and stepped into the hall. Her face was blanched of color. Though she tried to hide the stricken look on her features, she didn't hide it very well at all.

"She wants to see you now," she said.

She started to slip by him, but he wrapped a hand around her upper arm. "Zee, what is it? What did she say?"

"That's for her to tell you."

Zahra moved out of his grasp and headed down the hall to his bedroom. She disappeared inside and closed the door.

Odd that, Jaxson thought.

He entered the bedroom and went to his mother. She looked drained of all energy, not at all like she had before she dismissed them all but Zahra. Her head was cushioned against the pillows, her eyes closed. He paused at the bedside, watching her.

"Don't hover, son. Sit." She spoke without opening her eyes.

Jaxson sat on the edge of the bed where he had earlier. He noticed, then, she no longer wore her wedding band.

"What did you say to Zahra, Mother?"

"She wouldn't tell you?" Her voice was quiet, frail.

"No."

"Good." Her eyes came open then. She reached for his hand, turning his palm upward. She dropped her wedding band into it and then leaned back into the pillows once again.

"What is this?"

"I thought that obvious."

"Your wedding ring?"

"Yes."

His heart pounded in his throat as he stared down at the diamond and sapphire band. He knew what his mother was getting at, but he didn't want to think about that. Not yet. Marriage had never been on his radar. It had never been a possibility because the woman he loved was betrothed to another.

"I don't—"

"Marry her, Jax. Isn't that what you want?"

"Yes, but—"

"Then take the ring and go ask her. Before I die, I want to know you and the girl you've pined away for your entire life are married and that, someday, you'll have children."

He stared down at the ring in his palm, the weight of it heavy against his skin, even though he knew it only weighed an ounce or two.

"You are mates, yes?"

His gaze flickered up to her as shock rolled through him. "How do you know about that?"

"Everyone knows about that, son. Why do you think Fenwick is so hellbent on marrying her to Talal? The sooner they marry her to that idiot son of Herrick's, the sooner they can get her with child and force out Logan and your father. They are determined to take over the Council."

Hearing this, anger pounded through him. If it was true—and

he suspected, it was—then how did his mother know? Zahra mentioned her father was determined to get her back into the Hidden Lands to marry her to Talal. Now he knew why, and he also knew why she didn't want to do it.

"How do you know this, Mother?"

"Because I told her." His father spoke from the doorway. He closed the door and moved to stand next to the bed. He reached for his wife's hand and held it.

"You didn't mention this before," Jaxson said to his father.

"No, I couldn't in case Herrick found a way to listen in on our conversations. It was one of the reasons why I called you home."

Jaxson wasn't sure what to say. He closed his hand around the ring and put his fist in his lap, trying to make sense of everything.

"I've had spies in the Council for a while now. Since Archer's death, Herrick has been determined to oust Logan."

"Why?" Jaxson asked.

"Revenge," Nyles said. "Or didn't you realize Archer was Herrick's brother?"

"Half-brother," Isabella corrected.

"Yes. Same mother. Different fathers," Nyles agreed.

Jaxson stared at the two of them as though they'd grown a second head. He hadn't any idea they were related.

"That's why Herrick took over for Archer, why he's after Logan and the dragon relics, why he wants to break the curse first," Jaxson said.

"Yes," Nyles said with a nod. "If he gets his hands on the relics, if he breaks the curse first, he intends to overthrow Logan and take over the Council."

"But not just the Council," Isabella said. "Tell him, my love."

"He wants to become High King and return the Hidden Lands back to the glory it once was when the Ancients ruled," Nyles said.

Jaxson had no words as he stared at his father. "I don't understand."

"It's very clear," his mother said. "He wants to rule all."

"And he will if he gets his hands on those relics first," Nyles added.

"Well, that's not going to happen. Logan has the Blood Stone and the dragon's tooth," Jaxson said. "All he lacks is the scale from a fire-drake."

"Not just any fire-drake," Nyles added. "A scale from a Rindhara bloodline."

"I know that's why he wants Zahra." He clenched his fist around the wedding band so tight, his muscles ached. "And why they'll have to kill me to get to her."

"There may be another option for them, though," Nyles said.

"And what is that?"

"Not what. Who," his mother corrected.

Nyles's lips thinned into a straight line. His face looked grim.

"All right, then, who?" he asked.

"Zahra has a sister."

Nemea. She, of course, would have the same magic as Zahra being from the Rindhara bloodline. She could also be forced to shift so they could take one of her scales. Even so, Herrick still did not have the Blood Stone or the dragon's tooth from the Gildhara. He still could not break the curse.

"Tell him the rest, my love," Isabella urged.

"It's not for me to tell, love."

"It is," she said, her voice weaker. "Tell him, Nyles. He deserves to know."

Nyles released her and ran his hand down his face, leaving a bloodless trail on his still grim face. If it was possible, he looked even grimmer.

"What rest?" Jaxson said.

"Before I tell you, you must promise not to let Zahra know I told you."

He didn't like the sound of this at all. "I promise."

Nyles took a deep breath and told him the truth about Zahra.

❧ 17 ❧

Jaxson left his parents' room. He closed the door behind him then leaned heavily on it. His stomach was in twisted knots. A queasy sensation had taken up residence, making him light headed. If he hated Fenwick before, he really hated him now.

And Nemea. They had to get to her as soon as possible. His mind was already working on a way to get her out of Fenwick's house and someplace safe, out of his and Herrick's reach. He didn't know how to do it without outright kidnapping the girl.

His fist was still clenched tight around the wedding band. He uncurled his fingers to see the stones had left deep impressions in his palm. His mother had made him promise he would ask Zahra marry him. She felt confident Zahra would say yes. He suspected it was what they had talked about before he was summoned to her bedside. His father suggested marrying her right away would at least halt the betrothal. There would still be the marriage contract to contend with.

As for the mating bond…well, Jaxson wasn't sure how to fix that. He wasn't sure what to do. He felt lost and bewildered at the thought that Zahra, his beloved, his mate, was no longer truly his.

He needed to talk to someone. He reached into his pocket and pulled out his smartphone. He dialed Logan. There was some magical thing about how they could still communicate with their smartphones across realms. Jaxson wasn't sure how it worked and didn't really care to know. All he cared about was that it worked.

Logan answered on the first ring. "Where are you? Rafe said you left New York."

"Someplace safe." He didn't want to tell him for fear there was a way Herrick could track him through his phone.

"I'll accept that answer for now. What's wrong?"

Logan knew him well enough to know he wouldn't call if there wasn't something wrong. He told him everything about his mother's illness had taken a turn, how Zahra could no longer shift and why, and his fear Fenwick would try to use Nemea to get a dragon scale. He spoke for a long time, letting the story spill out of him while Logan listened on the other end, not interrupting. When he finished, there was a long, deathly silence on the other end.

"You still there?" Jaxson asked.

"I am."

Another silence. "And?"

"That's a lot of information to process, Jax. First, I'm sorry about your mother. I always did like her. I knew she was ill but I didn't know she'd gotten worse."

"Do you think there's any way to reverse it? With the Blood Stone?"

"I don't know but it's worth looking into. If there's a way to save her, I'll do it."

"Thanks." He didn't know if his friend could help, but it gave him some comfort to know he'd at least try. "And about Zahra and Nemea?"

"This is definitely a problem. You need to get to her sister before Fenwick and Herrick decide to use her instead. You know what happened with Mia's father."

"Yes, but I would think since she's Fenwick's daughter, they wouldn't be so…" He paused, trying to think how to say it.

"So brutal? I wouldn't put anything past either of them. You know why."

He did.

"As for Zahra's missing dragon magic and what appears to be your broken mating bond…" Logan paused again, as though he were trying to think of a way to break even more bad news to him.

"What about it?"

"I've read a lot of the Ancients texts. My father was able to translate a lot of the Old Language from the books. In my search to find a way to break the curse, I've run across bits and pieces of information that seemed irrelevant at the time. I think there is some way to help her get her magic back," he said.

His hand tightened on the phone as he waited for his friend to continue. He clenched his jaw so tight, it ached.

"There is an old custom. I'm fuzzy on the details but you may be able to find something in your father's library. He loaned me several books from there a few months ago. There's something about a handfasting."

He'd forgotten about his father's library. His father was a book junkie. He had scoured old monasteries and churches and crumbling castles all over their realm looking for books that he could add to his collection. Some books had bindings that would fall apart when they were opened. A glimmer of hope sparked deep inside him.

"I'll see what I can find," he said. "What about the mating bond?"

"That I don't know. My best guess is you'll have to find a way to mate again," he said. "I'm sure that won't be too much of a burden." He chuckled.

"Thanks for your help, Logan."

"Good luck, my friend."

When they hung up, Jaxson immediately headed to his father's library. The room had often been a place of comfort for him growing up. Bookshelves lined every wall and were crammed full. In the center, there was a faded area rug and a small, round cocktail table and two oversized leather chairs. When he was a boy, his parents used to sit there while he played on the rug at their feet.

Inside, the room smelled like old books and leather. He loved that smell.

He started with the bookshelf to his left. The task was going to be a big one and he had no idea where to begin. His gaze went over every title, every crackled binding as he made his way down the length of the bookcase. By the time he reached the last bookcase, his eyes were tired and gritty, as if he had sand in them. He had almost given up when he saw the one title staring him in the face.

Marriage and Mating Rituals of the Ancients

How did his father have this? He didn't know but he was grateful he found it. He pulled it off the shelf and headed to one of the chairs. As he sat, he opened the cover. It creaked from non-use. The pages were yellow. As he flipped through it looking for the handfasting Logan mentioned, he finally saw the word in the middle of a page.

It was then followed by a mating custom. He read through it, memorizing the details.

Jaxson closed the book and replaced it on the shelf. With the idea committed to memory, he decided it was now or never to try it with Zahra. Hopefully, she would agree.

When he opened the door to his room, he halted. Zahra slept curled up on his bed. She had unplaited her hair and brushed out her long locks. Waves of rose-colored hair was splayed behind her. She looked so peaceful. He didn't want to disturb her since they had a long last few days but he needed to try this handfasting and mating custom before he lost his nerve.

He sat on the edge of the bed and brushed his fingers through her hair. She must not have been in a deep sleep because her eyes came open and met his.

"You spoke to your mother?" she asked.

"I did."

"What did she tell you?"

"Everything." Despite his promise to his father, he had to tell her he knew the truth.

Her face paled. She swallowed hard. "Everything?"

He nodded. "I know."

"Then you know why I can't help you."

He stroked her cheek with the back of his hand. "I know."

"Are you angry?"

"No. I wish you'd told me."

"I didn't know how. But I didn't know all the details until today." She turned her head to look away. "I should have told you."

"I'd wondered why I couldn't mindspeak to you and why my inner dragon couldn't sense yours. Now I know why. Your memories, though. I could sense those."

"How?"

"I think there is some bit of magic still left in you or I wouldn't have been able to sense them."

"My father destroyed me and my magic." Her voice wavered with the threat of tears.

"We're not going to let him win." He leaned close to her and placed a light kiss on her cheek.

"I don't think I can get it back, Jax."

"I think you can."

At that, she turned and looked him, question deep in her eyes. "Do you think so?"

"There is an Ancient handfasting and mating custom I found in one of my father's old books. I'm willing to try it if you are."

Color rose high in her cheeks. "Handfasting? Isn't that...?"

"Marriage, Zee. I'm asking you to marry me." He reached into his pocket and pulled out his mother's wedding band. He held up the circle for her to see. "Will you?"

Her bottom lip quivered for a brief moment before she got her emotions in check. This was what was his mother wanted, he knew. But as he looked through the old book, reading the about the handfasting, Jaxson realized it was something he wanted, too. He had denied himself the idea of marrying Zahra for so long, he hadn't realized how much he really wanted to marry her. Or how much he really loved her.

"But the betrothal..." she started.

"Our handfasting, mating, and consummation will negate the

betrothal. We'll find a way to break the marriage contract."

Her face flushed again. He could see her mind working as she thought about it. "Are you sure? I'm broken."

"That's not a nice thing to say about the girl I love." He reached for her left hand and slipped the ring on her finger. "Will you marry me, Zahra?"

Tears danced in her eyes as a small smile crept over her lips. "Yes. A thousand times yes." He kissed her, deep and long. When he pulled away, he brushed the back of his hand over her cheek. She cleared her throat.

"How does this handfasting work?"

"I need a long piece of material." Excitement came into his eyes. "I have an idea."

He hopped up from the bed and went to his closet. He came out a second later holding an old tie. She got to her feet. They faced each other.

"Now what?" she asked.

"Now, you give me your left hand." He held out his.

They grasped hands. He draped the tie over their joined hands. He gave her a surreptitious grin. "This will be awkward."

With his free hand, he flipped one end over the top, then the second end over until the tie loosely bound their hands together.

"That will have to do," he said.

"What's next?"

"Next we say the words. I'll say them first, then you repeat." She nodded agreement. He took a deep breath. "I, Jaxson, promise you, Zahra, to be your husband. Blood of my blood. Bone of my bone. Heart to heart and hand to hand. You are mine and I am yours. I give you my body. I give you my heart. I give you my soul until our life is done."

Zahra watched him drape the old tie over their bound hands with a sense of wonder and shock. It was almost as though she were having an out of body experience as he said the words of binding. Her heart pounded so hard, she thought it was going to pound right out of her chest.

She was actually marrying him. She'd said yes. Not because it's what his mother wanted her to do, but because, deep down, it's what she wanted to do. She loved Jaxson. She'd loved him all her life. She wanted him for longer than she could remember, missed him when he left her. Now that she had him back into her life, she wasn't sure she wanted to let him go.

It wasn't the wedding she dreamed about when she was a little girl. She didn't stand before him in the big white dress. There was no music, no fanfare, no guests. Just the two of them. And as she listened to him say the handfasting vows to her, she realized it was exactly how it should be.

It was perfect.

And it would ensure they could be together. That no one could come between them.

"Now, you," Jaxson said.

She took a steadying breath.

"I, Zahra, promise you, Jaxson, to be your wife. Blood of my blood. Bone of my bone. Heart to heart and hand to hand. You are mine and I am yours. I give you my body. I give you my heart. I give you my soul until our life is done."

When she finished, they stood in silence. At last, he leaned toward her and touched his lips to hers in a sweet kiss that stole her breath. His lips barely brushed hers but as they did, something deep inside her stirred. Something she hadn't felt in a long time. Like a hummingbird's wings beating a thousand flutters at once.

Us. Forever.

She glanced down at their entwined hands. "Are we married then?"

"Handfasted," he said.

"Married," she corrected. She lifted her gaze to his. The look of tenderness and love she saw deep in his eyes nearly shredded her heart.

How had she been lucky enough to be with him? That he loved her as much as she loved him? That he looked at her as if she were the only woman in the world for him? A little grin lifted the corner of his mouth.

"Now let's see if we can get your magic back."

She watched as he unwound the tie from their joined hands. "How do we do that?"

"You have to ask?" He winked as he slid the material from their hands. "I make long, slow love to you."

Oh, gods. She couldn't stand the thought when all she wanted was for it to be hot, fast, and hard like before. She'd wanted it that way so she wouldn't have to feel as much, then. But maybe he was right in that it should take a while. He should take his time, make her remember what it was like to be loved and wanted again.

A breath shuddered out of her. That flutter she felt deep inside now glowed like the beginnings of an ember.

He undressed her with slow methodical movements. He barely touched her, his fingers grazing her bare skin as he removed first her shirt, then pants. When she stood naked before him, he brushed the pad of his thumb over her pebble hard nipple. Gooseflesh erupted on every inch of her exposed skin.

Never would she have ever imagined they would be here, in this moment. Handfasted—married—about to bond to each other once again, about to consummate their sacred vows, right here in his bedroom. It was the last place she thought something like this would happen. If someone told her three days ago she'd be back in Jaxson's arms, she would have told them they'd lost their mind.

But now, she stood before him wondering why he was still fully clothed. She reached for his shirt, slipped her hands under the material and over his cool skin. His skin was always cool to the touch, always a welcome respite to the burning heat that was her own. She had lost that, too, when her magic disappeared.

Slowly, though, that warmth returned to her. Either that, or her emotions ran hot and high through her. She didn't know if she should hope the little glimmering glow she sensed earlier was that of her magic. It would devastate her if it was nothing.

Her hands ran up and over his chest covered in a smattering of hair. She always loved the curve of his chest under her hands. She shoved his shirt upward. He complied by lifting his arms and letting her pull it off over his head. She tossed it aside.

Zahra slipped her arms around his waist and stepped into the circle of his arms. Skin brushed skin as they came together. Their mouths fused in a sweet kiss. His lips sipped her mouth as if she were a fine wine to be savored. One hand stroked the length of her hair all the way down her back.

It was the most delicious sensation she'd experienced in forever.

As they kissed some more, her fingers popped open the button of his jeans. She slipped her hands inside. A quiet moan rumbled his throat. He moved away, shucked his pants, kicked them aside, and then took her in his arms again. His fervent kiss sent heat pulsing through her down to the apex of her thighs.

Jaxson pulled her to him in a fierce move of possession and started to back her toward the bed.

"I thought you wanted to go slow," she teased.

"I am."

His voice rumbled around that glorious chest of his. She could feel the vibration of it through her. It made her head spin with delight.

Her knees crumpled when the backs of her legs hit the edge and she went down on her back. Jaxson wasted no time as he dropped down, pushing her legs apart. His mouth was on her a second later. She cried out when his tongue slipped over her dampness. Her hands fisted in his short hair, her nails scraping along his scalp with her pleasure.

She arched her back as her hips rocked against him. He slipped a finger inside her, then his free hand landed on her breast. She urged him on, harder, faster, and begged him not to stop, not to ever stop. It was what she needed, what she craved, what had been missing from her life all these years. Him. His love. His desire. His mouth and hands on her. There had been no other man who could make her want the way Jaxson did. No other man who could take her to such pleasurable heights. No other man who could make her come with a fiery look across the room.

He did that to her. He'd always done that to her. And she was certain he always would.

He removed his finger and planted a kiss on each inner thigh. The absence of his mouth on her left her wanting, left her pounding and throbbing for him. When he stood up, his tall form towered over her. Even in the shadowy darkness, she could see the desire, the need, the love sparking in his eyes.

She wanted to show him the same. She wanted him to feel the same as she did. She lifted up from the bed, her hands on his hips as she pulled him closer, closer still. Her tongue flickered out over the tip of his erection. Delight skipped though her at the dampness she tasted there. She sucked him between her lips, pulling his hips toward her as she tasted his engorged length.

Gods, she missed him, she missed this.

When they first came together, they were young inexperienced lovers. He'd been her first in everything. She had no idea how much she would like taking the length of him into her mouth until she'd done it over and over.

His hands fisted in her hair, tugging gently on her scalp. He emitted a deep groan as he gave her a nudge and pulled her away. With her hands still on his hips, she tilted her head back and looked up at him.

There was a slight smile playing at the corner of his mouth.

"You didn't like that?" She said it in her best innocent voice.

"Oh, I did. Very much. But if you don't stop now, I cannot be held responsible for my actions."

"Oh," she breathed, understanding what he meant.

"Turn over and stand on your hands and knees."

"Aren't you demanding?" She grinned as she complied, all too happy to do what he told her.

The mattress sighed with his weight as he got behind her, his hands on her hips, his fingers digging into her flesh. The tip of his erection teased her opening. She squirmed against him, a breathy moan escaping her with her need.

Unable to stand it another second, she tilted her hips and shoved backward into him. He grunted as he slipped inside her, filling her up. She cried out with her pleasure, the joy of him inside her pounding through her. She hadn't realized how long she'd carried the ache of needing him until he was there with her, sliding in and out of her in long slow strokes to the point it made her head want to explode.

Zahra fisted the coverlet and ground her back teeth together. The sensation of it all was too much and not enough. The glow in the ember burst into flame, searing through her with a scorching desperation.

"Harder, Jaxson. I need to feel you harder."

"No." He sounded so defiant. "I'll go harder when I'm ready."

But she was ready. Didn't he understand that? Didn't he sense how much she needed him to pick up the pace?

Suddenly, her dragon was there, roaring back to life with such force, a strangled cry escaped her. The heat of it went through her from head to toe, pushing through her. He must have sensed it, too, because he pounded against her. She knew she was close to finishing. She needed to see his face, to look into his eyes and know he was the one—the only one—for her.

"I want to see your face, Jax. I want to look at you."

She tried to turn her head, but he shoved her toward the mattress and fell on top of her. His hot mouth was her neck, whispering in her ear. "Not yet."

His body moved against her back. One hand snaked between her and the mattress. His fingers slid into her damp curls, touching her while he pounded into her from behind. Gods, it felt so good. He felt so good. But it wasn't enough. Even though he hadn't moved from her, it still wasn't enough. She needed more. She needed to wrap her legs around his waist.

The heat inside her intensified to almost unbearable. She whimpered, needed release. And suddenly he was gone from her. A cool breath of air kissed her exposed backside.

"Roll over," he said.

She happily complied.

His big body was between her legs as she opened up to him. But he didn't make a move to touch her.

She was aware of the throbbing of her heart, the painful pound of her pulse, the heat still pooling between her legs. Jaxson slid inside her, then out again, making sure she was aware of every inch of him. He continued, over and over. She wrapped her body around him and pulled him close, their mouths fused in a fiery kiss.

Her dragon magic burst through her the same time her orgasm did, flaring to life with a bright white flash and a loud reverberation that rocked her to her very soul. She flung her arms out to the side, her hands gripping the covers as her back arched and her body pushed against his. Everything burned from the inside out, her dragon magic surged through her, and suddenly she could hear everything going through his mind.

Us. Forever.

A groan of pleasure ripped through him as he shuddered against her before he finally stilled. He pressed a kiss against her temple and then immediately rolled off her. Cool air skipped over her sweat-dampened skin.

"Your skin, Zee…it's…glowing."

She lifted a hand and saw, in fact, her skin had a strange fiery glow to it.

"And it's hot to the touch." He reached a hand toward her but jerked it back before he could touch her.

She glanced at him, saw his skin was red as though he'd spent too much time in the sun. "You look sunburned. Did I do that to you?" Worry gnawed through her.

He glanced down and ran a hand over his chest. "I think you did."

"I'm sorry." She bit her lower lip.

"No. It doesn't hurt. It was unlike anything I've ever felt. I sensed your dragon come back, as though it broke through some type of shield or restraint. It roared, Zee."

She knew. She'd heard it in her head. She'd felt it through her entire body. "Are you all right? I didn't hurt you?"

"You didn't hurt me. I'm fine. Are you?"

Was she? She laid there, staring up at his ceiling, while he sat on the bed next to her. Her husband. With a tentative thought, she reached out for their mating bond. The flicker of it was there, a faint distant spark. Like it had come back to life. Somehow, she knew if they continued to be together, it would get stronger.

She didn't answer him. Instead, she asked, "Do you feel it?"

He was silent for a long moment, then he reached for her hand, grasped it. "The mating bond. It's there again. Very faint."

"Jaxson?"

"Yes?"

"I think we need to do that again. You know, to strengthen that bond."

He leaned down to her, his lips brushing over hers. "I think you're right."

❦ 18 ❧

She lost herself in him and he in her. It was dawn before they managed to untangle their tired bodies from each other. At some point, she'd slept, content in his arms as he stroked her hair and held her. It had been a long time since she had a sense of safety and security.

Since she stepped foot in the human realm, she knew, eventually, her past would catch up to her. What she didn't know was that both her father and the man she once loved would arrive in the same day.

Their mating bond gained strength the more they were together but it still wasn't as strong as it once had been. Maybe it never would be. Even if it wasn't, she was glad they had found each other again.

"Me, too, Zee."

She flushed. "You heard that."

It wasn't a question but he answered as though it were anyway. "I did."

Mindspeak was part of the mating bond. When she attuned to him, she could hear his thoughts, too. What she sensed there made her blush. He was never shy about his passionate thoughts about her. Even when they were young. He made it clear she was the only girl for him.

"Zahra, about your sister…" He paused, as if choosing his words.

"I'm lying naked in your arms and you want to talk about my sister?" Her tone was playful, but she sensed the worry gnawing at him.

"Not a great time, I know, but we need to get to her."

Zahra moved to a sitting position. Her hair fell over her shoulders. She was on instant high alert. Nemea meant the world to her. She was young, innocent, sweet. If anything happened to her, she would never forgive herself for leaving her behind.

"Do you think she's in danger?"

"I think she could be. Is she still living at your father's house?"

Zahra nodded. "I haven't communicated with her in a few days. We used to talk every week, but since…" She made a hand motion between the two of them.

"I know. I'm a distraction."

"A good distraction." She smiled. "I'm worried about her, too. I don't trust our father."

Something her father said came back to her.

You will force me to make unpleasant decisions.

She started to slide off the edge of the bed, but he caught her wrist. She gave him a questioning look.

"Not we."

Zahra was aware of the hard glint in his eyes. "I'm not staying behind. She's my baby sister."

"It's not safe for you. If your father even senses for a second your magic is back, he'll want you instead."

"Instead?" She repeated. "You think he's going to use my sister because I refused to help him, don't you?"

"Yes. And if they have a fire-drake dragon scale, then they'll go after Logan for the Blood Stone and the tooth."

"I'm coming with you," she insisted.

"You're staying here."

"Jax, please don't make me stay behind. If anything happens to her…"

He placed a finger over her lips to silence her. "Nothing will happen to her. I'm going to make sure of it."

While she trusted him and knew he would make good on his promise, being left behind was still not an option. She gave him her best pouty eyes. His shoulders drooped.

"Fine, you can come but you're going to stay out of the way and let me do what I need to do," he said.

"And what is that?"

"Whatever it takes."

Hearing him say that sent a flash of desire through her. She loved when he went all alpha dragon and took matters into his own hands. She leaned toward him, brushed a kiss along his scruffy jaw, loving the rough feel of it against her sensitive lips.

"I love it when you take charge."

"Is that why you agreed to the handfasting? Because I took charge?"

It hadn't really occurred to her until he pointed it out. His mother had insisted they marry, had insisted she say yes. And then what happened? Jaxson showed up with a ring.

"Your mother told me to say yes if you asked, so I did." She flicked her tongue over his earlobe. "Your mother sure is pushy."

"It's where I get it."

She giggled. "I can tell." She moved away from him and got to her feet, putting distance between the two of them. "What's the plan to get my sister?"

"I'm glad to see your one-track mind is still intact." He got up and reached for his pants.

As he pulled them on, she kissed his shoulder. "As is yours. I can hear your dirty thoughts, sir. It's time to focus."

"Now who's pushy?" He snatched his shirt off the floor and pulled it on over his head.

"I am. Let's go."

———⌀———

Being with Zahra made Jaxson lose all track of time. Those hours with her were the best hours of his life. Well, at least since they had last been together when they were young. Zahra was right, though. They were different people. They had grown up. When they were young, it was about getting naked. Now, it was about taking time to savor one another, to learn what each other liked and how. It had been everything from slow and easy to hard and fast.

He didn't know if the handfasting would truly make their marriage a real one. All he knew was he never wanted to be parted from Zahra again. That and when her magic flared back to life deep inside her, his dragon made it known it was pleased. It was is if it had uncurled from a deep hibernation, awakening for the first time in eons. He'd always knew it was there, deep in the shadows of his psyche slumbering away, but it had never bothered to come out. The second it realized Zahra was near, it purred. He promised his dragon-self he would never let her go. It seemed content enough with that.

Being with her the last few hours would never make up for the time they spent apart. Now that they were married, that she was his forever, he would spend the rest of his life making sure she was happy and she was his.

Getting her sister away from their domineering father was the first step. He knew how much Nemea meant to her. They had almost been inseparable as children. He wondered how she could leave her behind when she knew what a tyrant her father was.

After they showered and dressed, they headed down the stairs.

"Tell me something, Zahra. Why didn't you take her with you when you left the Hidden Lands?"

Her cheeks flushed as the memory flickered through her mind. "I wanted to, but I knew if I left with her, my father would never stop hunting us. Plus, I knew he always liked Nemea best."

"I don't think that's true."

"It is true. After our mother died, he favored her because she looks like her. She reminds him of her. He contracted me into a loveless marriage with a man I've barely spoken two words to because he doesn't like me."

He didn't know what to say to that. By the pained expression on her face, she was convinced it was the truth. It hurt him for her.

"And before you disagree," she continued, sensing he was about to do just that, "I know it's the truth because of the way he treats me. He may have loved me once, as his first-born daughter, but all that changed. It took me a long time to be at peace with that."

"Are you now?" he asked.

She nodded. "Yes."

"And yet you were still willing to go with him and follow through with the betrothal to Talal."

"I didn't think I had a choice. I didn't think…" She paused, motioned between them. "I didn't think we would happen ever again."

He brushed his fingers down her cheek. "We did and I'm glad."

"So am I."

"Now, let's go get your sister."

They slipped out of the house and into the early morning air. Both of them paused outside the door.

The sky was once a crisp, clear blue. The landscape was lush and verdant. The small village they lived in had been vibrant and full of color and activity. Zahra, Jaxson, and Logan had grown up in this village together. They played in the nearby glen. They had First Flight, where they all learned to take flight for the first time, at the Coliseum on the edge of the village.

Now, the village was mostly deserted. The houses were abandoned and falling into ruin. The sky was no longer that bright blue. Instead, it was gray tinged with a smoky haze that never seemed to go away. The land was no longer lush and green. Now, the land was brown and dying. Some of the lochs had dried up, leaving them without a fresh water supply.

He hadn't been back in nearly a year. She hadn't been back in much longer, so the shock had to be far greater for her than him. He looked at her, saw the pensive look on her face, the way she bit her bottom lip.

"I had no idea," she whispered. "How long has it been like this?"

"It's been slowly changing for a few years."

She pressed her fingers against her lips. Sadness etched her face. "Is it like this everywhere?"

"Yes."

"And this is the curse you were talking about?" she asked.

"It is."

"Breaking it will revert the Hidden Lands back to the way it once was?"

"We hope so," Jaxson said.

She dropped her hands to her side, her palms open and flat. He glanced down to see flames dancing around her fingers. In that instant, his dragon flared to life and banged against his skull, wanting out. It could sense her distress, her anguish, her fury. Her skin glowed, reminding him of the color of a fiery sunset. Reminding him of when her magic flared to life once again inside her.

"Zee, are you doing that on purpose?"

She lifted her hands, saw the flames. "No. It's because I'm upset and angry. I can feel the hot emotion pumping through me."

"So can my dragon."

"It can?" she asked.

"Yes. It senses your emotions. When you're upset, it wants out. It wants to rip into whatever made you upset."

She turned her head to look at him, a small smile playing upon her lips. "I think that's the sweetest thing you've ever said to me."

He suppressed a laugh, then reached for her hand. "Come on. Let's go."

They walked hand-in-hand, something they hadn't done in eons. Walking through the nearly deserted village was eerie, though, and unlike anything they had experienced together. Times had changed. Their lives had changed. Their world had changed.

And not for the better.

Zahra's house where she grew up was only a short walk from his. And beyond her house was where Logan grew up. They had all been close once. They would constantly sneak out together, lay on the grass in the glen, and gaze up at the stars with a million plans of things they were going to do, places they were going to see. None of that had come to fruition.

At the front of the small cottage, they paused. She tensed. Her tight shoulders lifted up around her ears. He could hear her shallow breathing and knew she was trying to find a way to control it. He squeezed her hand.

"Hey, I'll be right here with you every step of the way."

She cut him a glance, braved a smile and gave him a nod. "I know. I'm grateful for that."

At the door, she knocked. It seemed odd, he thought, that she knocked on her own door. That she wouldn't go inside and announce her presence. Apprehension wafted off her in waves as they waited for the door to open.

A minute later it did. The family butler stood on the other side with his nose in the air. Jaxson couldn't recall his name, but he definitely knew the sour face.

"Lady Zahra, this is an unexpected surprise."

She released Jaxson's hand, then pushed her way inside. "Is my father home? I want to see him."

"His lordship is otherwise indisposed," the butler said in his pinched, high-pitched voice.

"Tell him I'm here. I want to see him now," Zahra demanded. Once they were inside, she reached for his hand again, gripping it hard enough to convey the fear roiling through her.

The man lifted an eyebrow. He opened his mouth to respond.

"It's all right, Mervyn. That will be all."

Mervyn. That was the poor sod's name.

Fenwick said it as he exited his office and entered the entry hall.

The man gave a half bow to his employer and disappeared like a good servant. Zahra stiffened again, her bravado dissipating. Her father's gaze flickered from her to Jaxson and back again. His gaunt face had a look of disdain.

"To what do I owe the pleasure of your presence, daughter?"

"I've come to see Nemea," she said, getting right to the point, pleasantries skipped.

"I'm afraid she's not here." He didn't offer any more information.

"Where is she?" Zahra took a step toward her father, still gripping Jaxson's hand. "If you've hurt her—"

"Oh, she's quite safe." He didn't offer any more information than that.

Zahra had lost patience. She released Jaxson's hand and shoved past her father. She moved deeper into the house, calling her sister's name. She disappeared down a hallway, opening and closing doors with a slam. No doubt the bedrooms. Her father, meanwhile, stood in the entry with a disgusting smirk on his face.

Jaxson didn't like it one bit. His hand curled into a fist, ready to strike him.

Zahra returned, her face flushed and her eyes wild. "Where is my sister?"

Fenwick folded his arms over his chest. "Since you failed to show at our designated meeting point, I had to make other arrangements."

Jaxson sensed the fear flickering through Zahra.

"What does that mean?"

The smile spread on his face. "It means, dear daughter, Nemea is taking your place."

❧ 19 ❧

The terror that sliced through Zahra was something she had never felt before. Her knees went weak. The blood rushed to her head in a whoosh and for a moment, she saw nothing but black pinpricks dancing in her eyes. She stumbled backward away from her miserable father.

"What do you mean taking my place?"

"It will all be underway shortly. In fact, I should be going."

Her father tried to step around Jaxson but he blocked his path. The glare her father gave him would have seared holes through a lesser man, but Jax stood his ground. She loved him for that.

"What will be underway?" Jaxson asked.

"I do apologize for not informing you sooner. But Nemea has agreed to help us save the realm." He paused, gave her a pointed look. "Unlike you."

Her breath hitched. A cold fist pressed the center of her chest. "Are you planning to force her to shift so you can steal one of her scales?"

Her father turned that glare on her. It was a look she had seen many times as a girl when she was growing up. Then, she cowered. Today, she stood her ground. She lifted her chin a little higher.

"How do you know about that?" Fenwick asked.

"I know about everything. I know you're working with Herrick. I know you wanted me to marry his worthless son to further the family line. I know you are both plotting against Logan. I also know you're trying to get your hands on the other two dragon relics."

164

She did not like the dark look he gave her. The look of shear and utter hate. The look that said she knew way too much and she would pay for that. But she had to tell him. She had to let him know she was onto him and aware of his little coup. She had to protect Nemea at all cost. She didn't care so much about herself. She could handle her father. So could Jaxson. But Nemea was innocent in all this.

"Someone has been filling your head with lies." Fenwick gave Jaxson a scathing glance. "I can guess who."

"They aren't lies, Father, and you know it. It's the truth. I won't let you hurt her."

That smile, that disgusting smirk, played upon his lips. "As if you have a choice."

He hit her with a hold spell. It rendered all her movements useless but left her conscious. Jaxson lunged toward Fenwick, but he had been expecting that. He turned the spell on him next. She had been a fool to think she could come here, grab Nemea, and get out without incident. She'd forgotten how powerful he was and how willing he was to use that power.

"I do apologize for this horrific treatment of you both, but you give me no choice and I'm running late." He turned to look at Zahra. "Your sister's fate is out of your hands and now in mine. If you had done what I asked back in New York, this would be a very different situation. You and I both know that. As for him…" He cut Jaxson a glance. "I'm disappointed you still insist on hanging around this dragon trash."

Her fury surged through her, pulsing bright and wild and hot behind her eyes. She couldn't move or speak due to the hold spell. One thing he would never do was use his magic in the human realm. She knew that's why he didn't simply cast the spell on her before and drag her away. He respected the rules of the human realm.

"It pains me to leave you this way, daughter, but you gave me no choice. If you'll excuse me, I have to go now."

He stepped around them and exited the house, slamming the

door behind him. Zahra knew the spell would eventually wear off, but they didn't have that kind of time. She had to break through and get to her sister. She had to save her from Herrick before he stole one of her scales. She knew Nemea well enough to know the only way she would have agreed to help them was if they filled her head with lies.

The conversation with her father hadn't gone even close to planned. She had hoped she could talk some sense into him, she would see Nemea here and could take her with her when they left. But things were never that simple.

Fury built up through her, boiling her blood. Her dragon had come to life deep inside her and prowled the confines of her mind. It had only recently been resurrected, so she wasn't sure what type of mental state her dragon-self would be in. The beast had been suppressed for a decade.

Are you all right? Jaxson's voice flickered through her mind. It was comforting to hear him, to know he was there even though they could not verbally speak to each other.

Fine. Her reply was terse and she knew it.

She was too busy trying to control her unwieldy magic. All it wanted to do was burst through her, exploding like a collapsing star. Her inner beast was adamant it be let out to deal with the insolence. She had to remind the thing that the person who was insolent was her father. As much as she hated him, she didn't want him dead.

Even with her talking down the violence, her dragon would have none of it. Instead of slinking away to the dark recesses of her mind, it remained at the forefront of her mind, pulsing that brilliant, angry white light.

Zahra, you're fire. You can get us out here.

I know what I am, she snapped, and then instantly regretted it. She knew Jaxon tried to help. Then, in a more soothing tone, she added, I can't control it.

You don't have to. Not here in this realm.

Despite her bitchiness, he was still willing to help her, to speak to her. A breath shuddered out of her as relief sputtered through her. He was right. In this realm, dragons were not an unusual sight.

When was the last time you shifted, Zahra?

She thought back, trying to remember the last time she was able to do it. It had been so long ago she wasn't sure she remembered what it felt like.

Too long, she finally said.

His smile was a brush against her mind. Then let's shift together.

But how? The hold spell—

It can't hold us forever. He wanted to buy some time to put distance between us and him, he said.

Maybe Jaxson was right in that she could break free from the hold spell with her magic, that she could shift into her dragon-self.

We need to show your father he can't treat you or Nemea that way. The best way to do that is in dragon form, he added.

Doubt edged through her, pushing back the fury she'd felt with her father. I don't even know if I can, Jax.

His mind brushed hers. It was almost as if he'd brushed a kiss over her cheek. I believe in you. Now believe in yourself.

Indecision and fear flickered through her mind. It had been so long since she'd shifted, she was terrified of trying and failing. If she failed, how long would the hold spell keep them here?

She sensed Jaxson's magic flaring deep inside him. She cut him a glance, but saw nothing out of the ordinary. He still stood there, frozen in the same position as he was when her father cast the spell. He closed his eyes, the only movement she could see. And then he wiggled his fingers. He was using his magic to break free from the hold spell.

A bright flash of light surrounded him, blinding her. When it faded and she could focus again, he was crouched on the ground, his head down. She could see the muscles working along his back under his shirt and she knew any second now, his wings would sprout and he would shift.

Her breath caught in her throat as she thought about how

magical and wonderful it would be to see him transform from human to dragon. It had been too long since she'd seen him in that form and she wondered if he would still look the same as he did so long ago.

He lifted his head. Their eyes met. His azure eyes burned bright. He shot to his feet and ran for the door, flinging it open. It banged against the wall but remained open enough for her to see him change from man to beast. His bones popped and cracked with the transformation. Once he was in dragon form, his tattered clothes drifted to the ground as though they were scraps. He took to the sky, the beat of his translucent large wings the only sound she could hear.

Your turn, love.

I always did love your azure-colored scales, Jax. They're so beautiful.

His dragon hissed approval in response, white smoke coming from his snout to let her know he appreciated the compliment. But Jaxson, the man, was still in there and needed to coax Zahra, the dragon, into existence.

Your can do this, he told her.

Her eyes flickered closed as she took a deep breath, in and out. Her dragon sensed his was nearby and came to life, the magic burning like a flare deep inside her. She imagined breaking through the hold spell like punching through webbing and the second she did that, it released her. Her magic was there, big and beautiful and bright. She flexed her fingers, opened her eyes, and took off at a run.

As she ran out of the house, her body transformed from the girl into the dragon. Her neck elongated. Her body changed from human to dragon in a fluid motion that left her breathless. Her wings tore through her clothes and unfurled for the first time in years, flapping against the wind. Her shredded clothes were left behind her as she leapt from the ground and took flight.

That's my girl.

What little sunlight there was glinted off her yellow-orange scales as she banked left toward the sun, moving up, up, up, closer to it. She gained strength from the sun and soaked up the solar energy as she soared upward. He followed her in her ascent, staying close. So close she could sense his joy at seeing her in her dragon form. She hovered there, basking in the sunlight for as long as she could. She turned her big body and dove back toward the ground.

His wings flapped near her as he followed her. She hugged the rooftops and soared over the village as if she'd been set free from some terrible prison. Her magic throbbed and pulsed through her. Elation. Sheer joy. Wondrous delight. All emotions she hadn't experienced in such a long time, she almost didn't recognize them.

But all that disappeared when she saw the Coliseum and the High Council building not far from that reminding her of her true reason for shifting.

There's the Coliseum, he said.

She eyed it from her vantage point high in the sky and saw a small gathering there. Her dragon sensed her sister.

Zahra dove toward the building.

Jaxson followed her as close as he could. But she was fast. Faster than he recalled. He had no idea what she was planning. All he could sense was her fury.

Zahra was a wild child, a free spirit, the girl who always knew what she wanted and how to get it. When she made up her mind, there was no changing it. He loved that about her but he was fearful of what she would do once she got to the Coliseum.

She banked and took a nosedive right for it. She put her back legs down, her wings controlling her descent. She landed with a thud so loud, it made the ground vibrate. Jaxson alighted next to her. There was her father and his bodyguard, Bastian, along with Herrick, Talal, and Nemea. Her sister's eyes were wide and round as she stared up at both of them.

Zahra let out a roar so loud, it rattled the place and every building in the vicinity.

No one moved. And then he heard her father's voice.

Stupid girl.

A growl deep in her throat rumbled through her, evidence she had heard him, too. He knew if she shifted back to human form now, she would be naked. As would he. But she didn't appear to be ready to shift back. She took another step toward her father, leaning down so that her snout was right in front of him. She puffed out heated steam from her nose, clouding the air around him and the others. He didn't even flinch.

"Zahra!" Nemea gasped her name in surprise.

It had been years since he'd seen her younger sister. Nemea was not the little fresh-faced girl he remembered. She had grown into a woman. Tall, beautiful, with hair that cascaded into waves down her back much like Zahra's except in teal instead of pink. She had classic features with high cheekbones, a clefted chin that came to a point, and heart-shaped blood-red lips. Her bright green eyes were wide and round as she looked up at her sister in amazement.

She turned her big body to the side, lifted her massive tail and swiped it through the dirt, making a shower of dust all around them.

Herrick and Fenwick were not as enthralled as Nemea. Talal merely stood next to his father looking bored and annoyed at the whole situation. Bastian hung back behind them keeping a watchful eye on both dragons. There was a tense silent standoff. Jaxson shifted from one foot to the other, waiting to see what would happen next.

Nemea's gaze went from Zahra to their father and back again. "I don't understand what's happening. You said Zahra was never coming back, Father. You said she was banished."

He lied to her, Zahra said.

Yes, he agreed.

Zahra moved her head and lowered it to the ground in front of her sister. Her intense gaze was on the girl. Though he couldn't hear if they mindspoke to each other, the meaning was clear. She wanted her sister to alight upon her back.

Nemea took a tentative step toward Zahra.

"Whatever she's told you, Nemea, is a lie," Fenwick said.

Zahra huffed out another heated breath at her father, the steam rising around them all. Herrick stood next to him, annoyance on his cruel face.

Nemea paused long enough to look at her father over her shoulder, hesitating. She glanced back at Zahra who continued to hold her head down closer to the ground in invitation. Jaxson tried to tap into her mind, to see if they were communicating, but he got nothing.

Herrick stepped forward then, his gaze fixed on Zahra. "I thought you told me, Fenwick, that she refused to return to the Hidden Lands and that's why we had to go with the other girl." He motioned to Nemea as though she were nothing but a second-hand garment.

"The 'other' girl? What does that mean?" Nemea's faced flushed as she fixed her gaze on Herrick. It reminded Jaxson of Zahra when she was angry. Definitely a family trait.

"She did refuse," Fenwick said to Herrick, ignoring her. His voice was cold and hard.

Jaxson noticed then Bastian making his way from the back toward Nemea. He stiffened, keeping his watchful gaze on the man.

"Nemea also has fire-drake blood. I told you that, too," Fenwick continued. "She will do what we need her to do."

Nemea folded her arms over her chest. "And what is that, Father?"

Suddenly, all hell broke loose. Drakana surged through the Coliseum armed with obsidian blades. Two of them took hold of Nemea, grabbing her by the arms and dragging her away from Zahra. Several of them headed straight for Zahra, but she was too focused on her sister to care.

Zahra—

He started to shout a warning into her mind but that was as far as he got. Zahra saw them and reared back, her head soaring into the sky as two of them reached her. Her gaze was still transfixed on her sister. He could see her agitation, her frustration that two men dragged her away from them.

Jaxson had to do something. The fire bubbled up deep inside his throat as he turned his head and belched a ball of flame. It enveloped one of the Drakana headed for Zahra. The other didn't even seem fazed by the situation and kept running toward her. Before he could get another fire ball ready deep in his throat, the man with the obsidian blade lunged. He stuck the blade in one of her hindlegs. She roared in fury and pain and tried to kick the man off but he held on with both hands.

Jaxson realized then he dug the blade deep into her leg and was using it as a tool to remove one of her scales. With the tip of the blade, he pushed the scale out away from her body. Jaxson barked a cry and swung around, swiping the Drakana with the tip of his poisonous barbed tail. It crashed into the man's chest, the needles sinking deep into flesh. Jaxson jerked him away from Zahra, but the obsidian blade remained behind.

She staggered backward, stumbling on her hurt leg. The pitiful moans she emitted echoed through the empty arena. Even if he wanted to, there was nothing he could do for her while he was still in dragon form.

It was then he saw Bastian running toward her towing Nemea behind him. Somehow, Bastian managed to get her away from her father, Herrick and the other Drakana. As Bastian approached her, he released Nemea's hand. She placed both her palms on the underside of Zahra's belly, crooning soft words to her. It calmed her long enough for Bastian to grab the blade and yank it out of her leg. But in doing so, he dislodged the loose scale. It tumbled the ground as bright red blood trickled down her yellow-orange scales.

As Bastian clutched the bloodied blade, Nemea was already climbing up on Zahra's back. She reached her hand down for Bastian, who grabbed it and hoisted himself up behind her. A second later, Zahra was in the air. Jaxson took off right behind her, flapping his wings as hard as he could to get them away from the Drakana on the ground. Obsidian-tipped arrows flew past them as they soared higher and higher away to safety.

To freedom.

❧ 20 ☙

He didn't know where to go, so he led them to the only place he could think of. The family cabin in the woods. The very one where they had first mated. Only this time, there would be no romantic interludes. No snow keeping them locked inside in front of a fire.

Jaxson landed near the cabin and waited for Zahra to do the same. Her landing wasn't elegant at all as she stumbled with her injured back leg. It took several panicked moments for her to get her big body under control. Nemea and Bastian slipped off her back and got out of the way moments before Zahra crashed to the ground on her side.

After willing himself to calm, Jaxson shifted back into human form and then made a mad dash for the cabin door. He kicked it in with his bare heel and went inside. His frantic gaze went over the dust covered furniture. Surely, there was something he could use to cover up. He hurried to the bathroom, found a neatly folded towel on the shelf over the toilet and snatched it.

He wrapped it around his waist as he headed back outside to see to Zahra.

Her breathing was shallow. Her eyes closed. Nemea stood at her snout, her hands patting her trying to keep her calm. Jaxson went to her injured leg first and checked the wound. It oozed with that disgusting black foam and he knew the poison had already entered her bloodstream. There was only one person he knew that would have the antidote.

"Will she be all right?" Nemea asked, fear edged her voice.

"Yes, but we have to get her into human form as soon as possible. And we need the antidote for the poisonous blade," Jaxson said.

"There isn't one," Bastian said.

Jaxson cut him a glance and gave him a curt nod. "There is but we don't have much time."

"How do we make her shift back into human form?" Nemea asked.

"Her magic is unstable right now," Jaxson said, "so I don't really know the answer to that."

"Why? What's happened to her?" Nemea stiffened with fear and dread.

"It's a long story I don't have time to tell. I have to find Rafe."

Without waiting for an answer, he opened a portal and stepped through. The last thing he heard before the portal closed was, "Who's Rafe?"

Jaxson stood in Rafe's darkened living room with his hands clenched into fists as he waited for his eyes to adjust. The bedroom door flung open. A shirtless Rafe stood in the doorway, armed and ready to shoot. Jaxson held up his hands.

"It's me, Jaxson."

He lowered the gun. "What the hell are you doing here? I thought you were in the Hidden Lands."

"Zahra's been stabbed with an obsidian blade. She needs your help."

"Where is she?"

"The Hidden Lands. I can open a portal back there."

"Give me a few minutes to get the antidote."

He disappeared back into the bedroom. Jaxson could hear murmured voices as he spoke to Mia. A few minutes later he was back in the living room fully dressed with a medical kit in his hand. Relief sputtered through Jaxson and he knew Zahra would be all right.

Jaxson opened the portal.

ᘓ ᘔ

Zahra floated through darkness for what seemed an eternity. She dreamed her sister climbed on her back and then they flew away together up into the heavens away from their dreadful father.

She peeled her eyes open. It took some effort since it seemed as if they had been glued shut. When she finally pried them open, she stared at a wood-beamed ceiling she didn't recognize. Her mouth was full of cotton. Her head was full of lead. Her limbs refused to move. She couldn't quite remember what had happened to her.

What she could feel without question was the deep throb of her left leg from ankle to hip. The pain was like nothing she had experienced before. She groaned.

"She's awake!"

The female voice was familiar, warm, sweet, endearing. Zahra tried to lift her head but couldn't. Nemea's face floated into her line of vision. Her sweet, innocent face. Tendrils of teal hair hung down from the side of her face. The rest of her hair was pulled back and secured at the nape of her neck in a loose ponytail. She smiled down at her, the relief evident on her face.

"Thank the gods, you're awake." She crouched down next to her. Zahra turned her head, wishing she could lift her hand and touch her face, to make sure she was really there.

"Is this a dream?" Her voice rasped against the dryness in her throat.

"No, love." That was Jaxson nearby but she couldn't see him. She could sense his warm, powerful form in close proximity but she couldn't quite decide where he was in relation to Nemea or her.

"Get her some water, Nemea," Jaxson said.

She jumped to her feet and disappeared. A moment later, Jaxson was at her side. He perched on the edge of the cushion, the soft material sighing with his weight. He wore a black Henley she didn't recognize. Then it hit her. The dream of flying away with Nemea on her back wasn't a dream at all. It had been real. She had shifted into dragon form to save her sister. Bastian, her father's bodyguard, had gotten Nemea away from them and ran toward her. They both ended up on her back as she flew away.

Jaxson had also been in dragon form and flew away with her.

She tipped her head down to see that, thankfully, she was fully dressed. Someone had put her in an oversized cotton t-shirt and baggy sweatpants. She had no shoes. Or underwear. At the thought of that her face flushed hot. She hoped it was either Jaxson or Nemea who dressed her and she hadn't been exposed to whoever had been around when she shifted back.

"We found you clothes. Nemea dressed you." He gave her a weak smile at her relief. "You look better. How do you feel?"

"Like shit," she whispered.

He chuckled as Nemea handed him a glass of water. "Sip this."

She tried to lift up but didn't have the strength. Nemea was there, then, helping her up enough to sip the cold water. It hit the back of her throat, soothing it. Even that small effort took a lot out of her. She leaned back again, a breath sighing out between her lips.

"She's very weak," Nemea said. "Will she recover?"

"She'll make a full recovery once the poison is out of her system." She knew that deep, male voice, too, but couldn't place it. She could see his face in her mind's eye. Strong, wide jaw covered in scruff, silver eyes. His name escaped her.

"Thank you for helping my sister, Rafe."

Rafe. The exiled knight. Engaged to the queen of Andonia. Yes, it came back to her in a flash, then.

She peered up at the wood beams on the ceiling. A sense of familiarity washed over her. She knew this place. It wasn't her home or Jaxson's. She turned her head enough to get a good look at the living room. Well-worn furniture surrounded her facing the woodburning fireplace. The empty mantle was covered in dust and cobwebs.

The cabin. By the gods, he'd brought her to the cabin. She was perched on the three-seat sofa in the middle of the living room. She reached out a hand blindly trying to find Jaxson. He grasped her fingers in his, his hand closing over hers. Warmth cascaded through her with the comfort of him so near.

"You brought me here?" she asked in a whisper.

"It was the only place I could think to come that would be safe," he said.

She could read between the lines enough to know he didn't want to risk going back to his home in the village. Her fuzzy memory started to clear and she understood why he wouldn't be willing to put his parents in danger. Not with Drakana and an angry Herrick on the loose.

"How long have I been out?" she asked.

"Only a couple of hours. The poison hasn't been in your system too long, thanks to Rafe. Zee, do you remember what happened?"

"We were in dragon form. We went to the Coliseum to get my sister." She paused, dragging her lower lip through her teeth. He gave her hand a squeeze of encouragement. "Herrick was there."

"And his Drakana," Jaxson said, nodding.

"Right. They attacked us. Me." As if on cue, her ankle throbbed then. She remembered. The Drakana stabbed her with an obsidian blade. "I was poisoned with the blade."

"Yes. Do you remember anything else about the way he stabbed you?"

She wasn't sure what he was getting at. She shook her head. "Not really. Only that it felt as though he dug in the knife as deep as he could and…" Her breath caught. She met his bright blue gaze. "Oh, gods. What did he do, Jax?"

He took a deep breath. "He managed to get one of your scales."

Hot fear flashed through her, leaving behind black pinpricks of light in her vision. If she hadn't be lying down already, she might have fainted.

"Does Herrick have one of my scales?"

"We think so," this from Rafe, who hadn't left the room. He moved to stand across from her in front of the fireplace. "Logan's apartment in the city was attacked."

Her eyes flew wide as she looked at Rafe, then back at Jaxson. She knew he had a wife and baby now. "Is he all right? What about

Bree and the baby?"

"They're safe," Jaxson reassured. "They weren't home when it happened. But his place was ransacked. They were looking for the Blood Stone and the tooth, no doubt."

"Hopefully, Herrick and his men didn't get their hands on either?" she asked.

"No. Logan has them in a very safe place."

"Where is that?"

"Right here with you."

Logan stepped into the room and stood next to Rafe. Either she hadn't realized he was there or he had been in another part of the cabin. Looking at the two of them standing next to each other was like looking at a wall of dragon muscle. She would not want to make an enemy of them.

"Good thing I told Mia to warn him," Rafe said. "Otherwise, it wouldn't have been such a good outcome."

Zahra looked back at Jaxson. "So, we're all here, then."

What she didn't add was that they could finally break the curse. That is, after she shifted and gave up one of her scales.

"Then we should get on with it."

It took a lot of strength to push to a seated position. As soon as she did, her head throbbed. Dizziness swept through her. She groaned and leaned forward, putting her head between her knees.

"Not so fast," Jaxson said. "You still need to rest. And you're not ready for any action, yet."

"But the curse—"

"It's waited this long. It can wait a few more hours," Jaxson said. He wrapped an arm around her shoulders and helped her to her feet. "Let's get you to a bed so you can sleep off the poison. It'll help you heal faster."

Jaxson took most of her weight as she hobbled from the sofa through the living room. It hurt to put too much pressure on her injured leg. She was grateful for him. She didn't argue since he knew from experience what it felt like to be stabbed with one of those obsidian blades. Logan and Rafe still stood like sentries in front of the fireplace. Her sister stood off to the side of the room watching as they headed to the bedroom.

It was lucky Rafe was still around and had the antidote so close at hand. She wondered how it was he was able to have such a thing.

"He's ancient," Jaxson said, clearly hearing her thoughts. "He was the exiled knight, after all. I'm pretty sure he brought the antidote from the Old World with him."

"I'm glad he did."

"So am I or you, me, and Logan would be dead."

"He was stabbed, too? How?"

"Another long story. I'll tell you sometime." They entered the master bedroom. He helped her to the bed, easing her down onto the mattress. "I have to admit, you had me worried. I didn't know if Rafe was going to be able to help you or not."

She fell into the mountain of pillows with a sigh. Jaxson grabbed another fluffy pillow and put it under her injured leg, propping it up. It eased some of the pain.

"Why is that?" she asked.

"Because you were still in dragon form. We had to get you to shift back into human form before Rafe could treat you."

She stared at him a long moment as she thought back to the last thing she actually remembered. She didn't remember landing.

"So, you led us here?" she asked.

"Yes."

"And then what?"

"I opened a portal to Rafe. He came back through with me."

He perched on the edge of the bed and took her hand in his. It was almost as if he couldn't stand to not be touching her. The worry lines on his forehead concerned her. She sensed he didn't want to tell her any more.

To put his mind at ease, she placed her other hand on top of his and patted him. "Jax, you may as well tell me. Whatever you did, you did because you had to help me. I know that."

"He had to inject you with a changing serum. That's why you're so groggy."

She nodded, knowing that was the only explanation. He leaned toward her and kissed her cheek.

"I'll let you rest." He rose and turned toward the door.

"Jax, will you send Nemea to me?"

He paused, giving her a look of contemplation. "Are you sure you want to have that conversation now?"

He knew, as she did, they had to discuss their dysfunctional family. "There's no other time to have it."

He gave a nod and left the room. It wasn't long after he left that Nemea made her appearance. Despite her effort to look happy and relieved, Zahra could sense the worry gnawing at her. She held out her hand toward her and motioned her to the bed. Her sister didn't hesitate. She took her hand and sat next to her.

"Does it hurt much?" she asked, glancing down at her bandaged ankle.

Dear, sweet Nemea. Of course, she would worry she was in a lot of pain. It was part of her empathetic nature.

"Only a little. We should talk."

"Is it about Father and the others?" She gave her a surreptitious glance through her thick lashes. Apprehension laced her voice. "I was only doing what I thought was right."

She nodded and suppressed a smile. "I'm not angry."

Nemea puffed out a breath. "You're not?"

"No."

The relief was evident on her youthful face. "He told me I was going to help the Council with a very important task. He said I was the only one who could do it." She paused and gave her a surreptitious glance as she dragged her lower lip through her teeth. "He told me you were banished forever to the human realm."

A cold shudder went through her. What had her father planned if she hadn't broken the hold spell?

"He lied, didn't he?" Nemea asked.

"He did. He never banished me."

"Why would he say that, then?"

"Because he wants me out of the way. He knew you'd do what

he asked without question."

Horror and disgust flashed across her face as she contemplated Zahra's words. She swallowed hard. "He wanted me to shift into dragon form. That's why we were in the Coliseum."

Zahra nodded. "Yes."

"He said it was my duty as his daughter to help the Council," she continued. Her face paled. Her voice shook. "He never really said what he wanted from me in dragon form, though. He wanted you to shift, didn't he?"

"Yes, that and marry Talal," Zahra said. She sounded calmer than she felt saying it out loud.

A brief flicker of anger went over his sister's features before she got it under control. "Why is he so determined to marry you off to Talal? He's nothing."

Her dismissive tone made Zahra want to smile. "He's Herrick's heir. As the eldest daughter, it was a match to make sure that should we have a son, he would succeed Father on the Council. Just as Talal would succeed Herrick. He tried to make me return to the Hidden Lands with him."

"But you refused and that's when he decided to coerce me into helping him?"

"Yes. That and…he wants something else."

"What else could he possible want from me?" She practically snorted the words.

She didn't answer right away as she contemplated what to say. It was clear Nemea had no idea what they wanted from her. Before she could answer, Nemea had another question.

"You left the Hidden Lanes because Father was making you marry that bore of a man. Is that right?"

"Partly."

She hadn't really discussed it with anyone. Not even Jaxson. Oh, he knew she had left the Hidden Lands long ago, that it had to do with the betrothal to Talal and the horrible idea that Jaxson had left her and never wanted to see her again.

"He never wanted you to be with Jaxson." She said it so softly,

Zahra wasn't sure she heard her. "He hated you wanted to be with him as much as you were."

She knew that, even though he had never said it to her in so many words. There were things he did to try to keep them apart. When they had decided to disappear for the weekend, it had been to take her away from her horrible family life. Mating in this cabin hadn't been part of the plan.

"But I know you love him. Don't you?" Nemea asked. A flicker of a smile played upon her lips.

Zahra thought of the handfasting ceremony. The way the binding felt wrapped around their entwined hands. Her heart sped up at the idea they were actually married, that they would have each other forever. And no one, not even her beloved sister, knew the truth.

"I always have," Zahra said softly.

"I knew it."

They lapsed into amicable silence while Zahra contemplated whether or not to tell her about the handfasting. Her sister's gaze landed on her left hand and lingered there for a long time. Zahra resisted the urge to twist the wedding band off her finger. She remained still and quiet as Nemea reached for her hand. She ran her thumb over the ring.

"Is there something you want to share with me, sis?" She looked up at her through her thick lashes.

"Not really."

Nemea lifted her hand up between them. She pointed to the ring. There was an excited light dancing in her eyes. "Are you sure?"

"Oh, that." She swallowed the sudden lump in her throat. "That belonged to Jaxson's mother."

"And?"

"He gave it to me."

Nemea huffed out an exasperated breath. "And?"

"We sort of handfasted and got married."

Nemea flung her arms around her neck and squealed. "I'm so

happy for you."

"You're not upset we didn't have a wedding?"

Nemea held her at arm's length. "Gods, no. Father would have tried to stop it anyway. I'm glad you did it. And I'm glad you're married. It's obvious he adores you."

Zahra blushed to the roots of her hair. If even her little sister could see how much they wanted to be with each other, then she was glad they had gone through with it.

"Don't tell Father," Nemea whispered and then chuckled.

"I don't plan to."

"Good." She hugged her again. "Thank you for coming to get me."

"I couldn't leave you there when I knew what was going to happen to you." Zahra hugged her, hard. "I'm glad we got there in time and Bastian was able to get you away from them." She was probing, she knew. The memory of him running toward her dragging Nemea behind him would not leave her.

"He helped get me out of there." There was an almost wistful note in her voice.

Zahra hadn't noticed him with the others when Jaxson helped her to the bedroom. "Where is he?"

"He left. He said he had to return."

She sounded worried, but Zahra wasn't sure if that was because she was concerned he would reveal their hidden location or if it was something else.

Zahra didn't miss how Bastian grabbed her sister's hand and got her away from their father as fast as he could. It made her wonder about him. How loyal was he to her father? He'd come here and knew exactly where they were hiding. Her father told her in Bar Inferno he was one of his best men which said she didn't think they could trust him. Would he betray them and tell their father and Herrick where they were? She needed to warn Jaxson.

"When you landed and I saw you there…wow, Zahra. The sunlight hit your scales and reflected on them in a way I'd never seen before. You looked like a glowing fireball. It was incredible."

Wonder tinged her voice. "You were magnificent."

Zahra wondered if that was because her dragon magic had been suppressed so long. She felt the surge pound her when she broke through that hold spell. It had been violent and powerful and the most incredible thing she'd ever felt in her life.

"The only way to break the hold spell was to shift."

"But there's still something I don't understand," Nemea said. "Why would he want one of us to shift? What could he possibly hope to gain?"

Zahra took a deep breath, ready to tell her everything. "He wants a dragon scale. I don't think he's particular interested in which one of us he gets it from." She went on to tell her about the curse in the Hidden Lands, how they intended to break it, and Jaxson's mother's illness.

Nemea eyes were wide with shock. She pressed shaking fingers against her lips. "I had no idea."

"The toxic air doesn't affect all of us like it does Jaxson's mother."

"Then we need to break this curse as soon as possible to see if we can save her."

Zahra loved the determination in her voice. "That's what we're trying to do. But Herrick is determined to do it first."

"Because he wants sole control of the Council."

Zahra nodded. Even though her sister was young, she wasn't ignorant of politics. She frowned at the thought of Herrick and their father taking control.

"I know he's our father and all, but I think having him and Herrick in control would be the worst thing. They're only in it for themselves. They don't have the clans' best interests in mind."

Gods, she loved her sister. Hearing her say that made her want to squeeze her into another fierce hug. "I'm glad you see it that way, too."

"I was never blind to the way he treated you and your mate."

Zahra's head snapped in her direction.

"Oh, yes. I know. I can smell him all over you anyway." She

leaned closer and said, "I'm happy for you. I hope someday I have someone who loves me as much as Jaxson loves you."

"I hope you do, too, Nee."

She took a deep breath, gave her a winning smile and said, "So. How can I help you break the curse?"

✧ 21 ✧

"Are you sure this is the safest place for us?" Rafe stood at the fireplace leaning on the dusty mantle and brooding, unhappy being parted from his love. He stared down into the cold hearth, as though he willed it to erupt with a fire. Alas, it remained dormant.

Pent-up nervous energy hummed through Jaxson. It took all he had not to pace the length of the living room. Logan sat in the chair across from Rafe, his long legs stretched out before him and crossed at the ankles. He'd brought his father's journal and put the ancient tome on the cocktail table in front of the tattered sofa. Next to the journal was a red velvet pouch which contained the Blood Stone and the cold-drake dragon tooth covered in a white cloth.

Nemea had left Zahra after a while and now rattled around in the kitchen trying to find something to feed them. It appeared his father had intended to bring his mother here at some point. There was still unspoiled food in the fridge and pantry. Bree and the baby remained behind in the human realm with Mia. Rafe had refused to let her come due to her condition. They all knew there was a great battle to come.

"It's the only place for us," Jaxson said. "We can't return to my parent's house. I won't put them at risk."

"Coming here was the only option," Logan said. "You did the right thing, Jax."

"We need to figure out our next move," Rafe said. "We can't hide here forever."

Logan leaned forward and flipped open one of the journals. The aged spine crackled. "Once we have the final dragon relic, we can figure out how to break the curse. I haven't been able to translate this last bit of text. I think it's the chant we need to do."

Rafe moved from his position to stand next to Logan. He peered down at the book. "That looks like the Ancient Language."

"It is," Logan said with a nod. "One of the clan elders helped me with a lot of the translation. That's how I learned about the blood ritual and this mystical cave. But he couldn't help me with this part." He pointed to a passage at the end of the page.

"It's a spell," Rafe said.

Jaxson and Logan both snapped their head up at him.

"How do you know that?" Logan asked.

"I've seen this language before."

"Have you been holding out on me?" Logan wanted to know.

"You've never shown me this." Rafe pointed at the book.

"Fair enough. Can you translate it?"

Rafe crouched to get a closer look at the writing. He picked up the book, holding it up to his face, as if that would help him see it better.

"Some of the ink is smeared. That's probably why your clan elder couldn't read it."

"But you can?"

"I didn't say that." He never lifted his eyes off the page. He turned toward the light, tilting the book one way then another. "It's hard to make out but it says something about the Blood Stone." He paused as he ran a finger over the faded script. "Three drops of blood. No more." He looked at Logan then. "On the Blood Stone."

Logan jumped to his feet, flexing his hands as he paced the length of the small living room. "That's more than I knew before. Can you read more?"

"Yes." Rafe took the seat Logan vacated. "I need paper and pen."

Logan left the room in search of the requested items. Jaxson could hear him rattling around the kitchen and talking to Nemea. He returned a minute later with a pencil and napkin. He handed them to Rafe who gave him a quizzical look.

"Best I could do on short notice."

Rafe placed the book on the table. He studied it as though he were cramming for an exam as he scratched notes on the napkin. He crossed out a few words and rewrote. Finally, he put down the pencil and leaned back in the chair.

"I think I got it."

Logan stopped pacing. "What does it say?"

Jaxson leaned forward, his breath pooling in deep in his chest. He, like Logan, was on edge.

Rafe pointed to some of the text in the book. "This talks about the Dragon's Breath around the Whispering Mountain and how it hides it from the rest of the realms." He slid is finger down the page. "This talks about how Dragon's Breath is not meant to last forever." He glanced up at Logan. "I think your father may have known the Dragon's Breath would eventually poison the air. That's why it's cursed and why it's toxic."

Logan bit the end of his thumbnail, hanging on his every word. "And he wrote it down in the language of the Ancients because he didn't trust anyone on the Council."

"Except for my father," Jaxson pointed out.

Logan nodded agreement, then said, "What else did you find, Rafe?"

"This, I think, is the spell." His finger landed on another faded passage. "Ice infuses the Power. Fire lights the fuse. Gildhara, Rindhara, Elemental. Three drops of blood from these into the Blood Stone. Three drops of blood. No more." He paused, then said, "And then something in the Ancient language I can't translate."

"What is it?" Logan asked.

"Avok qaa."

As he finished, the Blood Stone inside the red velvet bag lit up, making it glow. They all exchanged a look of surprise. After a few seconds, it faded away.

"The Blood Stone lit up. What does that mean?" Jaxson asked.

Rafe shook his head. "I have no idea. Best guess is it has something to do with that phrase I can't translate."

"It's the spell. Ice infuses the power," Logan said. "That means the cold-drake dragon tooth infuses the Blood Stone with the power."

"Fire lights the fuse," Jaxson added. "If the dragon tooth infuses it with the power, then the fire-drake scale ignites it."

"And three drops of blood is the blood ritual," Rafe said.

"I guess that's it, then," Jaxson said.

"We have almost everything we need." Logan gave Jaxson a pointed look.

"Herrick already stole one from her. I'll ask her but I'm not going to make her do it," he said, knowing what was on his mind.

"You don't have to ask me." Zahra stood in the doorway of the bedroom, leaning on the doorjamb favoring her leg. "I'll do it."

Jaxson jumped to his feet, shaking his head. "No. You're too weak from the poison still. I won't allow it."

"You don't get to decide. I do. And I want to do this." When Jaxson started to object again, she held up a hand and continued. "Herrick has already come after the Blood Stone and the dragon tooth. He likely knows you opened a portal to the human realm. He'll be able to track that magic."

"Then we're all in danger here." Rafe glanced between Logan and Jaxson. "Aren't we?"

"It's possible Herrick and his Drakana will be able to track us down, yes." A bitterness swarmed in his mouth at having to admit that. He hadn't been thinking when he opened the portal to the human realm to Rafe. All he had been thinking about was saving Zahra. He looked at her now, saw the dark circles of fatigue under her eyes. "I couldn't let you die."

Before any further discussion could be made, Nemea entered the room carrying a tray of food piled high with sandwiches. She placed it on the cocktail table between them. Sensing the tension in the room, she broke the silence.

"No, you couldn't," Nemea said, having heard the entire conversation from the kitchen. "And for that I'm grateful. But, Zee, he's right. You're too weak. I doubt you can even shift right now."

"She can't," Rafe added. "The serum I had to use to shift her back into human form will suppressed her dragon magic for a while."

"How long?" Zahra demanded.

"Hard to say. At least for the next twenty-four hours. The poison should be out of your system by then anyway."

"We may not have twenty-four hours," Logan said.

Jaxson's stomach twisted into a nervous knot as he looked at his friend. He could almost hear his thoughts. They had the chant, the Blood Stone, and the tooth. All they lacked was the scale. He reached out to Zahra's mind with a tentative touch. She was exhausted.

"Zahra, as much as you want to help, you need rest. It took me days to recover from the obsidian blade when I was stabbed. You need to let your body heal."

"We don't have that kind of time." She looked at Logan. "If I can get you a scale, then what happens?"

"Then we go to the Crystal Cave in the Whispering Mountains to break the curse."

Determination set her jaw. Jaxson knew that look. "Jax, you can open a portal there, can't you?"

"Yes, but—"

"Then open a portal and take us there. I can sense my magic trying to recover. One we're there, I'll shift and you can take the scale and be done with it."

"No." It was Nemea that spoke up. "Listen to him, Zahra. You don't have the strength." She looked at Jaxson and the others over her shoulder. "But I do."

"Absolutely not." Zahra's voice was hard, commanding. "I won't let you do that."

"I'm a grown woman now, Zee." She gave her sister a fluttering smile. "You can't tell me what to do."

"It's not for you to do," she said.

Nemea weaved away her concern as she moved to stand next to her. "Enough discussion about the breaking of the curse and who is going to do what. We all need to eat and rest and then we can regroup tomorrow. Come on, sis. Let me help you to the sofa."

Reluctantly, she let Nemea help her.

"Then it's settled," Rafe said. "We'll plan to do this tomorrow. Logan, Jaxson, and I will come up with a plan on how this will go down."

"And what are we supposed to do? Sit around and be useless females?" Zahra didn't bother to hide the annoyance in her voice.

"No," Logan said. "When the time comes, Mia will join us. We'll need a drop of blood from her, you, and Rafe for the Blood Stone. So, you're not useless at all." He bent and picked up one of the sandwiches. "Now, let's eat."

He took a large bite, ending the discussion.

After they ate, Logan took Jaxson aside.

"I need a favor," he said, his voice low.

Jaxson glanced at Zahra who rested on the sofa, her legs stretched out in front of her. Nemea was in the kitchen cleaning up the food and dishes. Rafe took it upon himself to do a perimeter check.

"What is it?"

"I need you to open a portal for me."

His brows drew together. "Why?"

"Because I want to hide the journal and the relics. On the off-chance Herrick tracked you here, I need to make sure they're secure. I have a place in mind. Will you do it?"

He glanced at Zahra again, stalling.

"She'll be safe here with Rafe and we won't be gone very long."

"I'm coming with you then?" Jaxson asked.

He gave him a small smile. "If you don't mind."

"All right but let's make this quick." He didn't like being parted from Zahra very long.

"Come with me."

Logan waved him toward the second bedroom. As he went by the cocktail table, he snatched up the velvet pouch containing the Blood Stone, his father's journal, and the tooth still wrapped in a white cloth. He turned to Jaxson.

"Here's where we're going." He described the place. "Have you ever been there?"

"No, but with your description I'm sure I can find it."

"Good. If you'll do the honors."

"Before I do, you realize if I open this portal, the magic can be traced."

"I do."

"And you're willing to take that risk?"

Logan nodded. "I am."

Jaxson took a deep breath. "All right then. Let's do this."

He lifted his hands forward, his palms outward, and drew a circle in the air with one of his hands while the other remained still. Light sparked and crackled in the air between them. A second later, the portal opened to the destination on the other side. Logan didn't waste any time stepping through. Jaxson followed. As soon as he was on the other side, the portal closed.

They stood in the middle of what looked like a workroom. Dusty bookshelves lined one wall. An old desk was pushed against another wall under a grimy window. Tattered curtains clung to the wall and hung on either side of it. The wood floor was scratched and marred and had seen better days. A work table was across the room from the desk. One candle burned brightly, illuminating the ancient tome opened and resting there.

"Where is this place?" Jaxson asked.

"Remember the clan elder I told you about? The one who helped me translate some of the text of the journals?"

Jaxson nodded. Before Logan could reply, someone else spoke.

"Ah, so you've returned at last. I wondered when I might see you again."

The elderly man shuffled from around a corner. He was hunched over, an obvious hump in his back between his shoulders. His long gray hair hung to his waist as did his thin mustache and beard. Bushy eyebrows perched over onyx eyes in a pale brown face featuring a roadmap of wrinkles. He was dressed in gray and white robes that clung to his thin frame. He held a gnarled wooden walking stick helping him keep his balance as he approached.

"And you brought a friend this time, I see." His squinty smile showed off black and yellow stump teeth.

"I did. This is Jaxson. Jaxson, this is Ashe."

"Ashe," Jaxson repeated as he stared at the old man. "As in one of the Ancients?"

"That's right, sonny. You're a quick one, aren't ya?" He chuckled as he turned back the way he came, waving waved them to follow. "Come on. I know you don't have much time."

As they fell in step behind him, Jaxson leaned over and whispered to Logan. "He should be dead, shouldn't he?"

"I'm old, not deaf, sonny," Ashe snapped. "Nine hundred years, if you must know."

Logan cleared his throat and shot Jaxson a look that silenced him. "Ashe, thanks for letting us come here. I don't want to put you in danger—"

"Bah. I'm not afraid of a youngling who thinks he knows what's best for everyone."

He paused at an oversized door with a circular handle. He spun it clockwise and then grabbed it and pulled. It took some doing, but he finally got the heavy door open. Inside, was a vault. A table sat in the center of the room. No chairs. Shelving surrounded the table with various items covered in dust. It looked as if the room hadn't been open in ages.

"This Lord Herrick thinks he knows what's best for the clan, does he?" Ashe asked.

Logan nodded. "He does."

"And you plan to stop him with these items?" He motioned to the velvet pouch and the dragon's tooth.

"These and one other relic we don't have yet. He's already tried to steal them once. I don't want to take any chances."

"Wise of you." He motioned to a table in the center of the vault. "Put everything there."

Logan placed the tooth on the table, the pouch next to it, then the journal beside that. Ashe reached for the dragon's tooth and flipped off the covering. He gave a low whistle.

"This is what you need ground down?"

"Yes. Can you still do it?"

"I can. Give me a day or two, though, eh?"

"I can give you one day. That's all," Logan said, his voice firm.

A scowl crossed the old man's face. "Fine, fine. I'll have it ready for you tomorrow. And once you use it to break this curse on the Hidden Lands, then things will change?"

"That is my hope."

He gave Logan a thoughtful look. "I've seen the world change from being led by kings to the council system we have now. I've seen the worst of men and the best of men. I was around when Ienir the Great lived and died and tried to use to the Dragon's Breath to create a sanctuary of the Hidden Lands. I told him then it would fail. He didn't listen. Now, I'm afraid, it falls to you to repair it. When you're ready, let me know."

"I will try to make it right."

"And that's all you can do." He gave a smile then. "Best get back to your world, sonny, before you're missed."

"Thanks for your help."

"Before we leave," Jaxson said, "I have a question for you, Ashe."

"And what is that, sonny?"

"The toxic air is making some of our people sick. Once the curse is broken, will they heal?"

"Hard to say. Someone close to you is ill, aye?"

"My mother."

"There may be no helping her but if you can bring her to me, I'll see what I can do," he suggested.

Jaxson looked at Logan who gave him an encouraging nod. "You would do that for me?"

"Are you a friend of Logan's?" Ashe asked.

"Well…yes."

"Then you're a friend of mine. Bring her to me. Today if you can. I will examine her. When you return for the tooth tomorrow, I'll have an answer for you."

Relief burned through Jaxson. Relief and hope. He had not dared to hope his mother would somehow live and get over her terrible illness. But Ashe had given him that. Only one thing held him back.

"If I open more portals, Herrick could track us for sure," he said, mostly to Logan.

"I have a solution for that," Ashe said without waiting for a response from Logan. He closed his eyes and inhaled deeply, holding the breath deep in his chest.

"Dragon's Breath," Logan said. "My father used it to send me through the portal to the human realm." He turned to Jaxson. "Open the portal, Jax."

As he did, Ashe blew out the breath he held. White smoke concealed the magic as he opened a portal to his parents.

They stepped through the portal to save his mother.

❧ 22 ☙

As the evening wound down, and they figured out their plan for the morning, Nemea headed to one of the bedrooms while Jaxson and Zahra took the other. Rafe and Logan decided to stay in the living area and keep guard. Rafe took the oversized armchair by the fireplace while Logan stretched out on the sofa, his feet toward the door so he could keep watch.

As Zahra and Jaxson climbed into bed together, she couldn't ignore the throbbing pain in her leg. She knew they were right in that she didn't have the strength to shift. It still irked her. She'd finally made up her mind to help them and now she couldn't. Leaving it to her little sister seemed wrong.

"She wants to do it, you know," Jaxson said.

"I know." She knew he didn't have to hear her thoughts to know what was going on in her mind. "It doesn't seem right, though."

He kissed her forehead. "You're injured, love. Stop beating yourself up about it." He helped her into bed. "We have a big day tomorrow. Let's get some rest."

She nodded. He found extra pillows and propped her injured leg up, giving it a cushion and allowing her to rest from the pain. He settled next to her.

She thought about everything they had been through these last few days. Mostly the time with him had been a blur. One thing was clear, though. He wasn't going to let anything happen to her or her sister. She loved him more than she could ever say for that.

"Where did you and Logan go?"

"To secure the remaining relics." He balled the pillow under his head and turned on his side so he could look at her.

She gave him a quizzical look and tipped her head to the side. "Which is where?"

He cocked a grin. "I'm not at liberty to say. They're in a safe place. Safer than here." He reached for her hand, put his on top of hers. "I also moved my parents there."

"In this undisclosed safe place?" she asked.

"Yes."

He wouldn't elaborate. When she tried to probe his mind for more answers, he kept it closed off to her. He was good at that. Better than she was, in fact. There were times when she couldn't read his mind at all. Other times it was easy, though she suspected that was because he allowed her. At least their mindspeak connection returned with their mating bond.

"Jax?"

He hummed his response.

"Do you think this ritual thing will break the curse and clear the toxic air?"

"I hope so."

"What if it doesn't? What then?"

"Then we figure out what to do next."

She wanted to roll over to face him. She turned her head to look at him. He was on his side facing her, his eyes closed. His breathing had turned heavy as exhaustion set in. She could clearly see it in the lines of his face. She'd caused him a lot of stress since they found each other again in New York City.

"I love you." She didn't really expect an answer but she had to tell him before she missed the opportunity, even if he didn't hear her.

"I know. Now go to sleep." He never even cracked open an eye as he spoke.

She grinned in the shadowy darkness and let her eyes drift closed. She fell into a blissful sleep.

଼ ଼

A loud thump startled Zahra awake. In her half-asleep state, she couldn't discern what it was. She bolted upright, coming out of her haze and tried to figure out what she heard. Jaxson was already on his feet and running to the bedroom door.

"Stay here," he barked over his shoulder.

He disappeared leaving her sitting in bed with her heart racing and hot fear pumping through her. Another thump as if something rammed into the door of the cabin. The windows rattled in their frames and the walls shook. Nemea scurried into the bedroom a second later. She jumped on the bed next to her, huddling close.

"What is it?" Zahra asked.

"Drakana. They have a battering ram. I saw it through the window." Her voice shook. She pressed her fingers against her lips.

"Father?"

"I don't know. I didn't see him."

"Could Bastian have betrayed us?" Zahra asked, keeping her voice low.

Nemea shook her head before she even finished the question. "No. No way."

"What makes you so sure?"

"I just know, all right?" Her voice was terse as she said it.

Zahra took that to mean the subject was closed. But she couldn't help but think he may have had something to do with the Drakana finding them and attacking. She had no doubt her father was involved.

Another bang followed by a crack. It sounded like the front door blew open. Nemea squealed and crowded closer to Zahra. She glanced at her injured leg, trying to decide if they could make a run for it.

"What do we do?" she whispered.

Zahra was about to answer when she heard her father's voice. "I've come for my daughters."

Oh, gods.

"Help me up," Zahra said.

"But—"

"Do as I say." Her voice had a cutting edge.

Nemea complied and helped her out of bed. She shouldered her weight. The two of them hobbled out of the bedroom. As they made their way into the living area, the destroyed door caught her eye immediately. It hung off its hinges, sagging against the wall. The wood casing was cracked and splintered. Inside the door, her father, Herrick, and Talal. A wall of muscle stood between her and them. Logan, Rafe, Jaxson.

Fire ringed Rafe's fingers. Jaxson had somehow produced two obsidian blades. Where he got those, she had no idea. Logan stood on the other side of Rafe, his hands clenched into fists.

"Ah, there are my errant daughters. Come here." Fenwick waved them forward.

"Stay where you are, ladies," Jaxson ordered.

Neither she nor her sister moved. Fenwick shot Jaxson a death glare.

"Is that the way of it, then? So be it."

He stepped aside and allowed two Drakana inside. They carried someone between them and dumped him on the floor in front of the three men. Nemea's audible gasp rang in her ear.

Bastian was on the floor, his face a bloody mess. He had a black eye. Blood caked around his nose and trickled down the side of his face. Rope tied his raw wrists together. The skin was cracked and bleeding, as if he had been struggling against the bindings for a while. His shirt was stained with streaks of blood.

They had beaten him. He hadn't betrayed their location at all. He'd been tortured until he finally broke. She could see him searching the room and then his gaze halted on Nemea. He mouthed the words I'm sorry and suddenly Zahra understood why her sister was certain he wouldn't betray them.

They loved each other. Maybe neither of them realized it, yet, but clearly Bastian tried to protect Nemea. Maybe he'd always tried to protect her from their father. Zahra's heart broke a little for both of them. She had a new respect and understanding for Bastian.

He hadn't betrayed Zahra and Nemea. He had betrayed her father.

Fenwick stood next to Bastian who huddled on the floor. Herrick was next to him. There was nothing menacing about the two of them but Zahra knew there had to be a small army of Drakana outside the cabin backing them up. Even if they managed to escape out the back, it was likely a futile effort.

"What did you do to him?" Nemea fought to control the anger and fear out of her voice.

Fenwick's gaze landed on first her, then flickered to Zahra. "He refused to tell me where you were. I had to force the issue."

"You didn't have to hurt him." Tears clotted Nemea's throat.

"It was the only way I could get information out of him," Fenwick said. "There is a marriage contract to fulfill. I've come to collect." He gave Zahra a pointed look, then turned his gaze on Logan. "Then we will discuss the terms of your resignation, Chief Magistrate."

"There is nothing to discuss," Logan replied, his voice cool.

"Enough of this." Herrick unsheathed an obsidian blade from the holder at his waist. He knelt and held it against Bastian's throat. "Zahra will come with us and marry Talal immediately. You will give us the dragon's tooth and the Blood Stone."

"And if we refuse?" Logan asked.

Zahra liked him even more for including her.

"Then he dies."

"No!" Nemea cried out.

Zahra wanted to tell her to be quiet, but couldn't bring herself to hush her. It was clear her sister had feelings for the man but letting them know that was doing no one any good.

"I'm not handing over the relics," Logan said, his tone calm and matter-of-fact.

"And Zahra isn't marrying your son," Jaxson added.

"Then Bastian pays the price." Herrick pressed the blade into his skin, ready to slice but hesitating.

Nemea stepped away from Zahra, forgetting she had been the one holding her up. She nearly lost her balance and stumbled until she managed to balance on her good leg. She hobbled toward the chair and braced herself, taking the pressure off her left leg. She wanted to stop her sister, but she was already next to Logan. Her small hands were clenched tight into fists as she glared at Herrick and Bastian.

"Don't do this, Lord Herrick." Tears choked her voice.

"Killing him won't help you get the relics or Zahra," Logan said. "Besides, they relics aren't here."

Herrick narrowed his gaze. "I'm sure if I asked you where they were, you wouldn't tell me. Or I could call your bluff and kill the man anyway."

Nemea whimpered. Logan didn't back down.

"All I want are the two relics and fulfillment of the marriage contract. Then I'll be on my way. No one has to get hurt and no one has to die." Herrick nodded toward Bastian.

"You will never get the relics from him." The vehemence in Zahra's voice startled even her.

Herrick gave her a withering stare then looked back at Logan. "If neither of you will comply, then…" He paused.

"Then we're at an impasse," Logan said.

"Then we are at war."

Herrick declared war on them. His glittering gaze landed on Jaxson.

"Shall we start with your traitor father?" Herrick said. "I can have my men at your home in moments."

Fury surged through him as he thought of his father and his helpless ill mother. He had been right to suspect Herrick would try to threaten him with his parents. Smug relief replaced his fury when he realized he had been thankful for the forethought to move them out of the house and to Ashe's place.

Her mind touched his. *You knew.*

I suspected.

How?

Gut instinct. To Herrick, he said, "You can try but I don't think your men will find anyone home."

The man stared at him for a long, quiet moment as the words sank in. When he realized what Jaxson implied, his face flushed red.

"I should have killed him when I had the chance. His death would have been the finality your mother would need to succumb to her illness."

The pleasure in his voice at the thought of his dead parents sent rage through Jaxson. He could not stop the reaction he had when his dragon magic surged forward. The enraged beast inside him banged against his skull with a desperate need to get out. He flung both obsidian blades Ashe had given him at Herrick. He dodged them with ease which only served to enrage Jaxson even more. He rushed towards him, shoving him away from Bastian. His hands clamped around his throat before anyone knew what was happening.

In the distance, he could hear the commotion around him, the din of shouting voices. But all he focused on was his fingers pressing into Herrick's throat trying to crush his windpipe. He wanted the bastard dead.

Strong arms pulled him off Herrick. He stumbled backward. As his vision cleared, Jaxson realized it was Rafe. He wrapped his arms around his upper torso and kept him from leaping once again for Herrick who lay in a heap on the floor coughing and gasping for air.

"I will kill you," Jaxson said through gritted teeth.

"You…can…try…" Herrick said through his coughs and gasps.

Before anyone else could move, several Drakana stormed through the destroyed doorway. Two headed right for Zahra and grabbed her. With her injury, she couldn't fight them off. Rafe still held Jaxson back even though he wanted to surge forward. Zahra shouted an obscenity at the men, but they ignored her.

Jaxson shoved out of Rafe's grasp and went for her. If anything happened to her after everything, he would never forgive himself. But more armed Drakana stepped between them.

"Let her go, Herrick."

"Alas, I cannot. She is betrothed to my son. And I intend to see the marriage through."

Zahra's wide tear-filled eyes flew to him. He met her gaze, knowing what he had to do. It was the only choice left to him.

"Then I request matrim-duella," Jaxson said.

Nemea gasped. Zahra's face drained of color. Jaxson turned his gaze away and looked at Herrick.

"Are you mad?" Zahra demanded.

Herrick gave a gleeful grin. "A fight to the death?"

Jaxson nodded. "Winner gets Zahra."

The grin never left his face. "I will prepare my son. We'll meet at the Coliseum at dawn. Bring her. And that." He pointed to a near-unconscious Bastian before leaving.

Two men picked up Bastian and carried him out. The men holding Zahra dragged her away. As she went by him, she shot him a glare that told him exactly what she thought of the situation.

She was not happy.

As soon as they were gone, Logan said, "Are you sure about that decision, Jax?"

Before he could reply, Nemea said, "How could you let him take her?"

"He won't hurt her. He needs her alive and he's already got her dragon scale. And, yes, I'm sure. I can take him."

"He's right," Rafe said. "Talal isn't much of a fighter by the looks of him. Too scrawny."

"We'll get her back, Nemea. I promise."

She folded her arms across her chest and shot daggers out of her eyes. "You better."

"And," Jaxson added, looking at Logan, "We'll retrieve her

stolen dragon scale."

He gave him a faint smile. "What's your plan?"

At her father's order, the men loaded Zahra and Bastian into the backseat of a car. They took off through the woods back toward the village. She was furious with Jaxson for demanding matrim-duella. She didn't understand why he didn't tell Herrick the truth—that they were already handfasted. Unless he didn't want him to know the truth. She could think of no good reason for that as she twisted the wedding band around her finger, the anger burning through her. Her dragon magic threatened to ignite.

She wanted to let it. Oh, how she did. But her gut told her to hold on. To wait it out. As far as her father knew, she still didn't have it. She was helpless. She was still nothing but a pawn in his political game. Her father and Herrick rode in another car with several Drakana.

"I didn't betray you." Bastian's voice was quiet in the small space. "I wouldn't do that."

She startled when he spoke, her heart fluttering with the punch of fear. Bastian's face was a bloody mess. He looked awful. "I know. Nemea told me."

"I tried to protect her after you left."

Guilt and regret swept through her. She had once told Jaxson she couldn't leave her behind and yet that was exactly what she did. She was a selfish coward.

"Why did you?" he asked.

She didn't know how to answer, so she avoided it. "Thank you for looking after her all these years. I appreciate it." She paused, considering him. He leaned his head back on the headrest and closed his eyes. "Why did you do it? I thought you were loyal to my father."

"Your father…" He scoffed, a guttural sound deep in his throat. "He is only interested in his personal gain. Not Nemea. Not you. My loyalty shifted away from him a long time ago."

Her mouth went dry as she considered his words. He was in love with her sister and neither of them knew it.

"Whatever happens," he added, his voice rough, "don't let him win."

They came to a halt in the village at Herrick's modest home not far from the Coliseum. They hauled her and Bastian out of the car. Inside the house, the men took him away. She didn't know where and it worried her. The Drakana in charge of her practically dragged her with her bum leg up the stairs. She didn't complain. She kept her emotions in check when all she wanted to do was shift and burn them all to a crisp.

Even her father.

They took her to one of the bedrooms and shoved her inside, closing the door. A moment later, her father entered. He halted inside the door giving her a cold, controlled look.

"He won't win, you know."

She stared at him, her stomach twisting in a knot. It was what she feared most—that Jaxson wouldn't win. And since it was a fight to the death…she swallowed the sick feeling that crept into her throat. She couldn't think about that. Instead, she focused on the anger surging through her.

"You don't know that," she said at last.

"I do. And once this farce of a duel is over, you will marry Talal. You will do your duty as my daughter.

"I would rather die a thousand deaths that marry Talal."

He narrowed his eyes and gave her that look of disgust with which she was so familiar. "There will be no further discussions."

He turned on his heel and left the room, slamming the door behind him. Zahra blew out a breath. She sank to the edge of the bed, her hands shaking as she looked down at the wedding band. *Jaxson, what the hell were you thinking?*

She didn't get a reply, not that she really expected one. When she reached out with her mind to try to touch his, he had closed himself off from her. Frustration edged through her. He didn't want her to know what he was thinking.

All she could do now was wait for dawn.

⛬ 23 ⛬

Dawn came. Jaxson, Rafe, Logan, and Nemea arrived at the Coliseum as the sun peeked over the horizon. Jaxson tried like hell to talk Nemea out of coming. But she refused to stay behind at the cabin or go into the human realm with Mia and Bree. She had to be there for Zahra in case something happened. Jaxson didn't want her to have a front row seat to whatever happened, but he was unable to talk her out of staying behind.

She's the only family I have left, she had said.

That was enough to guilt him into letting her come.

The four of them entered the Coliseum on the north side of the building. In this place, young shifters learned to fly in First Flight. Jaxson, Logan, and Zahra had all learned to fly here when they were younglings. He never expected he would actually be here in a fight to the death.

On the other end of the arena was Fenwick, Herrick, Zahra between them, and Talal. As Jaxson glanced around the perimeter of the place, he saw armed Drakana positioned everywhere. Herrick's personal army, no doubt. He would never understand those who hated their own kind and served others, willingly hunting them down to eradicate them.

"I hope you know what you're doing," Logan said. The armed Drakana didn't escape his notice, either.

"I do." Jaxson sounded more confident than he felt.

They halted, the four at the other end a good distance away. But even from this distance, Jaxson could see Zahra wearing a white gown fluttering in the breeze around her legs. Her pink hair was loose around her face, a few tendrils blowing in front of her face every now and then. They had dressed her in the gown in anticipation of his loss and, well, that pissed him off.

"They think you're going to lose." Rafe's keen eyes caught everything Jaxson's had.

"They hope I'm going to lose, but I'm not."

How could he, after all? Rafe was right. Talal was a scrawny shifter with yellow hair, beady eyes, and a nose in the shape of a beak. He barely had any muscle tone. As Jaxson glanced between him and his father, he looked nothing like his father. His looks could only come from his mother's side, but he had no idea if he resembled her like since she died birthing Talal.

"Are you sure he'll have the scale with him?" Logan asked.

"No," he admitted. "But if I lose, Herrick will try to force you to turn over the other two relics. He won't want to waste any time breaking the curse and taking over the Hidden Lands. He's got to have it with him or nearby."

Herrick and Talal walked toward them. Jaxson headed his way to meet him halfway in the middle of the arena. Logan fell in step beside him. When he gave him a questioning glance, Logan flashed a grin.

"Just so he knows I have your back," he said, his voice low.

They halted in the center of the arena. Herrick gave Logan a cursory glance and then turned back to Jaxson with his full attention.

"The rules are simple. The matrim-duella is a hand-to-hand combat fight to the death. No shifting," Herrick said.

So, they could kill each other with nothing more than fists. It was one of the most primitive rituals of the Ancients.

"Understood."

Talal cleared his throat. "I request a champion."

"Granted," Herrick said before anyone could object.

"Wait," Logan said. "That isn't part of the rules."

"Oh, but it is. One party may request a champion if he feels as though he can't win in a fair fight." Herrick gave Jaxson a smirk.

"And so, Talal has requested a champion. Name him, my son."

"Him."

Talal pointed at Logan.

For fucks sake.

"I refuse," Logan said.

"If you refuse, then you forfeit and Talal wins by default. Are you sure you want to refuse?" Herrick almost couldn't hide his glee.

"Fuck me," Logan muttered under his breath. He gave Jaxson a glance. "Sorry."

"Begin when ready." Herrick and his son headed back to the other side of the Coliseum.

As they walked away, Jaxson turned to Logan. "You know he did that on purpose."

"Of course, I know. Two birds. One stone," Logan said with a sigh.

"There's no way I can kill you."

Logan nodded. "It's the same for me with you."

He looked at Zahra, meeting her furious gaze. He shut off his mind to her because he knew she was angry with him. When she learned he was supposed to fight Logan, he wasn't sure what her response would be.

"Any suggestions?" he asked.

Logan glanced back at the men heading back to the other side. Then his gaze flickered to the armed Drakana around the arena. "I'm working on it. They're going to keep a watchful eye on us so we probably should make a good showing of it."

With a sigh, Jaxson nodded. "I was afraid you were going to say that."

He squared off to his friend and put up his fists.

Zahra knew something was up when she saw the smug look on Herrick's face. Talal had followed him back to their end of the arena, leaving Jaxson and Logan in the center. Her gut twisted. Yes, something was definitely up.

"Your plan worked?" her father asked.

"It did."

"What plan?" Zahra demanded.

"With any luck, the two of them will kill each other. Then I can search for the other relics." Logan would not have them too far from him. He leveled his gaze at her. "You will marry my son today."

Zahra's head snapped back to Jaxson and Logan in the center of the arena. On the far end, her sister and Rafe waited and watched. Hot, pinpricks of fear went through her when her lover and her friend took a fighting stance.

"They're fighting each other," she realized. To the death.

"They are," Herrick agreed.

She turned her fury on him. "Because your son is too weak to fight Jaxson. You knew he'd lose so you made him call a champion. You son of a bitch."

"Zahra—"

"Shut your mouth, Father." She reeled on him. "I will not allow this to happen."

"You have no choice," Herrick said, sounding well pleased. "The rules of the duel have been decided and the champion selected. They will fight to the death."

She ignored him and kept her focus on her father. "Did you have something to do with this?"

"I know the rules of the Old Ways," he replied.

Her fury knew no bounds. Since her mother died, her father had been nothing but horrible to her. He'd lied to her and betrothed her to a man she didn't even like and barely knew. All for his own personal gain. She'd had enough. It would end. Now.

"You and I have unfinished business, Father."

He smirked, as if it was a joke. "And what is that?"

"You destroyed my life. You tried to destroy Jaxson's and Nemea's. Now I'm going to destroy yours."

He scoffed. "As if you could destroy me. I know you can shift again, but that doesn't intimidate me."

Her dragon magic flared bright deep inside her. "It should. And, for the record, I know about that, too. I know you tried to kill the mating bond between me and Jaxson. I know you tried to destroy my dragon magic."

"You gave me no other choice," he said. "You were wild, had no control over your magic. Or do you forget that?"

"I forget nothing."

Without waiting for him to respond, she let her dragon magic flood her. She lifted her hands, palm upward toward the sky. Fire danced in her hands. His eyes widened when he realized she had full control of her magic. He snarled in such a hateful, foul way it startled her. Frightened her. But she stood her ground.

All this time, Herrick and his son stood by and listened to their exchange. Now he grabbed his son and started to back away. As if he sensed something was about to happen.

An explosion rocked near the center of the Coliseum. The ground vibrated with such violence, it knocked her off her feet. She tumbled into the dirt. As soon as she landed, she rolled to her side and focused on the dust cloud rising from the ground. She could see flames billowing up from the ground. No sign of Jaxson and Logan. She couldn't see her sister or Rafe either. It took several minutes for the dust to settle, but then she saw them. Rafe and Nemea huddled against one of the inner walls. Logan and Jaxson getting back on their feet. Blood dripped from Jaxson's nose. Logan had a black eye. And both of their fists were red and raw. She hoped they were only doing it for show instead of trying to actually hurt each other.

Her heart rammed hard against her chest as she looked around the stands where Herrick had stationed his Drakana. One had a large weapon, still smoking from the end, as he lowered it. He'd missed them. It had been a warning shot. Next time, they wouldn't be so lucky.

"You bastard!" Zahra shouted. She wasn't sure if she was

calling Herrick or her father that. They were both bastards.

"You wish to fight me still, daughter?" Fenwick asked. "Then fight me."

He grabbed a fistful of his shirt and shredded it and the next thing she knew, he shifted into his powerful dragon form. He launched upward into the sky from the ground, the morning light reflecting off his black and red scales.

She balled her fists, snuffing the flames. The problem was, she couldn't shift yet.

Or could she?

She closed her eyes and concentrated on how the magic felt when it flowed through her, when she changed from human to dragon form. How her bones extended and popped. The way her wings sprouted from her back. The elongation of her neck. Her face changing into a snout and her body covered in scales.

When she opened her eyes, she realized, she'd shifted. Behind her, the fire snapped and crackled. It warmed her scales, burning through her in a way she hadn't felt in eons. Oh, gods, it felt so good to have that warmth push through her again. What her father didn't realize was that fire and sunlight gave her strength and energy. It was what made her what she was in dragon form. A true fire-drake.

Zahra launched her large body into the sky. She and her father flapped around each other, doing a careful dance. He reared back, his hind legs coming up with all his claws out. He dove for her, ready to sink those claws into her but she dodged. It took all his power to flap his wings hard enough to keep from crashing to the ground. He craned his body around and came after her again.

Her large diaphanous wings beat as hard as they could as she soared upward into the clouds, into the light. The early morning sun seemed at once so far and so close to her. She eyed it and headed straight for it, her father on her tail. So close, in fact, she could feel his hot breath wafting over her as he panted to keep up.

When she banked left, so did he. He flapped his wings harder with a loud whump, whump. He plunged to his right and crashed into her so hard, it stole her breath. She cried out which, in her dragon form, sounded like a loud growl-bark. Her wings wrapped around her body and she started a free fall toward the ground. She could feel his satisfaction oozing from him as she fought to regain control.

Bloody bastard.

Zahra spun out of control. Her wild heart thumped in her chest as she tried to regain control of her fear. She wasn't going to let him defeat her like this.

Finally, she managed to push out her wings and slow her descent, then turned and thrust her body upward. She saw him then, hovering in the air waiting for her to crash against the ground. Instead, she flew as fast as she could right for him. She ducked her head and didn't slow when she plowed the top of it, horns and all, into his chest. He emitted high-pitched squeal as she dug in her horns and pushed him up. Then she jerked her head to the side and flung him off.

She could see bright wet blood sliding down his scales from the puncture wounds in his chest as he fell through the air, his wings useless. He crashed against the ground outside the arena and skidded some twenty feet before finally coming to a halt against the base of a tree. She flapped in the sky, watching to see if he would rise again. When he didn't, she flew toward him and landed nearby.

She caught a glimpse of Logan, Rafe, and Nemea emerging from the arena. A few Drakana followed. No doubt sent by Herrick. But Herrick and his worthless son were nowhere in sight. Zahra approached her father with unhurried steps.

Fenwick appeared to be lifeless as he laid curled against the ground. She saw the two gaping holes where she'd dug in her horns. Fresh blood stained his scales. She sniffed the air, smelled the metallic tang of blood.

As she stood there, trying to decide what to do next, an overwhelming sadness hit her. She didn't want things to end with her father this way. She would have liked to have talked it out. Maybe they could have understood each other. Maybe they could have eventually come to actually like each other. It had been clear to her since her mother died, though, he didn't want anything to do with her. She never understood why.

Not that it mattered anymore. She had her own life to worry about it. A life in which he would never again be part.

She turned away and started to lumber off, the pain in her leg from where they removed the scale shooting through her. She knew it would take some doing to get her back into human form, but she wasn't worried about that at the moment.

"Zahra, look out!"

The shouted warning from her sister pulled her out of her thoughts. She turned her head in time to see the shadow of her father's giant form fall over her. He bared his razor-sharp teeth and, before she could take evasive action, he sank them into the side of her neck. The cry that escaped her sounded like a mournful wail.

His mouth clamped down hard on her neck. Hot blood spurted through the puncture holes into his mouth, turning his drool red.

Suddenly, another dragon kicked her father so hard, he released her. She crashed against the ground, her neck bleeding. Her eyes drooped from sudden fatigue as her mind tried to make sense of what was happening. She could have sworn she saw Jaxson in dragon form taking on her father.

It was the last thought she had before she passed out.

Us. Forever. She'd written that on the back of the picture he still had in his sock drawer. After she'd developed the pictures, she brought them to him and showed him the one she took of the two of them. He would never forget her beaming face when she showed him how it had turned out.

Not bad, huh? she said.

It's perfect. Like you.

I want you to have it.

I can't take your photo.

Yes, you can. I want you to have it. Now and always. She flipped it over and wrote the words that would forever be emblazoned in his mind. Because I love you.

He kissed her hard and fast with a sense of urgency he hadn't felt before. Let's run away together. Go somewhere no one knows us. Forget about the Council and our parents and everything.

She'd given him a sad smile. Jax, you know I can't leave Nemea behind.

All of this and more flashed through Jaxson's mind when he saw Fenwick clamp down on her throat. The mournful wail she emitted sent him into a rage. Before Rafe or Logan could stop him, he shed his clothes and shifted into dragon form. He used his back legs to kick the shit out of Fenwick, dislodging him from Zahra.

He flew to the ground and landed so hard the world vibrated. Jaxson landed near him, lowered his head, and roared his anger. Everything stopped and went deadly silent, as if the world held its breath waiting to see what would happen next.

Fenwick huddled close to the ground and turned his head, his black eyes glaring at him. Jaxson lowered his head to his level and met his gaze. He mindspoke to Fenwick.

If you ever touch her again, I will kill you.

Empty threats, Jaxson. You can't kill me any more than she can.

The snide remark made him lose all reason. Jaxson reared up, tossed his head back to the sky and emitted the loudest war cry he could. When he looked back at Fenwick, he was on his back haunches putting distance between the two of them.

Watch me.

Jaxson sucked in as much breath as he could, letting it pool deep in his lungs. He exhaled the puff of gray smoke right in Fenwick's face. It wasn't Dragon's Breath but it was as close as he could get. As a fire-drake, Jaxson knew Fenwick's scales would be fire proof. There would be no sense in using his fire to try to destroy him.

Fenwick didn't like his smoky breath response. He snarled,

baring his bloody teeth which did nothing but anger Jaxson even more. The dragon charged him, head down, and crashed into him hard enough to knock him back. He landed sideways, his body contorted in an awkward position as Fenwick pinned him to the ground, his snout inches from Jaxson's. He snarled down at him.

You were never worthy of my daughter.

His awkward position gave him the advantage. Jaxson flicked his barbed tail upward, embedding the spikes into the man's back. He reared back, roared his anger and pain. He jerked free and took flight, blood dripping down his scales and onto the ground below. Jaxson launched upward after him, determined not to let him get away. He knew Fenwick was headed toward the sun, trying to recharge his energy by getting as close as he could to it.

Jaxson's wings beat hard and heavy as he forced his big body to go higher and higher, faster and faster. As he neared Fenwick, he pulled up and kicked out his back feet. His talons tore through one his wings and he immediately started a dive back toward the earth. He couldn't control his descent as he tried desperately to flap his one good wing to regain control. He couldn't.

He crashed again, this time rolling over and over until he came to a shuddering halt against the wall of the Coliseum. The building shook, the walls vibrating and Fenwick was out.

Jaxson lowered to the ground, alighting as softly as he could. He placed his big body between Fenwick and Zahra, who was still out cold. He gave her a glance, saw Rafe and Logan and Nemea at her side.

Nemea placed her hands over the puncture wounds. Beneath her palms, a pale white light glowed. Her eyes were closed. Nemea used her dragon powers to stop the bleeding from Zahra's neck wound.

Herrick and his useless son were gone. Several of Herrick's Drakana remained behind, gawking as spectators at the dragon fight that ensued.

When Fenwick came to a rest, Nemea left her sister and hurried over to him. She placed a small hand on his snout and closed her eyes.

"His breathing is shallow. His pulse is erratic. I don't have enough energy left to help him."

Jaxson looked at Logan. My clothes?

Logan held them up. When Jaxson shifted, he'd shed them as quickly as he could to help Zahra. Now he turned his back to Nemea and shifted back into his human form. Logan tossed him his shirt and pants. He quickly dressed.

"Is she all right?" he asked Rafe.

"He bit her pretty hard. Nemea managed to stop the bleeding for now. She still needs medical attention."

"We need to get her someplace safe," Jaxson said. "Someplace away from here."

"What do we do with him?" Logan nodded toward the other dragon.

Nemea said, "He needs a healer and soon."

"He needs to die," Jaxson said, his voice hard and cold.

Her gaze flickered to him. "For whatever cruel acts he did, he is still our father."

"What would Zahra want?" Logan moved to stand next to Jaxson as he spoke. "Would she want him dead?"

Jaxson considered while Nemea pleaded with her eyes. It wasn't for him to decide what to do with Fenwick, was it? It was Zahra's decision to decide what she wanted to do with him. "We'll take him to a healer. Then he should be arrested for conspiracy and treason."

Nemea's face blanched as she realized the calamity of the situation. "I understand your position, Jaxson, even if I don't agree with it."

"He betrayed Logan, his Chief Magistrate," Jaxson said. "That cannot go unpunished, Nemea."

"He'll be tried for his crimes against the Council," Logan said. "If he's found guilty, it will be up to the adjudicators to decide his fate."

She stared him down for long seconds and then finally nodded.

"As you wish, my lord."

"Rafe, find a healer for both Zahra and her father," Logan said.

"Where am I supposed to take them?" He motioned between the two unconscious dragons.

"We can take them back to my family home," Nemea offered. "I know a healer we can contact for them both."

"No," Jaxson said, before anyone could respond. "Take them to my parent's home. No offense, Nemea, but I don't trust your father in his own home. We can still call on your healer, though, if you wish."

She, much like her sister, wore her emotions on her face. It was clear she didn't like Jaxson's suggestion but went along with it to keep the peace.

"What are you two planning to do?" Rafe wanted to know.

"Jaxson and I have unfinished business with Lord Herrick."

"You should let me go with you," he said. "I can do more to help you than be a babysitter for them."

"I don't need a babysitter." Nemea folded her arms over her chest, the look of indignation clearly on her face.

Jaxson ignored her. "I need you to protect Zahra and Nemea. You're the only one besides myself I trust to do that. I have a personal score to settle with Herrick."

"Don't we all," Rafe scoffed. He didn't look happy about having to be the one to stay behind. He nodded. "Fine, then. Go have fun without me. Good luck."

They arrived at Lord Herrick's house, which he'd left well-guarded. Jaxson and Logan easily took out the two guarding the front, stormed inside, and took out two more. Both of their fists were bloodied and cracked by the time they made their way through the house to the man's office.

The only person they found inside the office was Bastian tied to a chair, his raw wrists bound in front of him, his head hanging down with his chin on his chest.

Jaxson wasted no time as he went to the man and untied his wrists. He grunted something incoherent as he tried to lift his head.

"What did he say?" Logan asked.

Bastian tried again, but his words came out nonsensical.

"Not sure. It's clear Herrick isn't here. Help me get him up," Jaxson said.

Logan moved to the man's other side. Together, they lifted him out of the chair.

"Safe," Bastian muttered.

"Yes, you're safe now," Jaxson said. "Let's get you out of here."

"No." He huffed out a breath and nodded toward the wall. "Safe."

"I think he's trying to tell us there's a safe on that wall," Logan said.

Jaxson peered at the Van Gogh painting on the far wall. He let Logan shoulder the man's weight and went to the wall. He felt around the painting on one side. Nothing out of the ordinary. But on the other side, his fingers bumped against something that felt like a hinge. Surprise flickered through him as he pulled the painting back and revealed the safe on the other side.

"There's something in here. We need to get inside this safe," Jaxson said.

Bastian gave Logan a shove and stumbled toward the safe. He leaned heavily against the wall, his breathing labored.

"I can open it," he said.

"You know how to crack the safe?" Jaxson asked.

"Not crack," he corrected. "Open."

He lifted his hand and held it over the dial. His eyes closed as he concentrated. The dial began to spin. The metal door buckled. Bastian pulled it open. Inside, was Zahra's scale.

"You're an elemental," Logan said from across the room. "What's in the safe? I can't see."

"Zahra's scale." Jaxson reached for it, grasping it with a gentle hand. He pulled it out of the safe and held it as though it were a precious piece of glass. His gaze met Logan's. "We have the final relic."

❧ 24 ☙

A faint smile crossed Logan's lips. "Then it's time to retrieve the other relics and get to the Crystal Cave."

"Bastian needs medical attention," Jaxson said. "We should—"

"I'm fine," he interrupted, his voice stronger than it was moments ago. "Herrick won't be gone long. We should go while we can."

"Where did he go?"

Bastian gave a half shrug. "No idea. He left me here with a few guards and went to the Coliseum. He thought he had the matrimduella in the bag. It appears you didn't lose."

"It's a long story," Jaxson said. "Let's get back to the others. We should regroup and plan our next move." He was anxious to get back to Zahra.

"We need to get the other relics," Logan said.

Jaxson looked at him, his jaw clenched tight. He didn't know Bastian that well. He didn't know if they could trust him. Sure, he could open a portal here, now, and take them to Ashe to retrieve the tooth and the Blood Stone, but something about doing it here in Herrick's place seemed…off.

"You think you can't trust me," Bastian said. "I'd think that, too. I've been working for Fenwick for nearly twenty years. I knew his wife before she died. I watched his daughter's grow up. I would never do anything to put them in danger."

Jaxson knew he told the truth. He could hear it in his voice and sense it with his dragon magic.

"I believe you," Jaxson said with a nod.

"But you still don't trust me."

"I don't know you," Jaxson said. "All I know is you work for Fenwick."

"I work for him, yes, but I did it for a good reason," Bastian said.

"You did it for Nemea, didn't you?" Logan asked.

Bastian's gaze flickered from Jaxson to him and back again. His jaw was set in a hard line. Jaxson knew that was the real reason, though he was reluctant to admit it aloud. He understood. Perhaps Bastian was still coming to terms with his feelings for the girl. He wasn't ready to admit he had them and that she had them for him. The two were clearly interested in each other but hadn't found a way to express it.

"This is not an elaborate ruse," Bastian said, waving his hands up and down his beaten body. "I'm not a masochist. What I did, I did for Nemea and for Zahra. I tried to shelter them from their father. As the time drew near for Zahra to marry Talal, I could no longer keep her out of Fenwick's reach."

"And you got your ass kicked for it." Jaxson gave him a pat on the shoulder.

"I did."

"Commendable," Logan said with a lopsided grin.

"When she refused to cooperate, I knew he would set his sights on Nemea. If you hadn't showed up when you did, they'd have her dragon scale."

"He stole Zahra's." Jaxson didn't bother to hide the vehemence in his voice. "And for that, he'll pay."

"And soon," Logan agreed. "You're right, Jax. We should get out of here. Bastian, you're welcome to join us. I'm sure Nemea will be glad to know you're still alive."

He huffed out a breath and limped toward the door. "I doubt she cares that much."

But Jaxson and Logan both knew Bastian was wrong. Nemea cared quite a lot.

They followed him out, past the unconscious guards, into the dusky evening. It had been a long day and would probably get longer before they were done with the whole ordeal. All Jaxson wanted now was to get back and make sure Zahra was all right. His worry for her had gnawed him since he left her, though he tried hard to mask it. At least they had her scale back. He cradled it in his arm as if it were a fragile piece of glass.

Jaxson's parents' house wasn't far from Herrick's. All the Council members had homes in the same general area, including Logan. Apprehension swept over Jaxson as they arrived. He hurried through the small house looking for Zahra. He found her in his bedroom, curled on her side, her pink hair spread out behind her. Nemea jumped to her feet when he entered. Their eyes met. Hers still burning with that indignation.

"How is she?" he asked.

"The healer just left. She has several puncture wounds in her neck where he bit her. He said she was lucky. They weren't very deep. He cleaned and bandaged them. She also has a cracked rib and, he thinks, a concussion."

"He thinks?"

"Her pupils are dilated, but that could be from the shifting drug Rafe gave her. He didn't know." She headed for the door. "I'd like to check on my father now."

He caught her arm in a light grip as she brushed by him. "Nemea." He halted, unsure what he wanted to say.

She met his gaze. "You don't have to explain. I don't like my father sometimes either, but he is still my blood and the man who raised me."

He gritted his teeth so hard his back teeth ached. There was so much more he wanted to say about how Fenwick treated Zahra, how he betrothed her to a man for his own political gains, but he didn't. He kept his words to himself. She glanced down, then, and saw the scale cradled in his other arm against his chest.

"You found her scale?" she asked. "Where?"

"Herrick had it in his safe. Bastian managed to open it for us."

Light flickered through her gaze. "Bastian was there?"

"He's in the other room with Logan." Jaxson nodded toward the living area.

She didn't waste any more time as she hurried out of the room. Jaxson quietly closed the door behind her and turned to Zahra. Her back was to him. She hadn't moved since he arrived.

He moved to the bed and perched on the edge. Her eyes were closed, her beautiful face in repose. She had a fresh bandage around her throat. Seeing it sent the rage through him at the thought of the pain she must be in. He dragged his fingers through her tangled hair, gently pulling the knots free.

Zahra's eyes flickered open. She didn't turn her head when she whispered. "Jax?"

"Right here. Don't to talk or move."

She squeezed her eyes shut and stifled a whimper. "You're alive."

"I told you not to talk."

"You're not the boss of me." Despite her whispered voice, he could still hear the obstinance. "You idiot."

"I'm an idiot? Why?"

"You know why. You and your ridiculous duels." She coughed then. "Water?"

He glanced around the room, saw the pitcher of water and the glass next to it on the nightstand. With a careful hand, he placed her dragon scale next to it. He poured the water, then helped her sit up enough to sip it.

"I told you not to talk," he said again. "It can't be comfortable."

When she swallowed, she said, "It sucks." But this time she sounded stronger.

"Nemea was here. She said you were lucky the puncture wounds on your neck weren't very deep. And you have a cracked rib."

"And I have a horrendous headache." She reached up and massaged the skin of her forehead between her fingers.

"I'm sorry about the matrim-duella but I had to, love."

"Why didn't you tell him we were handfasted?"

"He wouldn't have believed it. He would have challenged me anyway. He wants me and Logan out of the way. That's why he pitted us against each other," Jaxson said.

"And that backfired."

He nodded. "It did. And I wanted it to be clear I intended to marry you."

"He has to know we're mated," she pointed out.

"If he does, so be it. I don't care who knows." He lifted her left hand and brushed the pad of his thumb over the ring that was his mother's. "Us. Forever. Remember?"

"Oh, Jax." She sniffed, a faint smile on her lips. Color rose in her cheeks as she blushed. It wasn't often he saw her blush. He liked it. "What happened with my father? I don't remember much."

He told her what happened after Fenwick sank his teeth in her neck. When he saw him clamp down her throat, he lost all thought of reason. He immediately stripped, handed off his clothes, and shifted.

"Did you kill him?" Her voice was quiet in the shadowy darkness.

"No." Though he wished he had.

"You should have."

"I don't think Nemea would ever forgive me if I had."

"I can handle my sister."

"There's more." He reached for the scale on the nightstand. He placed it on the mattress in front of her.

She sucked in a sharp breath. "You got it back." She reached out, dragging the tips of her fingers over the scale in reverence.

"We have all the relics now. We can break the curse. That is…if you are willing to let us have it."

"Of course, I am, Jax. I told you before I wanted to help. I meant it." Her eyes fluttered closed. She sounded tired.

He leaned down and kissed her cheek. "I'll let you rest."

He got to his feet and started for the door.

"Thank you."

"For what?"

"For everything."

"You're welcome, love."

He exited the room, quietly closing the door behind him. He found Logan and Rafe in the living room.

"Where are the others?" he asked.

"Nemea is with Bastian. Fenwick is sleeping in one of the spare bedrooms," Rafe said. "Still alive but not so well. He won't recover anytime soon after his fight with you."

"You left him along unguarded?" Jaxson asked.

"He's restrained and can't escape. As soon as he wakes, I intend to have him arrested and moved to a holding cell in the Council Building," Logan said. "I'll give my apologies to his daughters."

"You won't have to worry about Zahra," Jaxson said. "Nemea might have a strong opinion about that, though."

"You gave her back the dragon scale?" Logan asked.

Jaxson nodded. He could see hesitation in his friend's eyes. "She agreed to let us use it to break the curse."

The relief was evident on his face. "She has my thanks."

"So, what's our next move?" Jaxson asked.

"We need to retrieve the other relics. I told Ashe I'd return today." Logan gave Rafe a sheepish glance.

Rafe sighed. "I know what you're going to ask. You want me to stay here while you two go get them. I get it."

"I need Jaxson to open the portal," Logan said. "And you to stand guard over the dragon scale and Zahra."

"I know. Go on, then. I'll see you when you get back."

Logan gave him a nod, then to Jaxson said, "Open the portal, Jax."

"You aren't concerned Herrick can track us if I open it?"

"We'll be there only a few minutes," Logan said. "As soon as we get back, we get the women and head to the Crystal Cave. By the time Herrick manages to track us and the portals, the curse will be broken."

Jaxson took a deep breath. "I hope you know what you're doing."

"So, do I. Let's go."

Jaxson lifted his hands and drew a circle in the air with one. Orange and white light crackled in a circular motion as the portal opened. Logan stepped through first, then Jaxson, and they were right back in Ashe's dusty workroom. An eerie silence surrounded them.

"Where is he?" Jaxson glanced around, looking for signs of the old man.

"He'll be along shortly."

"Should we go find him?"

"No," Logan said. "We're supposed to wait here. He won't like it if we leave the room without him."

Jaxson lifted a brow. "I take it you've done that before?"

"And got a tongue lashing." Ashe's voice preceded him as he rounded a bookshelf and entered the room. He gripped his gnarled staff with his aged hand and gave them both a wide grin. "Come for the book and the relics, have you?"

"We have," Logan said with a nod.

"Well, no time to waste, I'd wager. Come on, then. Let's get to the vault room."

He headed back the way he came. Jaxson and Logan fell in step behind him. The door to the vault room was already open, evidence Ashe was expecting the two of them. He waved them inside.

The journal and the velvet pouch rested on the table. Next to it, a small wooden box with a clasp. It looked as though it had been hand-carved and sanded to perfection. Logan picked up the small box and flipped open the box. Jaxson peered over his shoulder. Inside was a white powdery substance.

"The tooth?" Logan asked.

"Ground down per your instructions, sonny. I hope it does what you need."

Logan snapped the lid closed. "Me, too. Thanks for your help."

A flashed of light from another part of the house startled them all. They looked toward the door just as Herrick and his son, Talal, entered. Herrick was armed with an obsidian blade. Surprise flickered over Logan's face. Jaxson turned toward the man and widened his stance. Both of them tried to put Ashe behind them, but he would have none of it. He stepped around them and then flipped his cane up, holding it in his aged hands ready to use as a weapon.

"So, this is where you hid them. It's ingenious, I'll give you that," Herrick said. "You see, Talal. I knew you could track the portal magic."

So that's how he found them. Talal could track portal magic. Jaxson snatched up the velvet pouch and the journal, not wanting to leave them exposed as an easy target on the table. He pocketed the Blood Stone. Herrick never took his gaze off him.

"And who might you be, sonny?" Ashe asked.

"Who I am doesn't matter." He turned his attention to Logan. "I know you took the dragon scale. I intend to get it back."

Jaxson clenched his fists. "You stole that from Zahra. You'll get it back only if I'm dead."

He flashed a grin. "If that's how you want to play, then so be it. I want the journal, the Blood Stone, and the tooth." He glanced around the room. "Where is the tooth?"

Logan smirked, his grip on the box tightening until his nailbeds turned white. "The tooth is no more."

Herrick narrowed his gaze. "What's that supposed to mean?"

Logan flipped open the lid to the box and tipped it enough for him to see the contents inside. Fury immediately creased the man's brow and his face turned red.

"What did you do to it?" he demanded.

"Nothing you need to know, Lord Herrick."

"Ah, so this is the illustrious Lord Herrick," Ashe said. He sounded less than impressed.

He snarled at the old man. "What's it to you?"

"You're an intruder in my home," Ashe said. "I don't like intruders, sonny. Especially ones that carry obsidian blades and threaten my friends." He moved forward, waving his cane.

Herrick waved the blade at the three of them. "Hand them over, Logan."

Then Ashe moved so fast, he was nothing but a blur. He knocked the blade out of Herrick's hand, then did a quick spin and smacked him hard in the middle of the chest with it. Herrick coughed, sputtered, and stumbled backward out of the vault room. Talal looked on, mute, with wide eyes as his father tumbled to the ground, his hand on his chest.

"You filthy animal. You hit me!" Herrick snarled.

"That's right, I did. You're lucky I didn't kill you, sonny," Ashe said.

Herrick climbed to his feet, eyeing the blade on the floor behind Ashe. Logan took a step back, as if deciding if he was ready to take on Herrick. Jaxson stepped between Ashe and Herrick, putting his hands into fists and lifting them up.

"This ends now," Jaxson said.

"You wish to fight me?" Herrick laughed. "I don't think so."

No one saw Talal move. No one saw the obsidian blade he pulled from his belt either. Not until he shoved it deep and hard into his father's side, right under the ribcage, and then pushed it upward. Herrick sucked in a sharp breath, his eyes going wide as he looked over at his son. Confusion was etched along the lines of his face. Talal's expression was nothing short of determined hate. Something must have snapped deep inside him. He pushed the blade deeper and harder into Herrick's gut, then twisted.

"Talal...what...?"

"That's for killing my mother," the boy whispered. "And for betrothing me to the girl I don't love. And all the other things you've done for your own personal gain."

He jerked away the blade. Herrick pressed his hand against the wound. Blood seeped through his fingers. He stumbled back and crashed into the door, leaning heavily on the jamb.

"You stabbed me," Herrick said in disbelief, staring with incredulity at his son. "My own flesh and blood...betrayed me."

"And you betrayed the Council," Logan said.

But Herrick was focused on his son. His astonishment turned to his own hatred. Little bubbles of spittle formed at the corners of his mouth. "You will pay for this, Talal. I will kill you."

"You won't," he said. "Because I had this made especially for you." He held up the blade, now shiny with Herrick's blood. "When you took over the forges in Andonia, when you thought you had everything under control, you had no idea I was plotting your murder."

Jaxson peered hard at the blade, trying to see what made it special.

"Most obsidian blades are forged with steel. Not this one. This one is purely obsidian. Meant to kill you…almost instantly." And with that, Talal smiled in triumph.

Herrick slide down to the floor, still pressing the wound bleeding profusely. His hand and shirt were covered in blood. His face had paled and turned pure white. His lips turned blue. His eyes were suddenly red-rimmed and bloodshot. The poison coursing through his veins worked fast. Faster than anything Jaxson had ever seen.

"You…bastard." Herrick uttered those final words before all the life drained out of him.

He was dead at the hand of his own son. Talal dropped the blade to the floor. He turned to Ashe.

"My apologies for our intrusion." He gave a low bow. "He forced me to track Jaxson's portal and bring him here."

"Where I come from, sonny, patricide is a criminal offense. Punishable by death," Ashe said. "Wouldn't you agree, Chief Magistrate?"

Logan was silent as he stared at Talal, considering. "Normally, yes. But there are extenuating circumstances in this instance, I think."

"There are. Be glad my father's reign of terror is over, my lord. I know I am," Talal said. Then he addressed Jaxson. "She's your mate, isn't she?"

It was the most Jaxson had ever heard Talal speak. In fact, he couldn't recall anything he'd ever said. Herrick had always done the talking and ordering.

Jaxson couldn't hide the truth. "She is."

"Then she belongs with you. As far as I'm concerned, the betrothal is broken."

Jaxson glanced at Logan who gave him a nod. "I'll make it official," his friend said.

"Well, I guess it's left up to me to clean up this mess." Ashe let out an exasperated sigh.

"We can stay and help," Logan offered.

"Yes, he is my father after all," Talal said.

But Ashe waved them all away. "Go. You have bigger more important things to do. I'll take care of that." He pointed at Herrick's lifeless body with the end of his cane. "Time to find my cleanup spell." With a sigh, he shuffled out of the room.

"Talal—" Logan began.

"I don't intend to follow in my father's footsteps," he said, cutting off Logan. "If that's what you're worried about. But you should know there are things he put into motion that cannot be undone."

"What kind of things?" Jaxson asked.

"Things like building an army of Drakana ready and willing to take over the Hidden Lands. He incited their fear, their rabid hatred of you and the clan system, Logan. And he had men willing to do whatever it took to see him named High King once again."

Jaxson shifted his weight from one foot to another. "No doubt there will be someone ready to rise to take his place."

Talal nodded. "No doubt. I wish you both good luck. I do hope you break the curse, Logan. It will do a lot to shift things in your favor."

"As do I," he said. "I'm sorry things turned out like it did with your father."

"What's done had to be done. Farewell." With that, he opened a portal of his own making, stepped inside and disappeared.

"Talal took the kill from you," Logan said. "I hope you're not too disappointed."

"Only a little," Jaxson admitted. "But I'm sure I'll recover. We should get back."

"Before you go, sonny," Ashe called from the next room. He stepped into the doorway and motioned for Jaxson to follow. "You'll want to come with me."

Jaxson had been so distracted with thoughts of Herrick and Talal, he had forgotten Ashe still hid his parents. He and Logan fell instep behind him. They wound their way down a corridor and up a set of stairs to a second level. At the top of the stairs, he turned left and headed down the landing, pausing at the last door on the left. He whisked it open. Jaxson stepped inside the room as his father jumped to his feet. His mother sat in a chair by the widow, her legs curled under her. She had regained some color in her cheeks and she no longer looked as frail as she had when he brought her through the portal to Ashe. She turned her head, met his gaze, and smiled.

He handed off the journal to Logan and hurried her side. She reached a hand up to him. He grasped her fingers in his. "Mother."

"I'm feeling much better," she said. "Ashe said once the curse is broken, I can return to the Hidden Lands."

"Are you cured then?"

"I'll never be cured. But once the air is no longer toxic, I will be able to breathe again. Like I can here in this place." She nodded toward the window.

The Blood Stone in his pocket felt heavy as he thought of the curse and all they'd been through to get to this point. He peered out through the grimy glass. The landscape was nothing he had ever seen before. In the far distance, a purple snow-capped mountain rose up to kiss a cloudless pinkish-blue sky. Just behind the window, a forest of black trees clustered so tight together, not even a ray of sunlight could pierce the shadows. His brows knit together in question. He turned to Logan and Ashe.

"What is this place?" he asked.

"You didn't tell him?" Ashe asked. Logan shook his head. The old man cackled. "Better explain it to him while I take care of that other business."

The other business being a dead Herrick. Ashe disappeared into the hallway, the only sound that of his receding footsteps.

When he'd gone, Jaxson asked Logan, "Tell me what?"

"Ashe is a bit…eccentric, Jax," Logan said. "An Ancient, yes. He didn't lie when he said he was nine hundred years old. He has a certain…old magic that isn't wielded anymore."

"That doesn't answer my question," Jaxson said.

"I'm getting there. Ashe is a master of portals. He knows more about them than anyone. Even you. He knows how to control them, how to open and close them between time and dimensions," Logan said.

"Time and dimensions," Jaxson repeated. He glanced again out the window as his gut twisted into a tight knot.

"Ashe is a magus, Jax," Logan said. "This place exists between time and realms."

His mouth went dry. "If Ashe is a magus, then that means…" He couldn't finish it. He didn't want to finish it. He didn't want to acknowledge it.

"So is Talal," Logan said for him. "And so are you."

"Did you know about this?" Jaxson asked his father.

He shook his head. "We didn't. Not until we arrived here. Ashe is very interested in you. He wants to teach you."

And what about Talal? Did Ashe want to teach him, too? Did Talal even know what he was? What kind of power he had? He doubted they would have answers to those questions. Even Talal. It was strange to think about, really, being able to wield a magic like that. Jaxson wasn't sure he wanted it.

His mother's hand tightened on his, breaking into his thoughts. "For so long, we didn't know what you were capable of. Now we have an inkling. My son, you are special. You should take Ashe up on his offer."

"I have to think about it," Jaxson said. Later. Much later. He needed to talk to Zahra about it before he made any decisions.

"You don't have to decide today," his mother said. "All you have to do now is break the curse."

Jaxson felt as if his mind was in a fog as he nodded. He would worry about everything else later. Right now, he had to get back to Zahra. He needed to talk to her.

"We have to get back." Jaxson slipped his hand out of his mothers and bent to kiss her cheek.

"Once the curse is broken, we'll be back," Logan added.

After they bid his parents farewell, he opened the portal back to his childhood home. The two of them stepped through.

$\mathcal{S}$ 25 $\mathcal{S}$

They arrived in the middle of the living room. Thankfully, alone. None of the others were around. As soon as the portal closed behind them, Jaxson whirled to face Logan.

"How long have you known about that?" he demanded.

"Not until the first time we went to see Ashe. I only suspected then."

"How?"

"There are certain…elements that make up the magic of opening a portal. Yours seemed different. I was right." It was clear his friend was trying to suppress a smile of triumph.

Jaxson narrowed his eyes in suspicion. He folded his arms over his chest. "How did you find Ashe to begin with?"

"Funny story that." Now Logan did grin. "I stumbled across something in my father's journal." He handed Jaxson the box with the dragon's tooth, then cradled the journal in one arm and cracked it open. He flipped a few pages until he halted at one with a star in the top left corner of the page. "Here my father mentions a specific spell that can cross time and dimensions. I'd never heard of such of thing, so naturally I had to try it."

"Naturally."

"Ashe actually found me," Logan continued, ignoring his comment. "Apparently, the spell is a call through space and time. A call that only a magus can hear. When I invoked it, Ashe opened the portal."

"And when you described the place to me, the first time we went…how did I manage to hit it just right."

"I gave you specific instructions using words from the spell. Ashe was on the other side waiting in case it didn't work. But it did." Triumph laced his words.

The kind of triumph Logan wasn't all too sure he liked. His friend had tricked him into using his portal magic and taking him to Ashe. But could he be all that upset about it when Ashe was able to cure his mother? No, he didn't think he could.

"I don't know if I want to learn more about being a magus," Jaxson admitted.

"It's all right if you don't. Ashe doesn't expect you to decide today. And anyway, we have a curse to break." His grin lit up the excitement in his eyes. "It's time."

"I need to prepare Zahra and make sure she's up for it."

Logan nodded, gave him a pat on the back. "We've waited this long. We can wait a little while longer if need be."

Grateful his friend understood, Jaxson made his way to his bedroom. He cracked the door a little to see her still resting on his bed. He closed the door and crept to her, pausing at the side of the bed and gazing down at her. He memorized her softened features, the way her hair splayed out behind her. She must have sensed him. Her eyes blinked open and she turned her head to look up at him. She gave him a faint smile.

"Hi," she whispered.

He perched on the edge of the bed, took her hand in his. "How are you feeling?"

"Better. Still tired." She inhaled a deep breath. "Did you get the relics?"

"We did. We're ready, Zee. Are you? If you're not up to it, we can wait."

She pulled her hand from his and reached for him, pressing her palm against his cheek. "No more waiting. I'm ready."

He cupped her hand against his face, relishing her warm touch. She had regained her color and looked much better than she had after the attack.

"Do you think this ritual will work?" she asked.

"I hope so. If it doesn't, then we'll return to the human realm and live out our days there." He started to tell her about Ashe and his ability to open portals across time and dimensions, but it didn't feel like the right time. Not now.

"Us. Forever," she said and gave him a sweet smile. "Before we go, Jax…" She hesitated, dragging her lower lip through his teeth. "If I asked you to do something, would you do it?"

"Anything."

"Take me. Love me."

He couldn't help but look at the bandage on her throat. "Are you sure you're up for that, now?"

"I need you. And I know you'll be gentle with me."

He needed her, too. More than anything. He would do anything she asked. He'd walk across hot coals for her. Hell, he was prepared to die for her.

He bent down, brushed a kiss over her lips. She reached up with her free hand and wrapped her arm around him, pulling her closer. He didn't rush through things, though. He did exactly as she wanted, letting her set the pace, letting her take the lead. While she slipped out of her clothes, he shucked his and then moved on top of her, keeping as much of his weight off her as he could. When he slid into her, her breath caught and then shuddered out of her in a long, wistful sigh. Her hips rocked against his in a slow, sensual rhythm that sent his senses reeling. Being inside her, with her moving beneath him, was the only thing he lived for. He would never get enough of her. Ever.

Their lovemaking was slow and gentle. When her climax shuddered around him, he let himself go and released his own need and desire. And when it was all over, he rolled to his side and held her.

They stayed cocooned like that for as long as they could. But, he knew, the others were waiting for him to make an appearance.

He helped her dress and then stand. She leaned on him, favoring her injured leg. She gave him a faint, brave smile.

"Are you sure about this? We don't have to do this now if you're not up for it," he said.

"I'm sure. I'm ready. Let's do it."

Nodding, he scooped her dragon scale off the nightstand where he'd left it and handed it to her. She cradled it against her chest with one arm. He helped her out of the room. Logan, Nemea, and Rafe were both seated in the living room. Her sister jumped to her feet when they emerged. Nemea rushed over and helped her limp the rest of the way to the sofa. Zahra lowered herself down to the cushion.

"Are you sure you should be up?" Nemea asked.

"I'm sure," Zahra said. "Besides, we have a curse to break."

"We'll need to open a portal to the ladies," Logan said to Jaxson. "Are you ready?"

"As I'll ever be."

With the threat of Herrick gone, Jaxson didn't worry about opening the numerous portals. One to retrieve Mia and Bree. They were both happy to be rejoining their husbands.

Logan hugged his wife. "I'm glad you came. Where's Elijah?"

"I wouldn't miss this for anything. He's safe. Meg agreed to look after him for a little while. I promised her I'd be back soon," Bree said.

Before Logan came into Bree's life, she and Meg worked together a long time at Bar Inferno. They were friends. Jaxson knew she wouldn't trust just anyone with her baby. Rafe folded his queen into his arms, holding her so tight he acted as though he would never let her go.

Jaxson moved to Zahra's side. He held a hand down to her. "Ready?"

"As I'll ever be." She slipped her hand in his and got to her feet, then glanced back at her sister. "Are you ready, Nee?"

She flushed, her cheeks turning bright red. "I...I've decided not to go."

Silenced descended in the room as everyone looked at her. This was news to Jaxson. He glanced at Logan who shrugged.

"Why?" Zahra asked.

She twisted a loose string on the end of her shirt around a finger. "Well...Bastian is here and still unconscious. If he wakes, I don't want him to be alone. I hope that's all right?"

"Of course, it is," she said. "We'll be back before you know it anyway."

"I have men stationed outside," Logan said. "In case any of Herrick's Drakana decide to cause more trouble. Two are guarding Fenwick."

Jaxson wasn't surprised to hear that. As Chief Magistrate, Logan took the safety of his people seriously. He picked up a backpack and slung it over one shoulder.

"I have the box with the tooth. Zahra has the scale. Do you still have the Blood Stone, Jax?" Logan asked.

Jaxson realized then he still had the velvet pouch with the Blood Stone in his pocket. He nodded and patted his jeans pocket. "Right here."

"Good. I think we're ready then." Logan glanced around at the faces in the room. "Let's do this."

Zahra blew her sister a kiss as Jaxson opened the portal to the Crystal Cave at the foot of the Whispering Mountains. He held it open while first Logan and Bree, then Rafe and Mia stepped through. Finally, he and Zahra stepped through the vortex and to the other side. The portal closed behind them, plunging the cave into total darkness.

Next to him, Zahra whimpered as she huddled closer to him.

The sound of a zipper opening echoed through the area, followed by movement, and then the cave flooded in a yellowish light from the lantern in Logan's hand.

The cave was huge. The ceiling soared upward so high Jaxson couldn't even see where it ended. It was nothing more than a black chasm overhead. There was a definite chill in the air. Zahra shivered next to him. He wrapped his arm around her shoulders and pulled her close to keep her warm.

"Where do we do this thing?" Rafe asked.

Logan knelt, rifling through the backpack. He brought out his father's journal and flipped through it, pausing on a certain page. He paused, reading over a passage.

"We're supposed to find the lake made of glass inside the Crystal Cave," he said.

"A lake made of glass? That doesn't make sense," Mia said.

"It must be a small pool of water somewhere," Bree reasoned. She glanced around the area, looking for some hint of it.

Zahra leaned all her weight on him. He could tell standing was hurting her injured leg. He moved his arm from her shoulders to her waist to hold her up as much as he could, taking her weight against him.

"Well, let's find this lake made of glass, then," Rafe said.

He didn't wait for instruction. He and Mia took off in one direction. Logan and Bree the other, leaving the two of them alone. Jaxson led her to a small rock outcropping. He helped her sit so she could rest. She stretched her leg out in front of her, taking deep breaths.

"Are you sure you're all right?" Concern edged his voice. He didn't bother to hide it. He wanted her safe. "If this is too much for you—"

"I'll be all right. Don't fuss."

"I'll fuss if I want to," he said.

"We found it!" Mia's distant voice rang out in the cavern.

Bree and Logan hurried back. He snatched up the backpack. "Which way?"

Jaxson pointed in their direction. "That way. We'll be along shortly."

Logan only paused a moment before he nodded and they went after Mia and Rafe. Jaxson could see the pain etched on Zahra's face and knew she wasn't strong enough for this endeavor. He decided then and there he wasn't going to let her walk anymore.

Without asking her, he scooped her into his arms.

"What are you doing?" Her demand was weak at best.

"Carrying you the rest of the way."

"I can walk, you know."

"Zahra, I love you, but shut up. You're clearly in pain. I'm doing this."

She snapped her mouth closed and argued no more but he could see the hint of a smile on her lips.

I love you back, she said into his mind.

They had so much to talk about when this was over. He wanted to tell her everything about Ashe and the portals. So far, he'd been able to shield that information from her by burying it deep into his mind.

The lake made of glass was a good thirty yards from their original position. Rafe, Mia, Logan, and Bree were already standing along the edges. It was, indeed, a glass lake.

Still, calm water reflected the surrounding cave rocks. It was a perfect shade of blue and so clear they could see right through it. It appeared to be bottomless. Rising up in the center of the lake was a smooth flat rock.

"That's it. That's the rock from my father's journal."

"What are we supposed to do there?" Jaxson asked.

"That's where the blood ritual takes place." Logan consulted the journal again.

"How do we get to it?" Rafe stared at the smooth surface with a critical eye.

"Let's find out," Logan said.

He handed the journal to his wife. He reached into the backpack and pulled out the box. He glanced at Jaxson and Zahra. She didn't wait for him to ask. She extended her dragon scale to him. He took it from her with a nod of thanks.

Jaxson lowered her down and placed her gently down on the rocks. Then he dug the velvet pouch out of his pocket and handed it over. Holding all three relics, Logan took a deep breath and approached the edge of the lake. He examined it for a long minute before finally taking a step. Bree sucked in a sharp breath.

They all did, really, as they waited. His foot, however, did not sink into the water. He landed on what appeared to be solid ground. Surprise flickered over his face as he looked back at first his wife, then the rest of them.

"It's solid," he said.

"Be careful," Bree warned.

He gave her a half a nod as he took another step. And another. Until he finally made it to the outcropping in the middle of the lake. He placed the dragon scale on the rock first. Then opened the box and sprinkled powdered substance from the cold-drake tooth over the scale. As soon as the dust from the tooth hit the scale, it began to glow and pulse in a pale orange light. Logan opened the velvet pouch. Knowing he couldn't touch the Blood Stone—for if he did, it would suck the blood from him—Logan shook the bag until the large red stone fell out on top of the scale.

"Bree, read the chant, please."

She said, "Ice infuses the Power. Fire lights the fuse. Gildhara, Rindhara, Elemental. Three drops of blood from these into the Blood Stone. Three drops of blood. No more."

"Mia, you first." Logan waved her toward him. He pulled a small folding knife from his pocket.

She glanced at Rafe who gave her a nod of encouragement. When she met Logan in the center of the lake, she held out her hand. He pricked her forefinger.

"One drop of blood, if you please, your majesty," Logan said.

She squeezed a drop of blood onto the stone. They could see a faint red glow in the stone. She then returned to Rafe's side.

"Now, Zahra," Logan said.

Jaxson reached for her to pick her up, but she batted his hands away. "I can do it."

His gut twisted as he watched her get to her feet in an awkward motion. She favored her left leg as she hobbled to the center of the lake. Logan pricked her finger. One drop of blood landed onto the Blood Stone.

The pale red light in the stone grew brighter.

Jaxson held his breath as he watched her limp back to his side. As soon as she was next to him, he wrapped his arm around her shoulders and held her close, letting her lean on him and take the weight off her leg.

"And now me," Logan said.

He pricked his finger. As his blood dripped to the Blood Stone, he whispered, "Avok qaa."

The light in the Blood Stone flared to life, illuminating the cave in a blinding red and white light. They all had to shield their eyes. Jaxson squeezed his closed. Zahra turned into him and buried her face into his neck. The light from the stone pulsed three times and then went eerily dark.

Nothing else happened.

Silence descended on the cave. They all looked at each other with bewildered expressions.

"Is that it?" Annoyance laced Mia's tone. Her lips thinned. "All that and for what? A light show? How do we know this worked?"

"Maybe something happened outside the cave," Bree suggested, hopeful. Wanting so much for it to work for her husband's sake.

Jaxson looked at Logan, who's face said it all. He was unsure the curse was broken. "We should check outside the cave."

Zahra pressed close against him. "I want to go home." She whispered it so no one could hear.

He sensed she'd had enough of being dragged through a cave for a blood ritual that may or not may have worked.

"You check," Jaxson suggested. "Zahra needs rest. I'm taking her back." He cradled her close while he opened the portal. "I'll be back."

He didn't want them to think he was leaving them to find their own way back. They stepped through the portal into his bedroom. He scooped her into his arms and took her to the bed.

"I'm so tired, Jaxson."

"I know, love. You can rest now."

She yawned. "Do you think it worked? It doesn't seem like anything happened."

"I don't know."

The truth was, he didn't really care much anymore. All he cared about was making sure she was okay and safe. She rolled to her side, tucking one arm under the pillow. He brushed her hair back from her face.

"You should go back to get them." Her voice was drowsy. He could tell she was close to falling asleep.

"I will soon enough."

Her eyes drifted close and then she was fast asleep.

Jaxson sat on the edge of the bed and watched her sleep for nearly ten minutes. He knew he had to return to the Crystal Cave to get the others back. And he would.

There was something he wanted to check first.

He walked to the front door of the house, pulled it open and stood there, staring at the sky for the longest time. Disappointment flooded him. Nothing had changed. The sky still looked the same as it had when they first arrived.

He wasn't sure how to break that news to Logan.

Despite feeling drained, he knew he had to open one more portal. He lifted his hands and engaged the magic.

Jaxson got them all back to his family home but no one spoke. Disappointment hung in the air between them all. Logan's jaw was set in a hard, grim line. He looked so dejected, not even Bree could console him. They all went their separate ways in the house. Rafe and Mia. Logan and Bree. Nemea was still keeping a vigil by Bastian's side. With nothing left to do or say, he curled up next to Zahra and slept.

It had been the best night's sleep he'd had in a long time.

He awoke to sunlight pressing the backs of his eyes. When he blinked them open, he stared at the window. The morning light filtered in through the blinds, leaving slats of light across the bed.

Zahra still slept. Rather than wake her, he slipped from the bed and padded out of the room. As he closed the door softly behind him, something niggled at him to go to the front door and look outside again.

He headed down the stairs to the front of the house and opened the door.

And stopped cold.

The world had changed.

No longer was the sky gray tinged with a smoky haze. No longer was the land brown and dying.

Instead, the sky was the brightest blue had had ever seen in his life. So bright, so blue, in fact he had to shield his eyes to look at it.

Instead, the land was once again lush and verdant. The village still looked abandoned with dilapidated houses falling into ruin but the air seemed clear. Clean. He stepped outside and took in a lungful of it, holding it for a few seconds before blowing it out.

"It worked." Logan's voice behind him made him turn. He stood in the open doorway, staring up at the sky in wonder. "I didn't think it would work. But it did."

"It did." Jaxson nodded. "Thanks to you, Chief Magistrate."

Logan swallowed hard, the emotion clear on his face. "My father's work is complete. We can finally come home for good now."

Jaxson clapped him on the shoulder. "He'd be proud of you."

"Thank you, my friend, for everything you did," Logan said.

"Glad I could help." And he was.

"I promised you a seat on the Council," Logan said. "It's yours if you want it."

Jaxson wasn't so sure, though. "I'll think about it."

"Fair enough." He gave him a nod. "I think I'll go wake my wife and tell her the news." With a smile, he sauntered away.

He was glad the curse was broken, the air had cleared, and everything would finally get back to normal. He thought of the promise he made to his parents.

It was time to bring them home. He opened a portal to Ashe and stepped through.

<h1 style="text-align:center">❦ Epilogue ❧</h1>

One month later

It was a whirlwind month. Things moved quickly once the curse was broken and Jaxson was back with Zahra. He didn't want to wait another second to officially marry her. They started planning their wedding right away. The ceremony would be in their home realm in Jaxson's family home.

After the curse was broken, the Hidden Lands began to heal and return to its former glory. Zahra, too, had healed from her ordeal with her father. Even Jaxson's mother was better after they returned home from wherever Jaxson had hidden them. He still hadn't mentioned it to her.

She hadn't pressed. She could tell the ordeal weighed heavily on him. There was more to it than the well-being of his mother, too, but she hadn't asked him about that, either. Something, though, was on his mind. Something he managed to keep hidden and from her, buried deep in the recesses of his mind.

The day had arrived. As Chief Magistrate, Logan would perform the ceremony. Nemea was her maid of honor. Rafe, the best man. Bree, the baby, Mia, Bastian, and Jaxon's parents would be the only guests.

A small, quiet little ceremony perfect for the two of them. She'd dreamed of her wedding day when she was a girl, but that dream had disappeared after Jaxson left her. She supposed that was why she took up wedding photography. Deep down, the dream of marrying Jaxson had been alive even if she didn't want to acknowledge it. They had talked at length about her career and life back in the human realm. She was more than willing to give it all up to stay with him. She admitted being back in the Hidden Lands suited her. It suited him, too.

Nemea managed to find their mother's old wedding gown. She spent hours cleaning it and mending it. To Zahra's surprise, it fit her.

She dressed in Jaxson's bedroom, commandeering it for her bridal suite. The sweetheart neckline scooped low, showing the silvery scars on her neck where her father had bitten her. She scrutinized it with a critical eye.

"Do you want me to use coverup on the scars?" Nemea asked as she fussed with the train behind her.

Zahra considered for a long moment, then finally shook her head. "No. It's part of who I am now."

She wore her long pink hair loose down her back. The blush colored gown complimented her hair color and her skin tone making her look like the perfect blushing bride. Nemea stood from arranging the train and stepped back. She met her gaze, tears standing in her eyes.

"Zee, you look breathtaking." She handed her the bridal bouquet.

"Thanks."

A knock on the door, then it cracked open. Bree poked in her head. She gasped as she came into the room, closing the door. "Wow. That gown is gorgeous."

"Do you think so?" Zahra asked. She'd argued with Nemea at first, telling her it was too old-fashioned.

"It's perfect." Bree hugged her. "We're about ready to start."

"I'm ready," Zahra said.

She had never been so ready to marry the man she'd loved all her life.

"I'll tell the others," Bree said. She whisked open the door and disappeared.

"It's too bad Mother couldn't be here," Nemea said, wistfully.

Before Zahra could reply, another knock on the door.

"Who is it?" Nemea called.

"Jaxson."

"It's bad luck to see the bride before the ceremony," she called.

"Let him in, Nee."

"But—"

"It's fine," Zahra said.

"If you're sure." She opened the door and stepped aside to let him in.

When he saw her, he hesitated. His eyes widened, surprise followed by joy flickering over his face.

"Nemea, give us a minute, will you?" Zahra said.

She slipped out of the room, closing the door. They stared at each other in silence for a long moment.

"I don't think I've ever seen anyone more beautiful than you are," he said. And his voice cracked a little.

"Do you like it?" She waved to the dress. "It was my mother's."

"It's perfect. You're perfect." He stared another minute longer then cleared his throat. "I needed to talk to you about something before we do this."

Worry flickered through her. "What is it?"

He reached for her hand. "You asked me before where I took my parents."

She nodded. "Yes, and you weren't ready to tell me."

"I am now. I know it's not the best timing, but—"

"Tell me," she urged, gently.

"It may change the way you feel about me."

"Nothing could change that," she assured.

He gave her hand a gentle squeeze. "Logan recruited one of the Ancients to help him translate the Old Language in his father's journals. His name is Ashe." He paused, looking down at their entwined fingers. She waited, allowing him to tell her in his own time. "Ashe is a magus."

Zahra's brow creased as she tried to remember the term magus and what it meant. She hadn't heard it in a long time. "A magus?"

"He has a special portal magic. He can open portals across time and dimensions." His gaze lifted to hers. "And so can I."

Mute, she stared at him, trying to make sense of what he was telling her. "You didn't know this before?"

"No. Ashe wants to teach me how to do it."

Her heart thudded hard. "Is that what you want?"

"I don't know. I was hoping you could help me with that." He gave her a sheepish grin.

"You've known since you returned with the relics, haven't you?"

"I didn't know how to tell you."

"It doesn't change anything about us, does it?" she asked.

"Of course not."

"You set out to help Logan break the curse. You did that. We did that. Now we can focus on the future. Whatever that future is. I'll be with you, whatever you decide." She took both his hands in his. "Us. Forever. Remember?"

He lifted her hand and kissed her palm. "Us. Forever. I love you, Zahra."

"I love you back." She leaned her forehead against his and pressed her palms against his scruffy cheeks, loving the way it felt against her palms. "Now, let's go get married."

And they did.

Sign up and get your free book!

I love interacting with readers and the best way to do that is through email. Sign up for my VIP Reader's List and get a free book, notifications of upcoming releases, join the review team and much, much more. It's a great way for me to connect with you!

You can get the free book by signing up at:
https://www.subscribepage.com/_VIP

Your privacy is important to me. I will never sell or share your email address.

Did you enjoy this book? You can make a difference!

Reviews are an indie author's most powerful marketing tool. Honest reviews help us get noticed by other readers and increase visibility in the marketplace. It's the best way for indie authors like me to be discovered by fabulous readers like you.

If you enjoyed this book, I would be ever so grateful if you could spend a few minutes leaving a review at your favorite e-retailer. It can be as short as you like. And if you're interested in joining my re- view team, email me a note to let me know! I personally answer every email I receive.

Thank you very much!

Also by Michelle Miles

Dream Walker
Call of the Dark

Age of Wizards
In the Tower of the Wizard King
On the Hunt for the Wizard King

A Ransom & Fortune Adventure
Highland Fling, Vol 1
Dead of Winter, Vol 2
The Citadel, Vol 3
Lord of the Underworld, Vol 4

Dragon Protectors
Desiring the Dragon Lord
Seducing the Dragon Knight
Tempting Her Dragon Bodyguard

Dream Walker
Call of the Dark

Guardians of Atlantis
Tempting Eden
Seducing Eve
Ravishing Helene
Guardians of Atlantis Box Set

Realm of Honor
One Knight Only
Only for a Knight
A Knight to Remember
A Knight Like No Other
Shadows of the Knight

Coffee House Chronicles
Talk Dirty to Me
Nice Girls Do
Have Yourself a Merry Little Latte
Take Me I'm Yours
Sex, Lust & Martinis

Forever Yours
A Little Taste of Heaven

Shorts and Anthologies
A Dance Among the Faeries, Short Story
Eorwulf, Short Story
The Soul of Sharah, Short Story
Sinfully Sweet, Short Story
Flights of Fantasy: A Collection of Short Stories

Watch for more at www.michellemiles.net

About the Author

Michelle Miles believes in fairy tales, true love and magic. She is the award-winning author of the epic fantasy, IN THE TOWER OF THE WIZARD KING, as well as the fantasy romance series, REALM OF HONOR, featuring knights and their ladies fair, and the paranormal dragon-shifter romance series, DRAGON PROTECTORS.

In her spare time, she enjoys listening to music, reading, cross-stitching and watching movies. Even though she's a native Texan, she loves castles, dragons, fairies and elves and is an avid Game of Thrones fan. She can be found online at Facebook, Twitter, Instagram, Pinterest, and Goodreads.

www.ingramcontent.com/pod-product-compliance
Lightning Source LLC
Chambersburg PA
CBHW071512110726
47908CB00003B/812